Carte Blanche

Blanche

A Michael Christian Mystery

MIKE SAAD

Carte Blanche

A Michael Christian Mystery

ISBN 978-1-7322499-4-3
Printed in USA

Dedication

I've had several partners in my police career, and the dangers we encountered shaped us individually and influenced us collectively.

Not all partnerships work out as well as we might hope. Others leave lasting marks on our identity and help form us. Avoiding the bad habits of some, while emulating the best characteristics of others, all play into shaping the person I became.

A few of my partners became friends for life, and the memories and the secrets we share form an immutable bond. This book is dedicated to three of my partners, all of whom predeceased me.

I worked with Jamie Rollo and Harvey Harris at the Detroit Police Tactical Mobile Unit, one of the finest tactical police organizations in the country. At a recent rededication of the unit, Detroit Police Chief James Craig said, and I'm paraphrasing his words, "The accomplishments and the statistics of this crime fighting unit have never been, and likely will never be, matched." Harvey and Jaime and I were a crew at the unit. It was an honor to be assigned to the unit and an honor to have these two fine men as my partners. We shared each other's secrets and we had each other's backs. These were noble and honorable warriors.

Tom Pennybacker and I worked together at the Wayne County Organized Crime Task Force, an elite and secret plainclothes unit, working under the direction of the Wayne County Prosecutor. Tom and I worked undercover, and managed a long-term investigation that resulted in dozens of arrests and convictions, ranging from dope dealing to art theft, from weapons smuggling to murder conspiracies. Tom's stability enabled me to become the character I was portraying without losing sight of the human being I was.

Gentlemen, the tours of duty we shared, and the depth of your friendship, will always be a part of who I am. Recalling our experiences still makes me smile. I wish we could get together and tell our stories again, some with outrageous laughter, and others in somber whispers. Your memory will live in my heart forever.

There are occasionally people who are on your team, who influence you more than they even know. While not "partners" as in law enforcement, their guidance is a constant. These are people who are wise from years of experience, and honest in their belief that doing good things is noble, despite what others might say. This book is also dedicated to Robert Healy, former Wayne County (Michigan) Prosecutor. Bob was assigned to the Wayne County Task Force and to my squad, as legal counsel.

His guidance, insistence on following the law, and keeping abreast with it as it changed over the years, ensured that our cases, some brought before the Citizens Grand Jury, always resulted in indictments and convictions. He was also one of the bravest prosecutors I had ever met. Bob was often side by side with arrest crews when executing warrants for homicide suspects, wanted for killing witnesses in drug cases. He was known, at times, to be "first in the door."

Bob, your personal guidance and your courage were an example to me. Many of the attorney's in my stories possess your inner strength and calm.

My wife Muriel, continues to be my rock. In every endeavor of mine, she says, *Sure* rather than asks *Are you sure?* She has given me room to grow and encouragement to try new things, including writing novels. She is my first proofreader and factual critic. Much of what you read on these pages has been influenced by her sharp eye.

Acknowledgements

My proofreader crew came through again, offering me their observations, comments and critiques and their sharp eyes in spelling, punctuation and grammar.

Tom Kowalski, Terri Kowal, and Pat and Dave Johnson, my sincere thanks for your valuable contribution in helping me get *Carte Blanche* to print. Besides telling a good story, an author strives to provide a "clean read" to his or her audience. Simple grammatical errors can distract from the flow of a good tale. Thanks for helping me get clean and enjoyable content to my loyal readers.

Working through the closures due to the Coronavirus, Peter and Caroline O'Connor, at *Bespoke Bookcovers,* got the draft of my cover to me on time, and captured everything I was going for in the artwork on the first draft. That makes three for three. Carrying the theme of the shadow figure on each cover, gives the Michael Christian

Mysteries the consistency and gravitas they need. Thanks for your consultation on that.

Any error or omissions are strictly mine and some of the grammatical errors are intentional on my part to maintain conversational tone.

Preface

The fact of the matter is, today's greatest nations weren't always great, especially when measured by today's standards. Rome and Egypt come to mind, and lesser known was the expansion of Iran in the fifth century of the Common Era. Even as the centers of world dominance shifted, the greatest nations had one thing in common, expansion through war, or resisting expansion through war.

When it came to growing its economic fortunes or strengthening its borders, no serious nation projected its might outward by offering olive branches They grew through war. The United Kingdom was no different. Whenever the flag of Britannia flew over a newly conquered territory, the country's financial and insurance giants followed to establish a means for trade to ensue. The United Kingdom expanded its might through trade routes paved with the blood of battles. And it wasn't always united.

For nearly two thousand years, Anglo-Saxons, Visigoths, Celts, Danes, Huns and Vikings battled for this grouping of islands.

1

And in the last century, Germany had a run at it too. And as the battles waxed and waned, the social landscape changed to reflect the new populace.

Since World War Two, there have been significant societal changes that set the stage for domestic violence as well.

England and its Emerald Island, Ireland, fought a bloody battle of domestic terrorism. Irish Catholics and Protestants fought each other for religious ideology, while England fought them for the same reasons, as well as for continuous governance of these buffer territories. As recently as the 1990s, the Irish Republic Army (IRA) conducted a decades old war of terrorism on its own people and on the police and military installations of Great Britain.

Bombings were commonplace and sniper attacks were a regular occurrence. The IRA once only focused its attacks on military and police installations. But as their efforts languished, they increasingly went after civilian targets. Their efforts were significantly enabled by weapons, purchased from the Middle East, particularly, Libya.

Another phenomenon occurred after World War Two. During that war, Muslims in India fought alongside British troops with great courage. Many were awarded the Victoria Cross, England's highest honor for valor. After the war, they migrated into England and assimilated into the culture. In the years between 2001 and 2009, their gradual growth in England became exponential. Their population grew nearly ten times as fast as non-Muslim populations did, with most settling in London proper. And the characteristics of the Muslim population changed to include a greater number of people of Middle Eastern descent.

Parliament's management of this explosion in growth was compounded by social subtleties that come with people fleeing a part of the world torn by radical violence, prior to and during these years. Not the least of these issues was that even within their own population, Muslims were fractured as to beliefs, life-styles and their religious-base laws of life.

In the late-twentieth century, another immigration phenomenon occurred. British and French intelligence believed that London, England was becoming a hotbed for jihadist terrorists, who were financed by, training for and planning attacks out of radical mosques. This view of the British Capitol was so commonplace that some French intelligence officers were known to pejoratively call it *Londonistan.*

Eleven hundred years prior to Michael Christian arriving in Wimbledon to conduct his investigation, Viking raiders terrorized Lundenwic. And two hundred years later, Charlemagne thought he was making peace with the Muslim Abbasid Caliph, Harun al-Rashid, who had marched his armies across Europe demanding submission to the name of Allah. The peace was dubious at best and short-lived, but the caliph sent the king an elephant as a gift. Neither the truce nor the elephant lasted very long.

This is the history and the setting that was waiting for Michael Christian, as he arrived in London to conduct his next seemingly simple investigation. What he stumbled on was about to rock one of the oldest surviving empires in the world.

3

This book is a work of fiction. It is set in a time when all these social and economic factors were actually in play. The author takes liberal license with historical events, including rumors, anecdotes, and unclaimed bombings and their attributions in the environs of London during this time, to create a story meant to entertain you, not educate you. Although many aspects of this story are based on actual experiences, remember, it's fiction.

■ ■ ■ ■ ■

EMILY LIVED IN THREE WORLDS. Her home life included her dog. Her work life included people she hated. But her brief, daily immersion into her fantasy life was alive with exciting characters.

Emily was exhausted, as she was each day when she got off work. It wasn't because working at the flower shop, where she spent most of her waking life, was physically grueling. In fact, she didn't mind standing on her feet all day. And even though the shop was small, it was fragrant with the scents of hundreds of fresh cut flowers. She could walk it at her leisure, or stand out back and look over the planted blossoms of hundreds more flowers. Those beauties waited their turns to be brought inside the store, admired, selected, and then delivered to new homes and businesses.

It was people who wore her out. Dealing with customers all day just drained her. Although she knew it was necessary, it didn't make her life any easier.

Men would walk into the shop, browse around a bit, wait for a moment, and then ask her what type of flowers she thought best for their special lady.

Then, when Emily asked all the right questions about the recipient, and personally picked the perfect arrangement, the man would want them

5

sent to an address other than his wife's. Those bastards.

Women asked for Emily's help as if she were a taxonomist who knew the genus and species of each bloom. Walking around the shop with a woman, who spent an hour undecidedly window browsing, then left without a purchase, just drove her crazy.

She desperately looked forward to getting home each day so she could finally relax. There, her first order of business would be to proudly parade Ringo around the dog park. He waited dutifully for her to return home before doing his business, because he was her *good boy,* and would never upset his *mommy*.

The Bichon Frise was a much more expensive breed than Emily could reasonably afford. She justified Ringo because she was single, had no children, and with her allergies to common dogs, a Bichon Frise was a proper indulgence which addressed each of her lifestyle issues.

Walking around her neighborhood park with Ringo, she felt important and maternal when others stopped to *gush* over her little baby. But until Emily got home, she was no one special, merely another invisible person, with a crushingly boring job, riding home on the Circle Line.

The Underground ride to her small walkup flat took less than half an hour, and the idle time wasted didn't matter to her. That was when Emily entered a fantasy world dominated by one of her fellow riders. It was, of course a different passenger each time. It wouldn't do to make up a new story for the same person each day. Emily lived vicariously in a make-believe existence that she conjured up about each one. And none of them was boring. She saw to that.

While most of her fellow passengers read the Daily Mirror, Emily created her cast of characters by closely watching their behaviors. Each person was private and kept to him or herself, and there was never polite conversation among the travelers, not even between couples. Like cattle, they herded together, and rode quietly, as if it was the proper thing to do. If they were not about to share themselves with her voluntarily, she would design their lives for them.

First, she perused them while they read their papers, or while others browsed over seemingly important notes from their burnished, leather briefcases. She was especially interested in those who just looked vacuously out the window, oblivious to their fellow human beings, each with a personal story to tell. But not Emily, she knew there were stories to tell and she was their storyteller.

And that was the game she played to pass the time. She built her stories based on what she saw in someone else's persona. After she first looked them over, she'd scan them again, looking for the most interesting character. And her game would begin.

She'd start by guessing if they were married or single. Often a wedding ring would be obvious, but then Emily would take it a bit further. She wondered if they were happily married, and usually she guessed not. Then she would look them over to discern their innermost secret. *Why weren't they happy? What would their lives be like if they could live out their dreams?*

Perhaps there was a lover for a forlorn woman, maybe an older man, or maybe a much younger one, or maybe a neighbor's wife. Or maybe it was just two wives who found solace in each other. And Emily would imagine the more sordid scenarios in rich, erotic detail as she rode, often blushing in her wicked creativity.

She would look at the men and wonder if they were wealthy, and then imagine how they came by their money. In each case, she was sure some inappropriate activity made them rich. And she just knew there was an even more devious pursuit on which they spent their fortune. And she would allow her imagination to fill in all those sleazy images as well.

Today, there was a young man that caught her eye. He seemed odd for some reason that she couldn't place, so she decided to explore him further. Maybe it was because he seemed over-clothed for the warm June day, or because he seemed to be biting his nails as if he hadn't eaten in a week. While evaluating him as her next likely candidate, he glanced up and caught her looking at him.

There was no pleasant look of recognition on his face, nor a congenial nod of acknowledgement that they had made eye contact. To the contrary, he stared deep and unblinkingly into her eyes, through the darkness under the bill of his cap.

In her small, little life, Emily never had anyone hold her gaze in such a manner, and it frightened her to her core. His look was menacing and lethally dangerous. He was warning her without uttering a word, and she knew exactly what he was telling her. She was unable to avert her eyes and was thankful when he looked away, toward the door of the rail car.

Quickly she looked down to the rubber-lined floor of the car, as much to make sure she didn't look at him again, as to try to recall that moment when he instilled such fear. Interestingly, she could not recall even one of the stranger's features. And although she could see his eyes in complete clarity, they seemed to be floating on a murky darkness in front of his unformed face. She imagined this must be like staring into the face of the grim reaper. She shuddered with a sudden chill, and pulled her sweater tighter about her shoulders.

When her Hammersmith station neared, she looked up and saw the man standing at the doorway with his back to her. She hoped he wouldn't notice her getting off at the same stop.

■ ■ ■ ■ ■

THE YOUNG MAN SAT NERVOUSLY, swaying gently side to side in the second of the six commuter cars, as they sped westward toward the Hammersmith station. He kept one hand on the top handle of his large backpack, steadying it between his feet, while he chewed on the nails of the other, going after some imaginary rough edge that never went away.

Although it was a mild spring day, he wore a lined jacket over a hooded sweatshirt that hung down just above his eyes. Under the hood, he wore a black ball-cap. He hated hats but it served its purpose, hiding the features of his face.

It was only a thirty-minute ride for him, but it seemed to take forever. He had walked the few blocks from his small warehouse and boarded the Circle Line, at the quiet Euston Square station, ahead of the afternoon commute toward Heathrow airport and the west London suburbs. He could have driven and gotten there sooner, but he didn't trust the roadways to be free of accidents or congestion. Once he completed his mission, he would switch to the Piccadilly line and continue toward Heathrow airport.

It wasn't easy to maintain his composure and not look tense. He was very well trained and unlikely to make a mistake, but that didn't make his task any less worrisome. Because he lived a relatively low-profile life, he didn't expect to be recognized out of context, but this aspect of his lifestyle was risky and dangerous, and any mistake could end up getting him identified, if not killed.

He thought back on how he had long ago given up worrying about the consequences of his acts or having guilt feelings.

In his younger years, he was a soldier of Faith and piety, and he let his religious convictions justify his actions. Others had splintered off the true path of his religion and now they were engaged in bitter war.

His people had been welcomed and then abused by the British because of politics, but mainly because of his religion. Thus, there would never be, in his mind, any reconciliation. He considered Britain's treatment of his people and their hostility to his religion, as acts of war, if not outright genocide. His original goal was to pester the British until they gave his people their land, free of British influence or rule.

Over time though, his belief system changed. Now he admitted that he was involved in a lifelong battle with the British military and the police force. And yes, even with the British people. He hadn't given up his Faith, but he was a warrior of a different kind now, a patriot in some broad general sense that he couldn't put into words. He would worry later about collateral damage. At least that was how he rationalized what he was about to do.

Truth be told, he actually enjoyed what he did. He couldn't bring himself to say that he enjoyed killing, even though he reveled in the bloody consequences of a mission well completed. He also came to realize, that he didn't care if this war ever ended.

When he was just a teen, his leaders had seen something in him, a spark of fervor. But when he looked back on that point in his life, he saw only hunger and hopelessness. Regardless, they invested time and money training him. He was trained in the art of incendiary and explosive bomb-making by members of the IRA engineering department, run by Patrick Gerard "Paddy" Flood, a man whose perfectionist style he admired.

He had also seen how failure was rewarded, which made him extra careful. It wasn't that he was unwilling to give his life for his cause, he told himself, but he would rather live to fight another day. He knew this battle would be a long one, and he wanted to be around to see it through.

Wars are not fought in a day, battles are. One bold skirmish after another. And he intended to

11

fight those battles until he brought his enemies to their knees, single-handedly if necessary.

On the map over his railcar's door, a bulb illuminated the next tube stop on the Circle Line, Hammersmith. He swung his backpack gently onto his shoulder and stood in the doorway, letting other riders congregate around him. Looking at the reflections in the window, he could see that the woman who stared at him earlier was approaching the door also. He had wanted to be just an anonymous person in the crowd when he stepped off. She was going to be a problem.

■ ■ ■ ■ ■

HE WALKED WITH THE CROWD until their gradual dispersal left him on his own. From the corner of his eye he watched the woman in the mousy-grey sweater and the brown skirt, as she left the station by the north entrance. She walked past the black cab stands and continued up Butterwick, crossed the busier Hammersmith Street and approached the Blind Squire apartments facing it.

A dog, in the second-story, front window, seemed beside itself, as it yapped and circled on the sill. The woman further agitated it by waving to it and calling out, over and over, "Ringo, mommy's home!"

He stood back into the shadows and watched her enter the building, while at the same time seeing the dog scamper from the window. He now knew where to find her.

He returned to the Hammersmith station across the street and bought a cup of coffee and his ticket to Heathrow, on the Piccadilly line. He then casually walked toward the north exit doors.

Once he was outside, he strode back toward her apartment. Hopefully, he thought, the Squire was still blind.

He practically ran into her though, as he approached the steps of her building. Fortunately the woman was terribly distracted by the dog, which had wound its leash around her ankle as she walked down the stairs to the sidewalk. He concealed himself alongside the apartment stoop, as she tried to extricate herself, and then followed her to a small wooded park.

There were only a few others in the park at this time of day, and most of them were casually walking their dogs. The woman seemed more intent on people-watching than paying attention to her dog, as she turned onto a narrow, tree-lined path.

It was the perfect moment.

As the yipping dog ran ahead a good ten paces, the man stepped in behind her, slammed his hand over her mouth and lifted her off her feet and backwards into the woods. In her panic, she thrashed about, letting go of the leash. Ringo, sensing his opportunity, abandoned his mommy and ran off down the familiar path.

The first thing the stranger did was to throw Emily onto her stomach on the gravelly ground. Her legs thrashed wildly, trying to push him off her. He then grabbed her by her hair and slipped his other

13

arm under her neck, cutting off air to her windpipe, and the blood to her brain from her carotid artery.

His strength was overwhelming and Emily could no longer struggle or scream. She cried out for Ringo, but no sounds escaped her mouth. She could see him in the distance sitting in his window perch barking happily as she walked to him.

But soon, her view changed, and a shadow appeared like a black picture frame around Ringo. He had stopped yipping and now sat still, no longer jumping around in joy. He seemed more like a photograph of a long-deceased loved one, the kind of picture you place on a coffee table in the corner.

Then someone turned off the lights and Emily could no longer see him, or hear her own silent screams.

It didn't take but a few moments until her thrashing stopped and she was unconscious. The man unceremoniously flipped her over, and with powerful, trained hands, forced his thumbs deep into her throat, crushing her windpipe, making certain he had squeezed the last bit of life out of her, even after she had stopped breathing.

Though her eyes were still open, he wouldn't have noticed the bright red pinpoints of petechia his strangulation would cause. He was too busy checking her pockets for identification. He found nothing but her room key. That would make identifying the body more difficult and time-consuming for the police. He rose, tossed the key as far as he could into the thicket, looked about, adjusted his backpack and casually walked a different path out of the woods.

In less than ten minutes he was back at the Hammersmith tube station. Walking in, he bought another coffee, and sat in the middle row of five, pew-like, bench seats, where he waited calmly for his train, thinking back to another similar moment.

■ ■ ■ ■ ■

IT WASN'T DIFFICULT FOR HIM to get the introduction he needed to the IRA's General Headquarters, Engineering Department. Hezbollah and Libya had been providing arms to them in such quantities, that it was concluded by British Intelligence there were enough weapons to arm the IRA for a decade. The challenge was for an Engineer merely to come down to meet him. North Ireland was nearly five hundred miles away. They said it would be easier for him to get into Ireland than for them to enter England.

But he knew the IRA was already staffed and hiding throughout England, based on the many bombing campaigns they had already pulled off. He would pay them well, if they would meet him closer. Besides, he was interested in meeting with only one of them - the famous Patrick Flood, known as Paddy, the lead bomb-maker of the IRA, or one of his direct reports.

Up to this point, Hezbollah dealt mainly in weapons for conventional warfare, it was how they fomented dissent and how they lined their coffers. But he knew he could never survive a conventional war. His objective was to create terror and live to repeat the process.

His goal was simple enough. Leverage the relationship, and as much money as it took, to learn the secret of simplified bomb construction. The IRA was very well known for their ingenious use of commonly accessible materials that were low-cost, easily transportable and highly destructive. That is what the young man needed. With the funding he was receiving, he would have access to large quantities of materials, allowing him to build many units and move them to targets throughout England, with ease.

At first, the meetings were held in parks in the bay area of Cardiff, Wales. The engineer chose the location because Cardiff had multiple small airports and cheaper flights. They would be unnoticeable in such a metropolitan community. That worked for the fledgling bomber because it was only about one hundred fifty miles from London. But once he negotiated the amounts of the cash payments to the IRA, the meetings moved to a small empty warehouse and the training began.

The methodology was much easier than he thought it would be, and he wondered why his people had not worked this out on their own. His teacher was patient with him, but wrote nothing down and would not allow his student to do so either, insisting the he commit every step to memory. Then the engineer insisted his student repeat out loud, and at every meeting, each step he had been previously taught.

He was taught the chemical names and which would burn the skin or not, which were highly flammable or explosive and what the difference was. The instructor explained the exact boiling points they needed to achieve, and what happened to the chemical composition and bonding requirements of the liquids as they change from fluids to pastes. The young man was not merely being taught how to mix things, but was being given a recurring lesson in their chemistry.

He was not allowed to touch any chemicals for the first entire week. His mentor merely took each component step and repeated it several times a day, building on the previous day's work. He added a new lesson at each subsequent meeting. While they waited for individual liquids to heat correctly, he was made to verbally repeat the process up to that point. His training, by rote methodology, went on over and over, day after day.

At first he resented being treated like a child. Soon, however, he came to realize that using this process was not attempting to belittle him, but was a way of training him in the way that engineers think – methodically, deliberately, objectively. His teacher reminded him that the process of bomb making was not merely a recipe, but a chemical reaction that takes place in its own time, at its own pace. He said that any attempt to change either the process or the speed could produce different results, some of which could be fatal.

The young man was, if anything, a survivor. He decided he could contain his urgency, considering the outcome he needed. And the IRA was being paid to transfer his knowledge to him and this seemed his instructor's way of earning his keep.

Before long, he realized that he was learning and recalling, in exact detail, the steps he had been taught. His teacher seemed to sense it too.

They worked with the detonator process first. And when the trainee made and ignited his first small detonation charge, he was secretly thrilled, but revealed his joy only with the slightest of smiles. The usually composed Irishman, however, seemed pleased and gave him a slap on the back, as a measure of satisfaction. The young Arab man hated him for it.

When they acquired their first supplies of household products that would form the explosives, he knew that his teacher was ready to proceed to the next stage, and he was ready as well.

In time the student learned how to pack all the elements in a sealed container to create a pressure against the release of the explosive force, thereby magnifying the effect. He felt they were very near to the test phase of a full explosive device and he had to admit to a sense of excitement.

He recalled how his first test was a letdown for him. They had driven deep into a large, flat grassy field past the northeastern suburbs. There were no structures, and they hadn't passed a person or an animal in over an hour. It was a desolate part of the country. The teacher removed the device and a shovel from the rented van. Handing the shovel to him the Irishman said, "Dig here," pointing to a nondescript spot in the field. The young man felt this task was beneath him, but knew an IRA engineer would never stoop so low, regardless how much he was being paid.

An hour later, he had dug a hole four feet by four feet by four feet that looked like a small grave. He was made to set the device in it, along with the alarm clock actuator. They set the timer for fifteen minutes, got in their van and drove almost a mile away and waited. Within minutes, there was an explosion accompanied by a large plume of dirt and smoke rising from the hole. They quickly returned to the site to examine their handiwork.

Their sixty-four cubic foot hole was now an excavation almost ten feet deep, and sixty feet wide. There was absolutely no debris from the bomb visible anywhere. "Oh, it's around," the engineer explained, but it's in many small pieces, hundreds of feet away. Given the radial explosive force, only a few pieces could possibly fall straight back to the ground."

The student looked around in secret disappointment. He knew this had been only a test of his first device. But he hadn't constructed it or set the timer. Nothing had been destroyed and no one had been killed. He couldn't wait until he could build and set such a device, or its larger brother, in the City of London.

They drove back in silence. The instructor, noticing his student's sullen expression said, "Don't worry. You'll get your crack at it. We're almost through with your training. All that remains is to work with you on storing the materials so their chemical structure doesn't change or interact with the others."

The young student of bomb making had no way of knowing that that his teacher was also a British Intelligence, MI5 informant, a traitor to the IRA.

Within twenty-four hours of returning home from their final training session, This engineer met the fate of many traitors to the IRA. His own leadership detained him in an interrogation safe house for days. With only a little bit of coercion, they got hours and hours of recorded confessions from him, detailing each instance where he had betrayed the IRA and informed to his British handlers.

When they had all they could get from him, the IRA bundled him up, took him for a ride, and then they put a bullet in the back of his hood-covered head. The exit wound left a gaping hole in his face. His dead body was unceremoniously dumped in a field, where several other IRA informants had been left for discovery. The engineer's abduction and murder were all that prevented him from ratting out his secretive Arab student to British Intelligence the next day.

■ ■ ■ ■ ■

ONE MINUTE BEFORE HIS TRAIN'S scheduled arrival, the young man removed the lid from his coffee, took several slow sips and replaced the top. He rose and walked nonchalantly to the Piccadilly platform line, boarded the train and headed westward toward the airport, just one more traveler among thousands that day.

His backpack remained behind, pushed underneath the bench seat, in the fifth row, in the center of the Hammersmith Station, on the Piccadilly Line.

■ ■ ■ ■ ■

He had no intention of remaining on board the rest of the way to Heathrow Airport. As he got off at the Hounslow East station, he smiled to himself and walked the two short blocks to the church, where a car had been parked for him. Kneeling down, he found the key under the left front tire, as planned. He sat confidently behind the wheel of the stolen car like he owned it, started it, slipped it into gear and drove slowly from the lot.

By then, news had already spread to the people of Hounslow East, of an explosion having taken place at the Hammersmith Station. All Hammersmith inbound and outbound trains were halted.

The British news media and local politicians, without any corroborating facts, would soon be awaiting the standard Irish Republican Army claim of responsibility for the bombing. And the local newspapers would be demanding immediate arrests and retaliation. Not that arrests ever followed the bombings. There may have been an assassination or two of IRA members, but no arrests.

Without a shred of evidence and while the damage was still being assessed, politicians would seek out any press camera they could find. Each wished to be either first or loudest to associate the incident with the homegrown terrorists of the IRA.

The Special Branch of the Metropolitan Police and MI5, the domestic intelligence service, were going to be even busier than usual. And the bureaucrats who ran those organizations would be spending countless hours explaining to the Prime Minister and the Parliament why no arrests would be immediately forthcoming. But they would have one clue.

The bomb signature was that of a dead IRA engineer, not that of a young man self-described as *The Messenger*.

■ ■ ■ ■ ■

I RELAXED IN THE WELL-DECORATED office of the General Counsel of Transeget Industries, waiting for him to return. The framed certificates, hanging on his walls, spoke to the credentials of one of the most powerful corporate attorneys in the country, *Juris Doctor* from Harvard Law, *PhD in Finance*, from Harvard Business School, The National Law Journal's *Lawyer of the Year* award, and the American Bar Association *John H. Pickering Award.*

Patrick Flannery was a highly recognized, but practically invisible giant among lawyers, and Barry Brinton, CEO of Transeget Industries used the best executive search firm in the country to find him. Then, having done so, Brinton threw an executive compensation package and a senior leadership role at him that were irresistible. Flannery took the job as General Counsel, moved to New Jersey and never looked back.

He currently ran an in-house law department of over 150 lawyers and a multi-million dollar outside counsel budget that put legal resources at his disposal all over the world. With all that talent, I found it curious that Brinton would have me meet with Flannery to help him solve a problem.

Flannery stepped back into his office carrying two cups of coffee. "Black, right?" he asked. But I could tell he had already asked someone and knew the answer. "Thanks, Pat. Black it is." I answered. And I waited for him to open the conversation.

"So, tell me Michael, do you ever get tired of traveling all over the world at the drop of someone else's hat?"

There had been many times I asked myself that same question, but it seemed that for the past several years, every trip I took was exciting, if not dangerous, in some way. And truth be told, other than being separated from my wife, I relished each opportunity to travel.

As I was framing my answer for Flannery, he said, "Don't tell me. To be perfectly honest with you, if you told me you hated the travel, I'd just as soon not know, because I'm asking you to take another trip. This time for me."

I didn't think he asked me to his office to invite me to play racquetball with him. Someone somewhere had either gotten himself crossways with the authorities or somebody had abused the company in some fashion, and I was being asked to go make it right. It's what I do. I fix problems that someone else in the company made. "Glad to help, Pat. What can I do for you?" I asked.

"We've had a theft in London and I need your help in solving it."

Disappointment rushed through me, as a lot of thoughts began to run through my head. I took a moment to get a grip on them. I had plenty of people on my staff, and I had third party resources all over the world, to handle the more mundane things, like theft.

Flannery pressed on, "I imagine you're thinking that this might be below your pay grade. And maybe it is. But I need your talents, Michael, your international experience, and frankly, I need someone who is not an attorney to step in for me and throw our corporate weight around. Barry said you were the guy. So here we are."

"Then I'm your guy. What happened?" I asked. If my boss had already made the call, then I wanted Flannery to know that I was all-in, without him having to twist my arm. In my mind it was a moot point. Whatever had happened didn't matter. If Barry Brinton said I was *the guy*, then I was already making mentally sure my passport was in order.

Flannery came from behind his desk and sat in the leather wingback chair next to me. "I'm not sure what the timeline is, but someone has stolen blank checks from our London office, forged the signature and cashed them through a third party."

I was regressing and indeed thinking this was below my pay grade. This was a routine investigation that practically anyone on my staff could handle. But I waited. There had to be more.

He continued, "There are two things that make this case uniquely yours, Michael. First is the dollar amount. The forgeries totaled over three-hundred thousand pounds."

That caught my attention and it must have showed. "Yes," he continued, "Over a half million dollars. And the other thing is that it took our auditors in the States to catch it. Therefore, as far as I am concerned, everyone in that office is suspect, even our London Office Manager."

Flannery was right. The theft of the half million on its own didn't necessarily make this a case I might take, but it was at a dollar threshold that would have a lot of executive eyes on it. Nor did the fact that an office manager might be on the suspect list mean that one of my team couldn't handle it. But combined, I could see where Brinton and others would want someone at my pay grade to be directly involved. I mentioned my concurrence to Flannery.

"There's one more thing," he said. "And this is the kicker. We're dealing with Barclay's bank over there and I've already spoken with their senior vice president of business relations. He was very polite but in so many proper English words told me that the loss is our fault for not securing our blank documents."

I could tell that Flannery had already lined up the legal rebuff to that claim by Barclays, and I wondered what their response was. I was personally interested, especially since I ran one of the world's largest corporate security functions and Barclays was claiming insufficient security design or implementation. "What was their reply when you told them our property had been stolen regardless of our security measures?" I asked.

"That's where you come in, Michael." Flannery replied. "If I engage in a protracted dispute on legal terms at this point, or if I use legal counsel in London, then Barclays can refuse to talk openly. We will end up in litigation and our half million will be tied to a judicial decision, years down the road, rather than to some good common sense. And that's why you're the guy, Michael. I want you to find out who stole our money, how they did it, and to make sure neither they nor anyone else can do it ever again. And then I want you to get our money back, even if you have to knock some sense into Barclays. Brinton assures me that if anyone can do that, you can."

I was still a bit uncertain about my role in this, given anyone on my team could handle the investigative aspects, management suspicions notwithstanding. But I could see that Flannery and Brinton had already made up their minds. I rose.

"I'll make arrangements to get over there right away. I presume, by now, the office manager is aware that the money is gone and it is okay to talk with him?"

"Yes," Flannery said. "He's aware. And he also knows that we have been giving him the cold shoulder on this. We have not included him in our discussion of next steps, or the fact that you are coming over. How do you want to handle that?" he asked.

"I think I'll wait until I get there to introduce myself." I replied. I had already experienced several clashes with management, who had been made aware of my pending arrival, only to find out later they had hidden or changed information, or briefed witnesses. In essence they had set the stage against the investigation to protect their political asses. It wasn't as if they necessarily had participated in the offense, it was just that they didn't want such a black mark on their watch. Sometimes surprise had its advantages, especially when management couldn't be trusted until proven trustworthy.

"Since this is an investigation that just might end up in litigation," I added, "how about we use the process that makes me an agent of the law department, working in anticipating of litigation? That way, my investigation notes and the witness statements might be protected from discovery. If your team can prepare the briefing letters informing employees that my investigation is in preparation of possible litigation, and that they are bound, as a condition of employment, to cooperate fully, I'll carry them with me when I leave," I offered.

Flannery got up from his chair, and walked back to his desk. He picked up an executive presentation folder and handed it to me. "I didn't want to be presumptuous," he said, "but here is everything you just asked for, naming you as my agent. And I have addressed a separate "to whom it may concern" letter to Barclays Bank, naming you as speaking on my behalf."

He continued, "And since you are my agent, Michael, speaking for me, I want you to know that I'm professionally pissed off at Barclays. So, you have total carte blanche to handle this any way you want. You don't have to call back here for permission, and don't worry about ruffling any feathers, theirs or mine. Just fix this and get our money back."

Flannery had just given me a blank check to work an investigation in London and to play hardball with Barclays. But he also let me know that he wanted to come out the winner on this one. I'd try the easy way first, of course. But it was nice knowing that I could do what I had to do, to get this resolved.

I rose from my chair, thanked Flannery for his vote of confidence, and assured him I was on my way, as soon as my office could make the travel arrangements.

■ ■ ■ ■ ■

JOANNE WAS MY ADMINISTRATIVE MANAGER who saw to my travel arrangements. In fact, she managed my entire work-life both on the road and in the States. If you wanted to see me, you went through her to get on my calendar. Unless I had to give a presentation, I was usually made aware of my calendar appointments on the evening before the events, including any briefing I needed to make me more effective. She took care of everything, including reminding me of important dates, like my boss's birthday. I'm sure she knew my wife, Alice's birthday also, but I was on top of that myself.

Whenever I needed to go somewhere, I merely told her where and when I needed to be there. She saw to everything else, air, hotel, car, driver or other transportation, spending money, and any special requests.

If necessary she could get me on any one of the corporate jets or helicopters. Joanne was very well connected to Brinton's executive manager, but we didn't pull that ace out unless it was absolutely necessary. Seeing as this trip to London wasn't urgent, it wouldn't require me to reserve a corporate jet. I'd be traveling first class anyway, which took some of the sting out the six or seven hour trip.

It was my intention to leave on the first available flight to London tonight or tomorrow, but I'd leave that to Joanne. Leaving in the morning was late afternoon in London. Add travel time and I wouldn't get there until late evening. I've also taken the evening flight and arrived in the early morning, exhausted, but boots on the ground and ready to go.

I explained the trip to her and she brought my calendar up on her computer. "You have four appointments today. Do you want to keep them or should I reschedule?"

We went over them together and none was so pressing that they couldn't wait another week. I disliked having to cancel anyone, because it was so difficult bringing people in a global corporation together, to begin with. But this kind of shuffling went with my job. We agreed to reschedule them.

Joanne asked if I knew the names of the employees, so she could get their personnel file details for me. I reviewed the letters Flannery had prepared. There were several sets of each, all on his executive stationary, with the impressive, embossed company logo in bright color. Upon closer inspection, I could see that there was an introductory letter made out individually to each of the employees in the London office. That would definitely help if there were to be any resistance to my work. Joanne could use these names for her call to Human Resources.

I knew she was wired into HR and would have those files for me in short order. She promised to have some travel options for me before lunch, so I left her to her devices.

I checked my watch and noted it was almost nine-thirty a.m. in New Jersey, so it would be two-thirty p.m. in London. That gave me some time to make a couple of calls to some friends across the pond.

As soon as my trip details were in order, I would call Alice, and let her know I was heading to London.

■ ■ ■ ■ ■

IT WAS QUIET IN CLARE'S small London flat. Somewhere in the background she could hear the throaty rumble of the black cabs outside her window and an occasional muted voice. But in her bedroom, all she could hear was the slow and rhythmic sound of her breathing. She inhaled deeply and could still smell their sex on her body. The intoxicating scent filled her small, one-room apartment and it thrilled her as she pushed back the thought of returning to work. She had been alone for barely two minutes and her heart, though calming, was still pounding loudly.

Clare considered herself just an average young woman, not a fashion model or an actress, and not an overly attractive twenty-six-year-old. She was pretty in a simple way. She had nice, clean facial lines, a good complexion and a nice smile. She kept her brown, short-cut hair clean and her shampoo left it smelling fresh. She hadn't always used a perfume, and frankly found it an unnecessary expense. But since they began dating, if that's what it could be called, she felt it necessary to spray some on when she returned to

31

work after her lunch break.

Her body was tight and held no extra fat, but by the same token, she didn't think anyone would call her skinny. She had small but obvious breasts that didn't need a bra, and she knew it was one of her better attributes. She felt empowered by them and was no longer bothered when her nipples showed through her blouse.

So it came as no surprise to her anymore, when someone flirted with her. Although she was embarrassed the first time a woman tried it, she felt more complimented than offended. In truth, her taste ran toward young men, just slightly older than she was. And the twin brothers who just left her bed had just turned thirty. They were perfect, even if they were culturally different.

Their relationship didn't start out as a threesome. In fact, they were office mates who shared the close proximity of working in the same place and seeing each other daily.

Their office, at Transeget Industries, consisted of three sections of space about eight hundred square feet each, separated by half-wall partitions. Clare's sturdy, wooden desk sat alone near the corner of one of those large spaces, which also included a small work-station for a shared printer, a copier and a fax machine. There was also a six-foot worktable that housed a postage stamp-machine, a label printer and the bins for each employee's mail and correspondence.

Next to hers was another open area, along a row of windows that looked out over the gardened courtyard of their one-hundred-year-old building. There was also a ten-person conference table with chairs, and its opposite long-wall held a station for making and serving tea, coffee, snacks and working-lunches. Although there was a small sink and a refrigerator, all the employees usually left the building at the same time for the daily lunch hour.

The brothers shared the next space, which was more of a bull-pen of desks, with half-walls for phone privacy. They were all part of an eight-member, small, administrative services team that handled customer inquiries or minor trouble calls. They routed major trouble calls to the proper sales or field agents. They were also authorized to handle the costs of quick service calls and repairs, and to pay contract workers out of their general fund.

Clare worked for the vice-president of operations as an administrative manager, pretty much running all nonprofit-generating aspects of the business. And although her boss held what was considered quite a prestigious position, his generous office was merely a large, well-appointed, open area, with a mahogany desk and matching arm-chairs, in the corner of the two windowed walls.

If it weren't for her having to open the office door each morning and stay behind to lock it up each evening, it was the perfect work-life for her. Her boss's role was to keep the operations on budget and to meet and greet the major corporate clients in and around London. So, she had plenty of unsupervised time.

Practically all the corporate papers were locked in his desk or in a small credenza behind his desk chair. Only he and Clare had the key to his space and his cabinets.

In all, there were less than a dozen employees in the twenty-four hundred square feet. Clare didn't think anyone would call their group a family, but they were surely close enough to know much about each other's lives, at least about most of them.

The brothers pretty much kept their company to themselves, but worked diligently.

With the exception of her boss, nearly every man in the office had, at one time or another, tried to open a relationship with Clare. But she found it easy to rebuff them, especially the married ones. At one time she worked out the logic that it might be safer to have an affair with a married man, because there would be no strings attached. But as she listened to her girlfriends talk about theirs, they all said they would never date a married man again.

So when the first brother approached her, as she was preparing tea one morning, she thought nothing of it. His conversation was light and breezy and non-threatening. In fact, she was drawn to his lilting and crisp middle-eastern accent, which gave his words a certain rhythm. Looking back, she would be lying if she said she wasn't also attracted to his lean, muscular body.

Clare couldn't say when it happened, but their conversations soon turned to an agreement to head off together for lunch at the local pub. They had a full hour for the mid-day meal, even more if they wanted, since their time was only casually monitored. Soon, it was the three of them sharing lunchtime - Clare and the two brothers.

Their conversations were light, friendly and filled with humor, of which the brothers seemed richly possessed. They could easily make her laugh, and they pranked her regularly about which brother was which. Clare felt she was pretty good at guessing, but frankly, they were identical twins in nearly every feature. They often fooled her to the point she would find herself stealing glances at them, as she tried to see if there was any difference she could discern.

Their lunch dates soon turned from an occasional once-a-week event, to going out together more frequently. And before long, they were meeting daily.

When they first started taking lunch together, they paid for their own meals, but within a couple of weeks, the brothers began taking turns paying for Clare's. At first she objected, but soon found it flattering that someone would do that for her, so she acquiesced.

Clare wanted to reciprocate in some way for the new friendship that was developing. She could not afford to buy three lunches, not even just once a week, so her plan to return the favor was simple and prudent, given her limited income. Although she normally walked to and from work, her apartment was only three tube stops and less than ten minutes away, if she was in a hurry. So, she decided to make the three of them a light lunch in her apartment, instead of going to a deli nearby.

She prepared tea-sandwiches with hard-boiled eggs and others of thin sliced cucumbers, salmon and dill. She also prepared a light dessert. When she was through with the prep of the various fillings, she refrigerated everything until the morning. At that time she would set the spreads in pumpernickel and marbled rye breads without crusts, cut them into tiny wedges, then wrap and refrigerate them until lunch.

Her small studio apartment was clean and neat, and she was not embarrassed to have friends over, even if her bed was in the eating area. It wasn't uncommon for small city flats to be laid out in this manner. She was so excited for company that she could hardly contain herself all morning.

The next day, when Clare proposed they head to her place for a lunch surprise, the brothers heartily agreed and each laughingly took an arm as they whisked her to the Underground station.

Now, six weeks later, her heart still pounded as she recalled how one of the brothers stood between her and her small refrigerator, keeping her from getting to the sandwiches. Keeping eye contact with her, he slowly raised her face to his and lightly kissed her. Although she had secretly longed for it, and this was totally unexpected, she felt no need to resist, melting into his kiss with her lips and her body. But then she was startled as the second brother wrapped his arms around her waist from behind, and leaned his body fully against hers, pressing his lips to her neck.

What happened next was totally spontaneous, as they tore each other's clothes off and stumbled to her bed, kissing and caressing her every step of the way. She had never experienced such an overwhelming rush of sensual pleasure, all over her body, at one time.

After that initial encounter, lunches were always the same, with the three of them having sex together daily. Afterwards, if they ate at all, she would sometimes serve sandwiches. Other times, one or the other of the brothers would run out to a local market. Upon his return, they'd hurriedly eat whatever he bought before they headed back to work. On other days, they would quickly change back into their clothes and head back to work without a noontime meal.

She knew her relationship was the stuff of fantasies, and desperately wanted to tell her closest friend. But the boys had insisted, with no uncertainty, that it was impossible. They were Muslims and it was forbidden for them to be with her like this, so their affair must be kept a secret. It really didn't matter to her that their faith was so different from hers, not that she was a religious person anyway.

But times were changing in London and some Muslims were believed to be hostile to non-Muslims, and others were believed to be outright seditious. None of that mattered to Clare who truly enjoyed their time together and had no intention of walking away from the intense pleasure they repeatedly provided her.

Keeping their secret was fine with her, but it was the most exhilarating experience she had ever had in her young life. When she was between them, her senses were on fire. She felt more alive than she ever thought possible, and she truly wished she could share it with someone.

■ ■ ■ ■ ■

THE EXECUTIVES WHO DEPLOYED MY services traveled in style. But in corporate America, there is a pecking order that determines who has their own luxury jets, sitting in a hangar *just in case* they might have to use them. Others, had access to the corporate fleets, but could be bumped off, depending on their status in the company. Others got to fly and stay first class all the way, but on commercial aircraft.

I made it a practice to travel at the same level as my clients. In many cases, I was put aboard executive helicopters to whisk me off to fix some local emergency. In others, like in this case, where I was traveling for the General Counsel, I made sure I was traveling in style.

Sitting on top of the 747-400 Jumbo Jet gave international travel a whole new meaning. Although the plane seated over four hundred people in this configuration, only twenty-two of them sat in the upper level, accessible by a set of private stairs. These seats were spacious, with a nice distance between them, and the British Airways flight attendant service, already world-class, was a cut or two above that, up here as well.

Although I caught two meals and two movies up there, by the time I got to the hotel, I couldn't remember the meals or the movies. The flight across the Atlantic was just the way I liked it, uneventful. And best of all, it got me to my hotel well before the breakfast hour.

Joanne had my room booked at the Grosvenor House Hotel, which was just opposite Grosvenor Square to the south and practically across the street from the U.S. Embassy, which would be my first stop. My south facing, sixth floor suite gave me a great view of the Square, and the room came with concierge level amenities. So, I had coffee and some rolls sent up while I grabbed a refreshing shower and shaved again. Odds were, however, that other than a possible meeting in the living room or dining room of my suite, I wasn't likely to get to use the nicer features.

Joanne knew I favored the Grosvenor for its history, premium services, and its proximity to the Embassy. It didn't hurt either that I could grab a black cab outside the door on any day or night, and the hotel was only a handful of blocks from the Bond Street Tube station at Oxford Street.

I walked out the entrance and looked eastward into a bright morning sky, quite an anomaly for this springtime of year. The streets were still wet from an evening rain. My suit coat flapped open and my tie blew carelessly in the warm breeze on my face. I was on my way to meet the State Department Regional Security Officer at the U.S. Embassy.

Meeting with these guys had proven so helpful in my investigations around the world, that it became my first stop on nearly every trip. Not only did they provide bread and butter information about the latest conditions, but my clearance very often got me more than the average citizen could get, just walking in off the street. I had called ahead and gotten a fifteen-minute meeting with Herb Lawrence, the RSO attached to the U.S. Embassy in London.

Herb's was a high-profile position with heavy security responsibilities for our Ambassador and other Embassy officials in the UK. The latest attacks by the Irish Republican Army on British soldiers, police and infrastructure placed danger just a step away from our highly visible government officials.

Although we had positive prior contacts with each other, I could tell that getting a quarter of an hour of Herb's time, on short notice, from his staff was a gift. Someone, somewhere had gotten rescheduled or was going to get a shorter audience with him. I knew how lucky I was and I intended to capitalize on my time. Mine was merely a courtesy call for a low-level investigation that didn't, this time, involve any aspect of espionage.

I was ten minutes early for my eight o'clock appointment, but was ushered right in to his office. It was obvious that I hadn't been his first appointment of the day. He was in full-on, high-energy mode.

He walked around his desk to greet me as I entered. "Michael, how nice to see you again. Sit, please sit," he said, as he turned to a coffee set-up. "Black, right?" he asked, as he poured us both steaming cups of coffee from a silver carafe and rushed to place them on a low-boy table between two chairs. "My first of the day," he quipped as he took a careful sip. "So, tell me what is it about a theft that brings you to London? I know something's up, or you'd have sent someone else." Lawrence didn't get where he was by being unobservant.

"You're right, Herb. As you guessed, I'm here at the special request of our General Counsel to try to get our money back from Barclay's. Seems they accepted some forged check signatures and now they don't want to replenish our account. They're playing hardball by their own rules, rather than the Banking Industry's.

"Flannery, our lawyer, wants a buffer between Barclay's and the Law Department to hold off any litigation. He figures I could kill two birds with one stone, handle the investigation and handle the conversation with them." I saw Herb screw up his face at that.

"What's up?" I asked.

"The United States is Great Britain's largest trading partner," he said. "And Barclay's is the UK's largest financial Institution. The country's history and Barclay's go practically hand in hand. For centuries, wherever the UK expanded its territorial reach, Barclay's was hot on its heels to set up a financial infrastructure to advance trade for God and Queen.

"We maintain a close but delicate relationship with Barclay's, to keep a balance that facilitates our trade agreements."

I wondered why that mattered to me. The amount of money we had at risk was statistically insignificant by comparison.

"I'll be nice." I told Herb.

He chuckled. "I've heard about how *nice* you can be, Michael. Try not to get locked up while you're here."

"I'll do my best," I smiled. "I know we're short on time. Is there anything I should be aware of? I really only plan to be in town a few days, mostly visiting my office team for some interviews and then a run over to Barclay's to see what they have to say for themselves."

Herb hesitated, as if he was trying to find the right words. I didn't know him as a man to tread lightly in conversation. He could be diplomatic or direct, but he usually wasn't at a loss for words.

"Look," he said. "You and I both know that you are not licensed in the UK to conduct investigations. But that is neither here nor there to me. Just don't get in trouble. It may even be a good idea to hook up with a friendly constable to serve as your 'shield', if you know what I mean."

I knew what he meant. I was officially here to conduct a corporate, private investigation. But when it came to British citizens, they had their rights protecting them from corporate and law enforcement investigations, which could only be conducted by duly licensed or authorized British citizens. My next official courtesy-stop would be to the Putney Constable station, where our office was located.

He continued, "There's something else. There's really not much you can do to change your risk posture, but our brothers over here have seen an increase in shooting attacks on soldiers and constables, and bombings by the IRA lately. This year alone, we've had three bombings in the area – and all three were really close-in."

"In January there was a satchel bombing on Downing Street, not too far from here. And in April, an explosion occurred just about three miles from here in the metropolitan area. It was a damn truck-bomb, Michael. There was massive damage, three people were killed, nearly a hundred injured, and that was *after* a warning to clear the area."

"And just yesterday, there was another bombing at a Tube station in Hammersmith about three miles the other way from here. That incident had no advance warning, but luckily, no one was killed. The yield on the bomb was pretty low and most of the passengers had boarded their cars or had cleared the station. In that one, the device also had all the earmarks of an IRA explosive device.

"I'm afraid if you are looking for local help, you may find all the constables and Special Branch guys are going to be tied up on these latest attacks.

"Both parties in Parliament have been in

session, scapegoating law enforcement and the intelligence branches, because they have been ineffective in stopping the bombings. And of course it makes great political fodder to stir up their voting bases, with each group trying to show their constituents how much they are doing to stop the atrocities.

"The fact is that neither local law enforcement nor the intelligence agencies are going to be able to bring this to a conclusion. And although only a political solution is going to work, there isn't a soul in that bunch with a practical plan.

"And a final bit of advice," he continued. "If you hear a government warning to clear an area, get the hell out as fast as you can. These guys mean business and most warnings are followed by an actual attack, a bombing of some kind."

Well that surely wasn't the kind of briefing I was expecting and I didn't know quite how to digest it. I rose and extended my hand, "Thanks Herb." I offered lamely. "I'll keep a low profile and will try to stay out of the Tube."

"I wouldn't go that far," he said. "But if you hear the warning ..."

"I know. Get the hell out of there." I replied. As I was escorted through the sign-out process and out the front doors, I thought to myself, *how did this majestic and beautiful country find itself in this dilemma*?

The morning was still fresh and the sky was bright. It was time to head over to our Transeget office just outside London. But first I wanted to dig into a light breakfast in my room, as I laid out my plan for the day. That would give me time to review the personnel files once more, and figure out an explanation for the constables in Putney.

■ ■ ■ ■ ■

THE INVESTIGATION PROCESS IS PRETTY straightforward in cases like these. Introduce yourself to the guy in charge. Find someone who could walk you through the financial payments processes, find out where the checks were kept and who had access to them. That would usually be an employee or a subcontractor. Interview the staff and begin eliminating suspects. Interrogate the suspect, get the signed admission, make specific recommendations for tighter controls, and then head back home. Really simple, in its outline form, actually.

Of course, the local manager would always ask how they should handle the guilty employee. It amazed me how most of these upper level guys had no stomach for making tough decisions on their own.

Oh, they could fire someone or lay off a bunch of workers, for sure. But send them to prison? Not so much. It was always better for them to be able to say, "Christian said we should prosecute them." But I always turned that decision back on them after giving them as many legal and practical talking points as I could. I almost always ended it with, *They're your people, it's your call.*

I picked up the pace back to the Grosvenor House. I had a few hours to grab a light snack and formulate my investigative approach. That would get me to Putney just before their lunch.

■ ■ ■ ■ ■

I LAID THE NINE FOLDERS on my desk and looked at the jacket labels. One vice-president, an office manager and a half dozen or so other staff members.

I knew there were internal controls over such things as access to the office, access to cash and access to financial instruments, like the stolen checks. I needed to find out who had access and whether or not the internal controls were well implemented. So often, they were by-passed to make life easier for the workers. Overriding security was a common event.

There was an electronic access control system at the office. If it was functioning, it would record the entry of all the employees and any maintenance workers who had been granted after-hours access. That would give me some patterns to look at. There was no requirement to present an access control card to the reader when exiting, and there was also the likelihood that employees could piggyback into the space, confusing the obvious record as to who was there or not.

The blank checks would be most likely stored in a lockable desk, credenza or file cabinet. I doubted, given the small size of this office, that they would have a full safe. It would be easy to find out who the key holders were, because there was a Transeget internal control requirement to note such information, along with formal mentions of when keys were issued and to whom. Spare keys also had to be noted with an explanation as to why a replacement was called for.

All that would be left for me to do was interview the most likely suspects, based on access privilege. I was pretty good at getting a final suspect to give an admission statement. And with the additional compelling force of the General Counsel's letters, they pretty much had no choice. All I had to do was decipher if they were telling the truth or not.

Because this was a small office with few employees, the interviews would proceed a lot faster. There was no way to know if someone may have a lot to tell, or if someone might take a bit more convincing to admit to the theft, but interviewing five or six folks was a lot faster than interviewing fifteen or twenty.

As I projected how this might go, I figured I would get to Barclay's tomorrow, with my investigation notes and an admission in hand. Then we could begin the slow dance of getting our money back. I might even extend my time here a bit and take in an opera or a play tomorrow night and do some shopping the next day, before heading back to the States.

I used the in-room phone to call the Putney Constabulary to see if I could get a meeting with a Detective. When I explained the nature of my visit, which was basically a courtesy call to let them know I was in their area on a routine matter for Transeget, I was politely told to stop by and, if a

Detective was available, they'd meet with me. *Quite accommodating*, I thought.

I packed my notes and files into my briefcase and headed down to the concierge. I needed to know whether it was better to take a black cab or the tube to Putney.

■ ■ ■ ■ ■

PUTNEY WAS A PRETTY GOOD-SIZED town, which surprised me for some reason. I was expecting a small village, given that it's a suburb of the town of Wandsworth. The ride took only about 30 minutes and the police station was only a couple blocks from the Tube stop.

The constable station was quite a surprise. Located on a busy downtown thoroughfare, it was light and modern and occupied a small but efficient, ground floor corner office space, in a larger office building. The front door was unlocked, and neither the reception area nor the back offices were protected by bulletproof glass. How different than in the States.

I approached the front desk, introduced myself and presented my business card to the desk sergeant. I could see that being in corporate security didn't impress him, regardless of the title on my card. Trying to be flattering, I said, "Back in my days on the Detroit Police Department, I would never have guessed that someday I'd be standing in an office of the Metropolitan Police Force." That had the effect I hoped it would.

"You were a police officer in Detroit, in the States?" he asked. I nodded in the affirmative and he reached down and shook my hand. "It's an honor," he said. "How can we help you?"

I asked if there was a detective constable I could talk with briefly, just to check in as a matter of courtesy. Promising to find out, he left the front reception area and walked out of sight to the rear.

In a few brief minutes, the sergeant returned, accompanied by a man in his late 30s, dark black hair, wearing a dark grey suit that hung on a body that looked more like a squat fireplug. If he had been another foot taller, he could have passed for a professional football player. As I learned later, he was a semi-professional rugby player and looked tough as nails.

He leaned toward me and extended a hard hand, "Marley," he said. "Detective Inspector, David Marley. C'mon back." And with that he motioned for me to follow him to the back office area.

He pulled his chair around from behind his desk and sat across from me as I gave him the ten-second overview of the case. "So," he repeated. "How can we be of service?"

I really didn't have a request for service and his overly friendly offer caught me pleasantly off guard. "I'm just here on a courtesy call, Inspector, but thanks for your offer. My plan is to run over to our office, interview a few folks, and hopefully crack this case this afternoon. From there it will be a trip to Barclays to get our money back into our account before I fly back."

He asked for and I gave him the address to our facility. "Do you know where that is?" He asked. I indicated that I didn't but was willing to take a cab.

He leaned over to the corner of his desk, grabbed his keys and said, "No need. I'll give you a lift."

It was as simple as that. We stood and walked out the back door to his black Jaguar sedan. It was a clean, but used vehicle and had no police markings on it. Marley, seeing me eyeing the luxury car, said, "It's an older one, and it's my personal vehicle." Although there were no markings on his car, he did have a blue, magnetic, roof-mountable, light for emergencies.

As we drove, I learned that, regardless of the good size of the town, there were very few cases that tied him to his desk, and being out allowed him to run an errand, "Just up the road," as he called it.

In our conversation, I learned that Marley, as it turned out, was also the head of the police security detail for Wimbledon, or as it was more properly known, The All England Lawn Tennis and Croquet Club, in the next large community to the south.

I was familiar with Wimbledon. It was one of the hallowed, major tournament venues for professional tennis. I was impressed. "Look," he said. "If you like, I can come in and handle some of the interviews with you and cut down on your time requirement. Then we can run up the road and drop off some things, and you can come with me." I had to admit, the offer to visit Wimbledon sounded intriguing. I'd love a personal tour of that place, and Alice would be so envious. But I needed to stay focused.

There was another matter as well. I was a bit worried about having the police involved at this stage of the game.

49

In the States, if a private investigator operates with, or acts under the color of law, he becomes a de facto *police agent* bound by the same rules of evidence as an officer. As a private investigator, I had no such boundaries, nor did I have to advise a person of his or her rights, when I begin to suspect them of being the perpetrator. At least that was the case in the States. I wasn't so sure about the rules in the United Kingdom.

I politely declined his help and he seemed to take it in good stride, saying he was going to drop me off and head up to the Club for a bit. We shook hands and I thanked him. As I turned to the entrance of our building, I turned all my attention to meeting our office vice president. The investigation began.

■ ■ ■ ■ ■

IT WAS NOT YET FIVE-THIRTY in the morning and the young man would be through here in a couple hours. Then, he would use the provided shower in the water closet to wash the smells off his skin and hair, even though there was only cold water.

Except for the hushed buzz of his small blenders, it was cool and quiet in the dimly lit storage area he rented off Caddington Street, near the Euston station. He had painted all the lower-level windows a pale, translucent blue on the inside, to keep passersby from looking in, while still providing some light.

He could afford a nicer location, but it wasn't necessary. Keeping secret what he was doing was more important to him than any minor discomfort. And being close to the train stations got him anywhere he wanted to go without resorting to using the truck until it was necessary.

Had he known though, he might still have picked another location. He was working less than six blocks from the offices of MI5, the British domestic intelligence-gathering organization, charged with terrorist oversight.

Fortunately for him, and although the government location was a secret kept in plain sight, their entire resource was focused on the IRA terrorist group operating out of the north, the people they thought responsible for the Hammersmith bombing. It was as if he didn't exist.

With singular focus, he watched as the three glass mixing-bowls rotated on their pedestals, with their speed on the lowest setting. Their wearisome whirring was barely audible, but he paid close attention to every revolution. Small Bunsen burners kept the liquid heated to the precise temperature he wanted, and he tested them regularly with a candy thermometer. He adjusted the burners as the liquid evaporated to a tacky residue. Too low and his entire process would be ineffective. Too high and the product could be wasted, not to mention there could be a catastrophic fire. He eyed the fire extinguishers he had placed throughout the small unit and wondered if he could get to any one of them if there was a fire. He mentally rehearsed the process for activating an extinguisher one more time, then pushed the thought from his mind.

His eyes crossed the room to his steel worktables. Nearby, neatly stacked on wooden pallets, were his latest purchases, bought from different stores, so as not to cast suspicion, or to create a memory of the purchase.

The five, twenty-and-a-half liter, commercial grade pressure cookers were still in their boxes, unopened. It wouldn't matter if they reached temperature correctly. It was only necessary that they could hold pressure and tightly seal the contents he was preparing in this very room.

On the opposite wall, and also stacked on pallets, were twenty, twenty-five-pound bags of ammonium nitrate. It was simple to acquire this common fertilizer for plant nutrition, but he was careful to buy them at different nurseries as well. His main goal was to keep the fertilizer off the floor, dry and cool for now, and separate from any combustible materials.

Later, it would become the destructive propellant for his thousands of projectiles. The explosive force alone would do massive damage, sending a circular shock wave outward at supersonic speeds, rendering nearly everything nearby into shreds or shards, pushing them along at murderous force.

He walked over to the wooden barrel that contained the bits of metal. There were small but case-hardened nuts and bolts, double-ought buckshot pellets, thick-shanked roofing nails, and sharp-cornered blades of steel, no more than two inches long. The shrapnel pieces were acquired from scrap yards or bought from different hardware stores.

He had regularly dampened the contents of the barrel to ensure they were rusting properly on their surfaces, and they were. Besides traumatically shredding bones and flesh, he was going for the next level of havoc, toxic infection. This time, he was going after victims, not just buildings. His goal was to create fear and a sense of helpless frustration. Terror begins when lives are at stake, and when people feel unsafe, not merely when structures are blown up.

It was all so simple, so effective, so deadly.

He had switched out the mixers' metal blades for flatter plastic paddles, to allow the bowls of peroxide to condensate more evenly, while at the same time reducing the unlikely possibility of a spark, to zero. A small window fan blew quietly nearby, sucking the air outward to keep the vapors from becoming overwhelming, and to prevent the residue from concentrating too soon.

At the other end of the room, he was doing the same with common acetone, or paint thinner. He walked deliberately back and forth between the two blending tables, watching the activity with the skill of a lab chemist. Soon they would be ready to be mixed.

It was a long, slow and deliberate process, but he was a deliberate man. There was no room for hurry in an activity where any hasty mistake could be fatal. He was on edge throughout the entire process, but it was a controlled nervousness that he channeled, to ensure there were no errors.

Although the final Tri-Acetone, Tri-Peroxide solutions would become exponentially more volatile, he knew how to keep them safely separated until the time came to combine them into the explosive detonator TATP, just as his instructor had taught him. Then they would be ready for his next mission, and so would he. One more field test, then soon the whole world would realize that no one was safe.

While he waited, he prayed.

■ ■ ■ ■ ■

THE THREE MEN DIDN'T REALLY expect anyone else to be in the building. Nevertheless, they took precautions about every aspect of this side of their lives, and spoke in hushed whispers. Indeed, it was entirely possible that MI5 or MI6 might be listening in, but they doubted it. There was no way the authorities would have the guts to try to obtain a warrant to listen, much less record a conversation, especially theirs.

Times had changed in London since the beginning of the Muslim immigration. Tens of thousands of Muslims had gone from having no places of worship to having the British government subsidize, if not outright finance the building of mosques.

High-level British officials attended mosque openings with pomp and handshakes, celebrating an emerging brotherhood that would never occur. And liberal officials now rebuffed every attempt by the more conservative voices that accused radical Muslims of recruiting for a jihad against the West. It was even considered racist to use the word *terrorist* and *Muslim* in the same sentence, even with the qualifier of *radical* to distinguish from other

54

Muslims. And coordinated efforts by Muslim lobbyists around the world ensured their representatives stoked the fear of xenophobia, to keep law enforcement agencies at bay.

No, there would be no one listening or recording, especially not here. And there was one more element in their favor. All the resources of the British government were focused on the IRA bombings.

This mosque was where the Hezbollah operatives, under the protection of their Imam and the cover of the mosque, planned and financed their proxy warrior. The meeting was merely to update the Imam about their last deposit into a separate mosque account, which, by law, was not reviewable.

The twins smiled and bowed, whispering, *ma al-salamah,* "with peace", as they left the Al-Irschad Mosque.

Once they got outside they spoke in whispered tones. "Do you think he suspects?"

"No. If he did, we would be dead by now. I do not believe he knows about us keeping a part of what we steal for ourselves. And he seems not to care how we get it. He takes Iran's and our money and uses it as he pleases, whatever that is."

"That is not what I meant," said the other. "Do you think he knows about her?"

There was a moment of silence. "No. If he did, all three of us would be dead. He has left what we do, and the way we operate, to our own invention. And that works to our advantage. But he has his limits. It is best if he never has reason to suspect our connection to her."

The brothers walked through the alley to its

opening at the sidewalk, before heading the few blocks to their home.

■ ■ ■ ■ ■

MARLEY DROPPED ME AT THE front door and drove off on his errands. Before I went in, I stood and looked at the dark brown, brick façade of this older building. It was beautiful not merely because it stood as a testament to its history, but because it was a visual compliment to its construction crews. The brick had never been sandblasted to clean it, yet the stones glistened as if they were new. The wood frame windows obviously bore many coats of paint over the decades, but they seemed to have been applied with care. And the glass within them bowed with age.

Transeget's Putney office was a second-floor walkup. In the States, the visual demonstration of corporate success was to have your business housed in a beautiful, new building of contemporary architecture. New and modern furniture of the latest ergonomic design would grace the interior space, while guests waited in a vestibule of corporate opulence.

Here, in the land of kings and queens, going back for millennia, success was measured by performance alone, and some of the most powerful people in the world were housed in office buildings, made-over from homes and apartments, that were over one hundred years old. Such was the case with TI's offices.

The wooden stairs leading to the second floor office were original, and bore no signs of repair or replacement, or damage from the intense Nazi bombings of World War Two. The dark hallway was fitted with a handrail when the structure was built. Skilled trades crafted the stairs and the rail, and neither squeaked a bit.

At the top of the stairs, I turned the knob on the door, marked with our name in gold gilt on opaque glass, and found it unlocked. This was supposed to be an access control door, yet the magnetic locking mechanism was not functioning. There was also a key override on the door and that was not latched either. Glancing at my watch I saw that it was still a bit into the standard lunch hour.

Figuring our manager might be taking his lunch inside, I pushed in the door and entered. I heard feet shuffling towards me from around a partition, and a young man, in business casual attire, soon came into view. He wore our TI logo embroidered on his black golf shirt, so I made him for an employee.

"May I help you?" he asked cautiously.

I glanced around inside at the neatly equipped office but didn't see anyone else. I handed him my business card and said, "My name is Michael Christian and I'm the head of security for TI. I'd like to speak with your manager. I don't have an appointment, but I'm sure he'll see me."

He looked at my card and took the time to read it carefully. He looked up at me and back at the card as if doubting its originality, or unsure how he should react to a stranger showing up without an appointment.

I was about to take the conversation down that path when he said, "I'm sorry, Mr. Hardy isn't in at the moment, but I do expect him back shortly. Would you like to come back? I could have him call you for a time when he is sure to be here." He began moving toward the door, as if inviting me to follow.

I kicked that idea around for a bit, but Putney wasn't exactly across the street from my hotel and I still wanted the element of surprise. "If you have a place for me to sit, I'd prefer to wait, thank you." I stepped by him and walked inside the office with him following close behind. As he closed the door behind me, I turned back to him and asked, "The electronic strike didn't seat on the door and I see that you didn't lock it. Why not?"

He looked at me, turned toward the door for a moment, as if the answer was written on a note and taped to the door, and then back to me before replying.

"A while ago, we turned it off during business hours." He explained. "It was becoming troublesome to always have to fish our access cards out of our pockets and use them to get in and out of the office. The loo is out the door and down that hallway. We always had to remember our cards, or we'd have to knock and disturb someone to get up and open the door, to let us back in. So, we asked, at a team meeting, if Mr. Hardy would turn off the system during the day. Besides, no one ever comes here to visit. It's an operation center, mostly."

I opened my arms at my side, with my body language saying, *and yet here I am*. He nodded, immediately getting it. I was doing an internal slow burn at the cavalier way management took the loss of nearly a half-million dollars, as demonstrated by the fact the damn door was still unlocked.

As if to move the conversation away from the topic of locks, he offered, "If you like, you can sit here at this desk, or in one of the lounge chairs. May I fix you a cup of tea?" He saw my hesitation for a moment and recognized, by my accent, that I was from the States. "We do have coffee also, but I would have to put on the water for a fresh pot."

I thanked him, deciding to sit at the desk, so I could organize my work papers while I waited. "Yes. I would like some coffee. Black, thank you." I wasn't so much interested in the coffee, but I noticed the amenities counter would require him to turn his back to me. I wanted to get the lay of the land as quickly as I could, while not being conspicuous about it.

I think he sensed it too, because he turned to look over his shoulder at me as I made myself comfortable, opening my briefcase and extracting my files. He finally turned away.

The office was set up primarily as a utilitarian space with a bullpen of workstations in the center, each equipped with a telephone, a computer terminal and keyboard. A set of plug-in headphones, connected to the telephone-set, was draped over each empty chair. The TI logo swirled slowly on every terminal, as the screen savers attempted to keep the glass from etching while they sat idle.

In the corner was a fairly large office area with a glass wall section, without a door, that I figured to be Hardy's. Sitting outside of that was a very orderly desk, displaying a multi-button telephone, propped next to a computer terminal and keyboard. This desk was different in that it featured a small bud vase with sprigs of larkspur, stock, and a pale, pink lily with blood red anthers. A small, lightweight cream-colored sweater was neatly draped over the back of the chair, instead of headphones. I guessed it was Clare's, the admin manager.

I didn't see a floor-safe, but along the far wall, the file cabinet lock buttons were all depressed. Somewhere in this room would be the storage container for one or two books of blank checks with four chits missing from their sequence. The checks were originally stolen from Clare's desk, but I wondered where they kept them now.

Looking through my notes, I found the Barclay's photocopies of the front of the forged checks. They were numbered *thirteen twenty-one*, *fourteen sixty-three*, *fifteen zero-eight*, and *fifteen ninety-four*. The four checks were not taken all at the same time. Or, if they were, the thief took them in random order from different pages in the book or books. I wondered if they were torn out or carefully removed along their perforated edges. One method would indicate haste, the other the deliberation of someone who knew he could take his time. I'd have those questions answered shortly.

I could hear the coffee finishing its brew and also heard the clinking of a porcelain mug being retrieved from a shelf. Soon, my reluctant host was walking the steaming cup over to me. As he approached, I said, "You know my name, but I'm afraid I don't know yours."

Again there was that hesitation, as if maybe he didn't want me to know, or perhaps he was still suspicious of my intent. I let him mull it over.

"I'm Nidal Halima. I staff one of the call center's trouble desks."

"What does that entail, Nidal?" I asked.

"Customers throughout England, experiencing lower level difficulties, call in to this office. Depending on the nature of the problem, I can walk them through a script we have to help them resolve their issue over the phone. If it is too complex, or requires a firmware fix, I take the order and route it out to our service department."

I recognized Halima's name as one of our employees, and glancing down at my notes, confirmed my understanding of its spelling. There was another employee here by the same last name.

I noticed that the phones weren't ringing. "Is this a slow period?" I asked.

"No," he replied. "During lunch hour, or when we are all in team meetings, we roll the phones over to an automated voice attendant where the caller can leave a message and we will get back with them as soon as we are able."

"Well, I'm glad you were here when I arrived, Nidal. Otherwise, I wouldn't know where to find the coffee while I waited." He knew I was alluding to the fact the door was unlocked during business hours. He was contemplating a remark, when I continued, "Did you not go to lunch today?"

"Yes, I did," he replied. "I have been out and came back early."

"Well," I said. "Don't let me interrupt you. Please feel free to go about your business. You don't have to entertain me."

As he sat at his desk, he turned to me and said, "It won't be long now. Everyone should be back in about five or ten minutes."

It was twelve-fifty so I guessed lunch hour ended at one o'clock. Looking at my watch reminded me of how tired I was from an evening flight across the Atlantic. I had been awake since five o'clock yesterday morning.

Within minutes, I could hear him talking softly into his mouthpiece, apparently back at work.

■ ■ ■ ■ ■

I OPENED MY NOTEBOOK AND made my first observation-based, investigative entries. *Office door unlocked. Insider or outsider theft? Where are checks kept? Why is N. Halima back early? Who else comes back early?*

Halima was right. Within minutes, employees began walking into the office, sometimes in pairs and some by themselves. Everyone took the time to look at me, then at Halima. He merely shrugged his shoulders as they passed, not indicating he knew who I was. But when the admin manager entered, he rose from his seat and approached her along with the man she entered with. He must have told her who I was because she made her way straight for me. I noticed, however, that Nidal grabbed the other fellow's arm and walked him back out the door.

"Good afternoon," she said. "My name is Clare Bennett. I'm Mr. Hardy's administrative manager. May I help you?" It wasn't lost on me that Halima must have told her I was here to see her boss, but she was going to hear it for herself. I actually gave her points for that.

Handing my business card to her, I repeated my introduction and continued. "I don't have an appointment, but I've traveled from the States to meet with Mr. Hardy, and as a heads up, you might want to clear his calendar for the remainder of the afternoon."

I could tell I offended her proper British way of doing business right off, by assuming a superior role in her chain of command, and showing up without an appointment. But I was making a point about how the investigation would proceed. It was going to be no nonsense, and no begging off from it because of "other commitments." I was sure she would convey that unspoken message to her boss as soon as he walked in the door, which was nearly immediately.

He was in his late-thirties well groomed, and well dressed. He wore a grey sport coat over the black TI logo golf shirt, like the rest of his team had on, all except Clare that is. His manner stated simply, *I run this office*, and the team seemed quite comfortable in his bearing.

He glanced toward me and realized he would have to walk right by my desk to get to his office. But before that happened, Clare walked up to him and hustled him off to the side. I could not make out the words of their hushed conversation, but I certainly understood the tone of her message. I did, however, hear him exclaim loudly, "What?" They talked a bit more before he made his way to his office without even looking at me. Clare returned to my desk looking a bit flushed.

"Mr. Hardy will see you Mr. Christian, but he has limited time this afternoon. You see, he has other appointments."

With that, she stood back from my desk as if to say, *Follow me*. I rose, gathered my notes into my briefcase, made sure I had a business card in my hand and followed her as she instructed.

I entered the spartanly equipped office and noticed that his minimalistic decorative style also went so far as to exclude diplomas, credentials, or certifications. There were no family or pet pictures. The message I got from it all was, *I am here to do business, not to get to know you, or you me*. That was fine by me. But it also said, *I don't feel personally connected to being here*.

I set my briefcase down on the seat of the guest chair, leaned forward and offered him my business card with one hand, while extending my other in greeting and introduced myself. He took both perfunctorily and motioned me to sit. He had yet to speak a word.

As I reached down into my briefcase I said, "I'd like to extend greetings to you from my boss, Barry Brinton. He asks that you extend me every courtesy." I knew Hardy was banking on the fact that his title outranked mine and that he would control the meeting pace and its time allotment. I took that card off the table by way of letting him know that I reported to the highest level in the corporation.

Then I set the next play in motion. "I also extend to you the personal greeting of our General Counsel, Patrick Flannery for whom I speak, and who has chartered this investigation." I saw his throat catch when I mentioned Flannery, and it caught again when I referred to this being an investigation. Now I had his attention. What I needed next was his total and honest cooperation.

I knew it seemed like I was hammering on him, but Hardy wasn't off my suspect list and he had told Clare to prepare me for a short day on the basis of other appointments. I didn't know if he had any or not, but it wouldn't matter at this point. I handed him the first of the letters.

"This is a formal statement of the investigation and of your role and mine. Please read it." Then I sat.

Hardy sat and put on reading glasses, as he deliberately and slowly read, then re-read the letter from Flannery. It was clear, terse and left no room for misinterpretation. The final lines advised Hardy he must sign the letter, which was merely an acknowledgement that he had read it, or resign from his employment with the company.

Hardy rose from his desk and walked to the edge of the glass wall. "Clare," he said. "Hold all my calls and cancel all my appointments for today."

He returned to his desk, signed the letter and said, "What can I do for you?"

Perfect.

I began, more politely now, continuing with some small talk to soften the mood a bit, because this was not an interrogation, at least not at this stage, and Hardy seemed openly cooperative. But now it was time to cut to the chase.

"So that we begin on an equal footing of understanding, I'm here to look into the theft of checks from your unused check supply, their subsequent forgery and the loss of nearly a half million U.S. dollars in value from our account at

Barclays. I'm also here on behalf of Flannery to try to get that money back into our account."

Hardy interrupted, "Do you really think you can get them to redeposit that money? They are one of the most powerful banking institutions in the world and act like it. Not only have they refused to put our money back into our account, but they have closed ranks to the point they won't even return my calls anymore."

I could see where that was going to be a problem, but that was down the road. "Let's focus first on the investigation aspects, Mr. Hardy," I continued.

He interrupted, "Please call me Darryn." He seemed sincere and open with his request, and didn't seem to be couching his invitation within a hidden agenda.

I proceeded, "As I reviewed the internal audit report and your call to our European counsel, you reported that at some unknown time, four valid, blank checks were stolen from your unused check supply.

"Subsequently a signature was forged, and they were cashed to a combined amount of over three hundred thousand British pounds, which is about five hundred thousand U.S. dollars. Is that right?"

"Well, yes, somewhat," Hardy answered. "You see, we have the exact dates they were cashed and the Barclay branch number. I didn't have that information when I called, but it now shows on the deposit record. But you are correct, I do not know when they were taken."

I was aware of that, but it was a good sign that Hardy was offering the details.

"Tell me about the signatures," I asked. To me

they all seemed the same, illegible. But maybe he recognized something about them.

He said, "I can't make out what it says. Most of the characters seem to be merely tight, wavy lines rather than letters."

He was right about that. The signatures were deliberately made in an attempt to obscure the identity of the maker. Barclays would have the original copies and they either might or might not release them to me for a handwriting analysis or sample comparison, if I ever came up with a suspect.

The four checks were cashed on different dates, but within a few days of each other, and at a Barclay's branch outside Central London.

I noted to Hardy that all four checks had been counter signed by a numbered account when they were deposited. "Any idea who that might be?" I asked.

"None," he replied.

Finding that person would be a solid lead, if I could get Barclays to release the information to me. I had to be careful not to walk into Barclays and ask for help with the case, if I planned to play hardball with them afterwards. I decided to leave that for later in the day.

"Tell me, Darryn, who has a key to the storage compartment for the checks?" I asked.

"That's simple," he said right away. "Only me and Clare."

He was right. It was pretty simple. He seemed pretty calm about inking himself back onto my suspect list.

"May I see your key," I asked. With that, he leaned back to the coat tree behind his desk, reached into his jacket pocket and pulled out a key ring. He leafed through the half dozen keys, separated it from the others on the ring and handed it to me. It was a small gold colored key, but felt like brass. It was stamped on both sides *WH* and beneath those two letters it was stamped *2A3*. I was reminded of the British and Canadian mail coding systems. I asked about the markings.

"WH is the furniture maker's mark, William Hands. They have been making office furniture in the UK for over a hundred years. My desk and Clare's are William Hands desks. The others are less expensive and more utilitarian.

"The *2A* is their desk model and the *3* is our key numbering system. My key is number three and Clare's is number two."

"Who has key number one?" I asked.

"Well, originally, I had number one, but I seemed to have lost it several months ago. I may have lost it at the gym, but I'm not sure. So, I took the spare from the key cabinet and logged it out to me."

I was encouraged to know that he had followed the protocol of logging the key to himself, but concerned that a missing key complicated the access issue. I had serious doubts as to how the key could have accidentally made its way off his key ring, based on the effort it took to get this one off.

"Let me ask you, where did you keep key number one, the one you lost?"

"Yes, that's the problem," he said. "I kept it on this key ring, just like the one I gave you."

Something didn't make sense with that. He either lost it, or conveniently reported it lost about the time the checks disappeared. I didn't have enough yet to press harder on that, so moved on.

"Tell me, why does Clare have a key?"

Hardy, leaned over to his right, opened the half drawer in his desk and retrieved a manila folder. He opened it, leafed through a few papers and handed one of them to me.

It was a bank document showing that Clare was an authorized signer for up to seven hundred and seventy-five British pounds. "This is for office administrative purposes," Hardy said. "I am often out on day-trips, or longer, and this amount, roughly one thousand dollars, keeps the office running for larger emergency purchases, like a printer gone bad, if you know what I mean?"

Clare having a key to the check-supply made sense. "In a moment, I'd like to see where the checks were stored when they were stolen. But first, I have just a few more questions.

"When I came here this afternoon, the office door was unlocked and I was free to enter. Fortunately, Halima was here to greet me. When I asked about it, he told me the door was not locked during business hours, including during lunchtime. Is that correct?"

For the first time since we began his interview, Hardy looked uncomfortable. "Yes," he answered quietly. "Several months ago, at one of our team meetings, a request was made to unlock the door during business hours. At first, I was reluctant to acquiesce, but the more we discussed it, the more it made sense from an operating perspective and it seemed good for morale. Leaving calls unanswered several times a day to open the door for visitors, or for employees coming and going, was a nuisance and a service disruption. We had never had a problem before, so I agreed. And things have been running without a problem ever since. That is except for the embarrassing moment when you walked in."

I thought to myself, of course you'd never had a problem. *The doors were locked.*

"Yes, there was that," I responded. "And that little matter of a half million dollars in checks walking out that door too. I do hope you realize that the unlocked door may have been a contributing factor to the ease of access." I wasn't going to let him off the hook that easily.

"So, here are couple things for you to think about Darryn. The unlocked door makes it nearly impossible for me to use access control records to look for any anomaly in activity that might help me isolate a suspect. I'm sure you can see the fact that your key mysteriously disappeared off your key ring, is problematic, as well.

"Those seemingly careless acts may have allowed an employee, with authorized access, to enter the building, or made it possible for some stranger, who had the balls or the knowledge, to just walk in through an unlocked door, and get into our space.

"Then, that same someone also found a key to the unused check repository, got in there, and stole four of our checks. That someone was awfully lucky to have found an unidentifiable key, with no address on it, and then managed to find our unlocked building, then knew where to look for blank checks. Does that seem to be about right?" I asked.

Before he could formulate his answer, I said, "I have one more observation. The person who stole and cashed the checks could be an employee, who is already authorized into our space and who has a key. Right?"

At that point, Hardy could clearly see that he and Clare were very high on my suspect lists.

"Yes," he stammered. "I mean, no! Clare would never do such a thing. She has worked for me for four years and I respect and trust her totally. And one more thing," he said. "I didn't do this and have no knowledge of anyone who would have or could have."

I wasn't surprised by his answers. Guilty or innocent, he practically had to give the same answers. The thing was, I almost felt, without any rational explanation, that he was telling the truth.

"Let me ask you Darryn, who brought up the idea of unlocking the front door?"

He seemed to be trying to remember accurately. His expression didn't suggest he was trying to fabricate an answer, but rather that he was trying to draw it up from his direct memory.

"I'm not sure actually." He said. "It might have been Nidal or his brother, Ahmad. But then, like I said, I'm not sure. It could have been anyone on my team. I don't keep minutes of team meetings." I made a note of the answer.

"Okay, Darryn. Let's move on. Where are the unused checks kept and where is the check register kept?"

He rose from his desk. "I'll show you."

I followed, grabbing my notebook and the next letter. I pretty much knew where he was going.

We walked outside his office to Clare's desk.

"Clare, would you get the check books for us please?" I noticed he said "books". At that point the entire work team had turned their attention to us. I sensed that by now, they all knew who the stranger was in their office.

Clare reached down to her lower right desk drawer and pulled it open. No key required. Hardy saw that at the same time I did and paled. "Clare," he asked urgently. "Why is the drawer unlocked?"

"Oh," she said, "I unlocked it when I came back from lunch. Otherwise, when I am out of the office, I lock it."

I interrupted. "Clare, I have something I want you to read and handed her the letter. I waited until she had a chance to read it completely before asking her to sign and acknowledge. She did so without any sense of pressure.

"Clare," I began. "When you go down the hall to the loo, do you lock your desk?"

She hesitated just that brief moment and she saw me notice it. "Clare, remember. You have to be completely honest."

"Most of the time, I do. Yes, of course," she answered. "But if everyone is here, I almost think we are all watching out for each other, so sometimes I quickly just run down the hall and back."

I noticed she was a smoker and asked her, "When you go out for a smoke, do you lock the drawer each and every time without fail?" I asked.

"Mostly," she replied. Then, "Yes I think so. Yes. Now I'm confused. I'd say yes. When I go for a smoke, I am gone a few minutes longer than just running down the hall, so I lock the desk. You have to remember that it is my work desk and I keep other things in that drawer because it locks, like my purse. So, while I may not use the check book for a few days, I keep it locked most all the time anyway."

That wasn't as clean an answer as I would have liked, so I decided to push a little more. "Clare, I want you to think a bit before you answer me. Is there anyone you know of who has expressed an interest in the contents of this drawer?"

She answered nearly immediately, "No. No one." That was too fast.

"Clare, I want you to go slow and *think* about your answer. Has anyone in any way, at any time, talked with you about the checks, your desk, your purse, the cigarettes or makeup in your purse, your keys, or why you lock or don't lock your desk?"

I watched her body movements, her face and eyes for signs of deceit. I saw her eyes reflex correctly as she tried to draw upon her memory, rather than try to make up an answer. That was a good sign.

But then it happened. Her recall mode changed to realization mode. And her eye directions changed from recall mode to a creative-response mode. Not a good sign.

She looked downward as she answered, then at Hardy, rather than me. "No," she said. I can't think of anything."

"Clare," I said looking directly into her eyes, "Are you sure? Anything even innocently asked about, or talked about, relative to the checks? This is very important. Was it someone in the office?"

She folded her arms across her chest, leaned back in her chair, stretched her legs completely straight toward me and said firmly, "No, I told you *No*. Why do you keep asking me?"

Hardy said, "She's already answered, Christian.

She said no one has asked her or talked about it. What more do you want? Would you like her to lie to you?"

I was furious that Hardy would interrupt me, but had to manage him properly. Of course I didn't want a witness to lie. But I didn't want a witness who was lying, or withholding what could be important information, to get off that easily from my questioning.

I ignored Hardy and turned my back to him as I talked with Clare. "I know you have more to offer Clare and you know it too." She didn't object. I pressed my card into her hand and said, "You can call my office in the States and they will see I get a message at my hotel, or you can call there yourself, if you are comfortable with that, and leave a message for me at the Grosvenor. Think about it some more. When you are ready, call me."

I stood and looked at Hardy and was ready to respond to him when Detective Inspector Marley walked into the office. He looked around the office until we made eye contact.

Although I was surprised to see him, it was a pleasant surprise. I nodded him over. "I didn't expect to see you here."

Marley replied, "What's up?"

"Darryn Hardy, I'd like you to meet Detective Inspector Marley of the Metropolitan Police out of Putney. Marley, this is Darryn Hardy, he runs this operation." I then turned to Hardy and said, "Let's return to your office."

The entire office was now aware that not only was there a Metropolitan Police Detective in the room, and that not only was I well aware of who he was, but I was managing the introduction. That ought to take the curiosity level up a bit.

■ ■ ■ ■ ■

AS WE ENTERED HARDY'S OFFICE, I quickly brought Marley up to speed. "The front door is unlocked all day and also when the office is unoccupied at lunch. There are only two key holders to the check storage area and I've had superficial interviews with them both, Clare Bennet, the admin, and with Mr. Hardy here.

"Darryn says he didn't do it, as does Clare. Oh, and Hardy reports that a couple months ago, his key disappeared and he is using a replacement. Since he didn't replace Clare's key, I am betting the lock wasn't changed. Is that right Darryn?"

Hardy's look betrayed the realization of his error by not replacing the lockset and issuing two new keys. The cost of that simple repair would have been less than one hundred dollars.

"What I'd like to do," I continued to Marley, "is to take formal signed statements from each of them to that effect. And let's explore what they perhaps may inadvertently be aware of about the behavior of others, or find out if they know something they aren't telling me." I directed that comment right to Hardy.

"David, why don't you talk with Mr. Hardy here, and I'll have another run at Clare, only this time in private." I turned to Hardy, "Do you have a place where I can interview her in private?"

"Yes," he replied. "Clare can take you to it."

Despite his rank, Marley seemed perfectly content in helping out. In fact, he seemed eager. I reached into my briefcase and handed him another narrow-ruled notepad and was reaching for a pen to give him, when he produced his own Meisterstuck Classique ballpoint pen. Again, I wondered about a Detective Inspector driving a Jaguar, and writing his daily notes with a pen that cost several hundred dollars.

Marley saw the question in my eyes and rolled the barrel revealing the logo of The Wimbledon Club. "A gift from the president of the Club," was all he said.

As I nodded and walked out to talk with Clare, I heard Marley say to Hardy, "Well now, shall we begin?"

When I turned towards Clare, I saw Nidal talking with her. He looked up as I approached and returned to his desk. Clare had obviously been crying.

"Are you okay?" I asked.

She nodded and dried her eyes with a balled-up tissue.

I went straight for it. She had information I needed and I had to figure out how to get it from her. I started out easy.

"Clare, we got interrupted when I was asking you about the checks. I'd like to see the check stock you have in that drawer."

This time, she reached for her keys. There were only two keys on a loop of woven yarn, formed into a mini lanyard and wrapped around her wrist. "Clare, what's the other key for?" I asked.

"That is the key to the front door. If the power

76

goes down, the doors fail to a secured mode and we need a key to override the lock to get in. Only Darryn and I have a key."

And there I was again. Only two key holders. If I were to presume that a key holder got in and took the checks, the first assumption had to be her or Hardy. Yet again the unlocked door factored heavily in the investigation. My investigation closing report would drive that home.

Clare withdrew one large leather-bound check supply book and one envelope of the same dimensions but not as thick as a full book. The envelope was unsealed.

The pages of checks were bound into the book on pegs screwed to the binding, while the numbered checks were attached to each corresponding register stub by a perforated edge. The process was pretty simple. Annotate onto the check stub the date, the payee and the purpose. Write the check amount on the register, and do the same to the check. Then tear out the check, leaving the stub of information in the book.

What was of particular interest to me was that there were two supplies of checks, one that had been bound into the ledger, and one that was still in its delivery envelope.

I asked her to show me from where, in the book, the missing checks were taken.

"This is our current register," she said. "It holds two hundred checks. Our current numbering sequence began with twelve hundred one and runs through fourteen hundred. My next check to write will be number twelve ninety-six."

I noted that the first missing check, number thirteen twenty-one, was stolen from this range.

She then lifted that book to put it out of the way. "Wait a moment, please Clare. Can you show me where the stolen check was removed?"

She put the book back down and riffed through thirty pages of stubs before coming to a page of blank checks on the next page. There were only three unmade checks. The missing one, the top one, corresponded to the first forgery and the stub had been marked "VOID". The thief had gone three quarters of the way into the book to steal the check.

It was obvious that this page had been handled many times and fingerprints might be possible, but unlikely. If I had to make a last ditch effort, I'd try, but I would need Marley's help running the prints.

"Have you discovered any more missing, other than the four that were reported?" I asked.

Again, she looked flustered.

"When was the last time you checked, Clare?"

Rather than answer, she began flipping through the remaining last pages of blank checks to the end of the register, the last number being fourteen hundred. There were no others missing.

She opened the unsealed envelope and withdrew a sheaf of unbound blank checks. I had to admit, seeing Transeget Industries name on the same financial instruments, as the words *Barclays Bank,* impressed me.

"These are the next in the sequence," she said. "Numbered fourteen hundred and one, through sixteen hundred."

"Why so many blank checks, Clare. I mean, you have over three hundred blanks. Do we write that many checks?"

"Well," she started, "It got to be troublesome and costly to order checks in smaller quantities. So, after the first order, we began doubling the quantity."

I didn't see the harm in being frugal, but with the large number of blanks on hand and weak office auditing and internal controls, theirs was a recipe for disaster, a half million-dollar disaster. Again, creature comfort and a negligible cost savings won out over good security precautions.

"Show me, Clare, the pages where the missing items were taken, but go through each sheet one at a time. I want to see if any more are missing."

Clare carefully turned each page until she got to the page with number fourteen sixty-three. Only the stub remained. The same was true for the other two checks. Each was from its own page, far enough apart as to create an unnoticeable gap.

This may have been a simple theft on its face. But someone had thought it out well enough to get away with it. What I didn't know was whether they were taken all at the same time, or just one or two at a time. I asked Clare to tear out a blank check for me and mark the stub "Evidence for Michael Christian." I had plans for that one later.

"Okay Clare, you can put them back."

As she placed the checks back in their drawer and locked it, I said, "I want to talk with you some more. Darryn said you know of a room where we can talk alone."

I stood and recovered her signed statement from Flannery, and placed it into my note folder. She rose from her desk, retrieved another set of keys from a teacup on her desk and a small note pad of her own, and led the way.

■ ■ ■ ■ ■

WE PROCEEDED TO A ROOM out the main door and down the hall, across from the loo, and entered what she called a *customer conference room*. "If a customer has a confidential issue or an angry complaint, we can talk with them in here more privately," she explained.

"Clare, I began as we sat. "I want to explain something to you, and I want you to pay close attention. Only two people in this office have the key to your desk, you and your boss.

"Yes, it is possible that someone may have happened upon your unlocked office door and entered to steal the checks. But it is most unlikely they could have guessed where they were being kept, and entered your locked desk, without breaking into it. Then there is the matter of knowing that there were additional checks in a non-descript envelope. I also happen to think, based on the forgery dates, that the checks were not all stolen at one time, but rather were taken over a period of time, perhaps one at a time. That would eliminate the option of someone just wandering by and getting lucky. Do you see where I am going with this, Clare?"

Clare's posture had gone from sitting upright and attentive to slumping with her shoulders down and forward, and she was wringing her hands as if they were cold.

I could tell she was under stress, not from being

interviewed, but from being accused. The blood had gone from her extremities to her internal organs in an involuntary protective mechanism. Yet she was not showing the signs of someone wrongly accused. She should have been pushing back against my line of questioning, hard. But she was not. She was listening for what I might say, and learning what I may already have by way of evidence.

"But I didn't steal the checks," she pleaded.

"I'm not saying you did, Clare. What I am saying is that there is very little likelihood that whoever did this, was able to pull it off without a key. You have a key and Hardy has a key. So let's focus on your key."

We went over her habits during the day when she might be careless with her key. But she seemed adamant that she kept the key on her wrist all day, and it was easy to see this might be the case, because they were dangling from her wrist as she spoke.

"What about when you are not at the office Clare? What do you do with the key?"

Clare's response at first seemed pretty tight. She even wore it home on her wrist and put it in a tiny wooden bowl by her front door, where it stayed until the next day when she went to work.

She was warming to my questions now and her mood changed, as did her posture. She was upright again and leaning forward, as if to anticipate, if not welcome my next question. Her pallor had changed back to pink again. It looked like she felt comfortable with her governance of the key, which in turn might remove her from suspicion.

"Clare, when you have friends over, is there any

chance that someone might recognize the key and what it is for?"

Her head snapped up with that question. "Guests? You mean company? Like for dinner or something?"

In the world of *behavior symptom analysis*, her reaction is known as a *gross body movement*, compared with her reaction to the other questions. It was nothing more than a signal for me at this point. But it highlighted the fact that there was something important worth exploring relative to the key and other people in her home.

"Where do you live, Clare?"

"You mean my address?"

"No, Clare, I'll get that from your file later if I need it. I mean do you share a home with family, or a roommate, for example?"

Again she seemed uncomfortable and shifted her position, leaning back in her chair.

"I live alone and rarely have dinner guests or company. I go home, have dinner, read a bit, then go to bed. If I am with others, it is to go clubbing. I like my privacy." When she said she liked her privacy, she looked completely away from me before returning her gaze to the floor.

It was obvious there was something worth pressing on, relative to others being in her home.

"Do you have any friends here at the office? I'm talking about close friends, rather than just work acquaintances. For example, do you go to lunch with the same crowd or for a quick drink after work, before heading home?"

"Well, no!" Her answer was louder than the other answers she had given and I knew was touching on some kind of nerve.

"We are all friends and yes, sometimes we might go out to lunch. I don't understand what that has to do with the key. I wear it all the time! We get along well. It is not like I'm having an affair with anyone, if that is what you are getting at."

It wasn't at all what I was getting at, but it now answered why she was so reluctant to open up.

"What about that gentleman you were talking with when I came out of Hardy's office the first time, you know, Nidal."

"What does it matter?" she answered defensively. "We are just mates, office mates. I am very uncomfortable with your insinuations. He was asking me about you. Your appearance here is most unusual and it was just typical office gossip, like *who are you*, and *I wonder what he wants with Hardy*. That kind of thing."

I knew about office gossip and, yes, I could generate that kind of curiosity. But I was observing a different reaction here. She knew Nidal much more intimately than she was comfortable talking about.

"Has he come to your home," I asked?

Clare thought back to this very afternoon when she, Nidal and Ahmad were both at her home, naked. Her sheets still smelled of their sex. She flushed uncontrollably at the thought, as she did each time.

"No, he has not been to my home," she lied. "That is none of your business, if he had been anyway. I am through answering your questions."

Clare was preparing to rise from her chair when I said, "Actually Clare, it has everything to do with your custody of the key. I could care less if you are having an office romance, but I need to know about the security of the key. When he comes over, do you remove the key from your wrist while he is in your home?"

"It doesn't matter if I remove it from my wrist or leave it on when we have lunch, Nidal would never steal from the company. We are together the entire time and I would know. Besides, it is always in my bowl when it is time to go back to work."

A hard knot had formed in the pit of Clare's stomach as she thought about the times that one or the other of the brothers might have gone out to bring back lunch, while she took a short nap in one of their arms, after their lovemaking. She could never admit this to anyone. Not only had the brothers forbidden her, but it would just be too terribly embarrassing. And she certainly wasn't going any further with this stranger who was accusing them of theft.

"I am through here, Mr. Christian. I have told you all I am going to. If you are going to have the company fire me, then do so, but I have nothing else to say."

"Alright Clare. We'll stop, for now. But if I have more questions for you, we'll be right back here, or down at the Putney police station. You may or may not have committed a crime, but you just might be an accomplice. I'm hoping that rather than you being a felon, about to go to jail for a very long time, that perhaps someone took advantage of you.

"I want you to think it over Clare. I've been doing this a very long time. And as I've told you, I'm neither surprised nor judgmental about your affair. But I do believe you are sitting on top of some very important knowledge that can help me resolve this.

"We'll stop for now, but I want you to ask

yourself how much trouble you may unwittingly be in. And now I am going to give you some advice, and I want you to pay very close attention. Do not talk over anything you and I talked about. This is a very serious corporate matter and our conversations are privileged to the law department. Do not share any information with Nidal or anyone else for that matter. Mr. Hardy is being given the same instruction, so you are not to talk with him about it either. I'll be here a while longer, feel free to call me, Clare. You and I both know you have more to offer."

With that we both walked back to the office in silence.

It was time for me to have a go at Nidal Halima.

■ ■ ■ ■ ■

AHMAD WAITED OUTSIDE THE BUILDING as long as he could before climbing the stairs to the office. He had just finished his smoke and had tamped his medwakh pipe on his heel, before heading back in. He enjoyed his tobacco for the quick buzz it gave him, in fact the very name of it, *dokha*, meant *dizzy*.

His father and uncles smoked the imported ground leaves in their pipes in the cafes and lounges, usually over demitasse and playing shesh besh. But he did not have the inclination to sit around wasting time. This blend was potent, worked fast and lasted. He would be high in just a few seconds, and stay that way for at least a half hour at his desk. Then he'd slip out for another smoke break and do it again. He wasn't addicted to it, he told himself. He had just come to appreciate the feeling he got when the chemicals entered his blood stream through his lungs. And why not, he found that he could work through the buzz.

He particularly liked to light up before and after their lunch with Clare. She started out innocently enough, but once she got turned on to the erotic sex play, she became intoxicating to him, just like the dokha. And although he denied being addicted to smoking, he knew he was addicted to Clare.

He scaled the stairs two at a time and almost ran into his brother coming out the door.

"I was just coming down to get you," Nidal said. "The head of security and a Constable are upstairs. They can only be here for one reason and if I am right, he will be talking to each of us, including you and me. He took Clare into the office down the hall, and I have no idea what she is telling him, if anything. And he was with Hardy for a while first. This was an eventuality we talked about. We have to leave now."

Ahmad was less sure, as always, "If we leave, we'll just be calling attention to ourselves and our work is not done. You were in there already. How would you explain just walking out?"

"Yes, but if we stay, we might contradict whatever Clare could have said, and get caught in a lie. That would point the investigator right to us. No, we must go, now. We can start over somewhere else under new identities. That would not be a problem."

Normally, he did not have the courage or ability

to think things through. But now, he argued, "I disagree," Ahmad said. "The American will be looking for some slip-up that proves we could have taken the checks. But there are no witnesses and Clare is very unlikely to admit that she is involved with both of us. We both know that. She is our alibi. Let us stick to most of the truth of that. We are with her at lunch and that is the truth, most of the time. Without proof, he can do nothing to us.

"Come, let us go back up."

Nidal was not the risk taker that his brother was. He was methodical and avoided detection by staying a step ahead of curious or prying eyes. They both knew that eventually someone would come asking questions about the checks and now that day had arrived. Maybe it was best to stick with the alibi that Clare provided. It was true and it was verifiable. If they had to, they could leave at any time.

"Okay," Nidal said. "We will go up, but let us stick to the fact that we just go to lunch together. Do not let him take it any further than that. Afterwards, we can get with Clare and work on the details to keep our stories straight, in case he comes back with more questions.

"But I promise you brother, at the first sign that we might be in danger, we are leaving, that very day."

With that, they walked back into the office.

■ ■ ■ ■ ■

AS MUCH AS A GOOD detective story seems to have excitement at every turn, I knew that most investigations plodded along through the evidence gathering and interview process, until someone told a lie contrary to the facts or made an admission. Then it was just a matter of pushing through their final objections and letting the truth come out. All that followed was the paperwork, getting good written statements and writing the final report. This case was going down that path. Soon I'd be doing a bit of sight-seeing then heading for home.

I knew Clare had some kind of guilty knowledge. She either stole the checks or was just horribly embarrassed to have been caught in an office romance with Nidal Halima. Maybe she was worried that Nidal actually could have taken her key and stolen the checks. Or maybe it was a combination of those. Either way, this was a paper chase as far as I was concerned, and I was already beginning to think about how I was going to deal with Barclays.

My interview of one of the other office workers lasted about five minutes. He had no access, was only mildly familiar with Clare on a personal basis, had never been to lunch with her, but was sure she would never have taken the checks. He described her as a *wholesome* girl. The kind you'd take home to your mother. I sensed perhaps there was a shy admirer in him.

Marley was moving at about the same pace. His

interviews were also ending quickly.

It was becoming apparent that only two people had legitimate access to the checks, and with all the workers in such close quarters, it would be nearly impossible for anyone to get into Clare's desk during working hours, without someone else noticing. Either Clare took them, or someone got in and stole them when the office was unoccupied.

I noticed that Nidal Halima was walking in with another guy, and I had to do a double-take. They were identical twins, completely identical. Only the clothes separated the way they looked. I was willing to bet they were a handful as young kids, confusing everyone with their identities.

A thought occurred to me.

I caught his eye and nodded to him. "Nidal," I said. "Have you got a moment?"

The two men separated and Nidal came over.

"Your twin?" was all I asked.

"Yes. My brother Ahmad also works here."

"We're talking with all the workers about the missing checks, Nidal, and I'd like to talk with you now." With that, I handed him his copy of Flannery's letter and told him to read it and sign it, which he did.

We proceeded down the hall to where I had talked to Clare. Knowing that Halima wasn't an authorized key holder, I decided to approach him differently.

"You know that only Clare and Hardy have keys to the office and to the drawer with the checks. Let's assume for the moment that neither one of them stole the checks."

At that he said, "Of course. They would not do such a thing."

"Let's work with that, Nidal. So, let me ask you, how would someone be able to enter the building, enter the office, get into her desk and take the checks and leave without being seen?"

He looked at me for a while, as if sizing me up, before responding.

"Well, as you saw when we met. Someone may have come in while the door was unlocked and no one was here and stole the checks then."

"Yes," I agreed. But that doesn't answer how they knew where to look."

Nidal stared at the wall a long a time again. I waited, wondering if he was trying to imagine such a scenario, or if his suspicion of my line of questioning was growing.

He thought for a few more seconds and replied, "Perhaps this was someone who was in the office on business, and Clare was making out a check to him and saw where the checks were kept."

"But," I said, "That doesn't explain how he was able to get into Clare's desk without a key. No, I think Clare did it, either by herself, or with an accomplice."

With that, Nidal became more relaxed and sat back in his chair. "Yes," he said. "I suppose that could be. One really does not truly know a person well enough to understand what motivates her to commit a crime, I suppose."

"Interesting." Was all I said.

"What is so interesting? That she could do such a thing?"

"No," I replied. "That you would give her up as a suspect so easily. Because, Halima, when I asked her if she thought you could have done it, she immediately rushed to your defense." Now I referred to him by his last name, to let him know that I was no longer accepting his flippant answers.

"Yes, Yes! Of course," Halima stammered. "It is because I didn't do it"

"No, that's not why. She told me she was in a relationship with you. She described it as a romance, where she came to know you, and knew you would not do such a thing."

"What? That is not true." Halima said.

I stopped him right there.

"Look Halima, I really don't care if you are having a relationship with Clare. It means nothing to me. All I am focusing on is the stolen checks. But I am not going to let you lie during this questioning. Were you having an affair with Clare. Are you still?"

And I was serious. I really didn't care. But if he was intimate with her and in her home, that would give him access to the key. It didn't explain how he could have gotten it from her without her knowing, but it moved him way up on my suspect list. Not so much for lying about the relationship, but for betraying Clare so easily. "Well, are you?"

"Yes, I am." He said quietly. "But that doesn't mean ..." I interrupted him.

"Did you take Clare's keys at any time?" I fronted him with that question because it was at the heart of the case. But more importantly, because I wanted to test his reaction.

His eyes immediately shifted from a position of factual recall to constructive recall, where he wanted to spin the truth of the answer with a falsehood. He shifted in his seat from leaning back comfortably to sitting straight up with his hands folded in his lap, defensively. He was definitely exhibiting suspicious behavior. He either took the keys or had some kind of valuable knowledge that I needed.

"I have answered you," Halima said. "I did not take the keys and I do not know who did. Maybe you were right that Clare took the checks. Why don't you focus on her and leave me alone. I have nothing more to say to you. You have no authority to fire me, so we are done here."

He was right. I had no authority to fire him, but I sure could make it happen. I did have more questions for him though, like *what days did he go to Clare's, how many times, did he know where she kept her keys*? And I wanted to ask if he and his brother ever spoofed her into thinking that Ahmad was Nidal? But I knew I wasn't going to get any further with him without additional leverage.

"OK, Nidal. We're through for now. But I may need to talk with you again, so don't wander off."

With that we stood and Halima walked out of the room without looking back.

It was time to press Clare one more time for details about Halima being at her home, but when I got back to the main office, she was gone and her desk was cleared.

I walked into Hardy's office with my back to the workforce, leaned over his desk and asked, "Where is she?"

He seemed surprised by my question. "She said she felt ill and asked if she could go home. So, I let her go. Why, do you need her again?"

As much as I thought Hardy had no part in taking his own checks, I was beginning to believe that he was seriously contributory through negligence. He just seemed to be taking the investigation too casually. It was almost as if, because it was the company's money and not his, that the theft was no big thing.

I turned back to the bullpen area to talk with Nidal again. Both he and his brother were also gone.

This was getting out of hand.

Marley was sitting at the desk I first used when I got there. He was reviewing some notes. "Did you get anything of interest?" I asked.

"Yes," he answered. "Two things. The first is that I agree with you. I don't think Hardy did it or has any knowledge. I just think he isn't competent in these matters. His mind doesn't look at people as capable of crimes. He just sees workers and tries to keep the peace amongst them."

"And the other thing?" I asked.

"Yes, the other thing was, that by the time I finished with Hardy, Nidal and Ahmad had left the office. I find that pretty telling. So much so, that I'd like to get a crack at them myself. Meanwhile, I talked with the remaining folks and found them pretty much unaware that the checks were even missing. They seemed out of touch in terms of access or knowledge."

I had come to the same conclusions. Hardy pretty much facilitated this mess by being too loose with his office's access controls. And although I couldn't see Clare as being a thief, I knew she was in some way complicit, either by intent or ignorance. And that led me to Nidal and Ahmad. They had just put themselves at the top of my list of people to press further. It was time for me to change tactics and to take on a partner.

"David, I'm guessing you and I are pretty much thinking the same things at this point. Nidal and

Ahmad are persons of interest to me, but I'll lose any clout on this, the moment I walk out this door." I said, nodding my head toward the unlocked office door.

"Normally, I'd run with this on my own, but given the brothers' propensity for flight, even from work, I think getting to them is going to be a problem. I could use some help with this."

"Glad you asked," he replied, without hesitation. "My whole station has been aware of this incident since it was first reported to us by your Mr. Hardy. He was, however, very clear that he was reporting this for insurance purposes and because of a company requirement, but he did not want an investigation to disrupt his workplace. While we found it a bit strange, it wasn't the first time a corporate crime was swept under the carpet by a company's management.

"When we didn't hear from your insurance carrier either, we moved on. Many of our superiors feel that corporate crime is victimless crime. Barclays didn't file a police report, so my guess is they feel they're covered for the loss. Either that or three hundred thousand pounds is beneath them and unworthy of their time.

"So, having said all that, how can we help?"

Again, there was that British willingness to partner with their American brothers in crime fighting. I loved it.

At this stage of the game, I was perfectly willing to prosecute whoever was responsible. Usually this is a choice I leave to the local manager, but in Hardy's case, I was taking it away from him. Whoever did this was going down, hard, even if it meant the investigation with law enforcement put us in the position of becoming police agents.

"I want to find out all I can about Clare, Nidal and Ahmad. I want to quickly find out if their addresses of record are good ones, and I want to talk with Clare and Nidal again and I want us to get to Ahmad first hand, also.

"Another thing I can use some help with is finding out who cashed those checks for the thief. We didn't get that info from Barclays and I know we're entitled to it. I want to interview the check payee. But I'm not ready to shake Barclays' tree yet to get the info.

"If we can background check the brothers and Clare, that's a start."

Marley just nodded. "That would be my starting point also. And yes, those things are possible. If you tried to get that information through an investigative agency, because it is a workplace case, you'd be violating British law. But working with us on a crime, we can make that happen. Why don't you give me a copy of what you have, and we'll use that as a starting point."

I walked with Marley over to the copy station and opened my briefcase. "Would you like a coffee, while we do this?" I asked.

"Help yourself," he smiled, as he walked over to the hot water pot, preparing his tea. I looked at the coffee pot that contained better than half a pot from what Nidal had made for me earlier. It was looking rather oily. I poured myself some of those dregs and set about making a full copy of our personnel files.

It really didn't take as long as we thought to copy the sheets with the names, addresses, dates of birth, and other personal identifiers that are common to employment files. But I also made copies of their resumes. Maybe something in them would stick out to the cops.

Marley stacked his copies and placed them in a file folder I provided. "Come with me," he said. "I still have that errand to run. Then we can head back to my station and get started."

I was pretty much at his disposal at this point, so I agreed.

■ ■ ■ ■ ■

AS IT TURNED OUT, HIS little side trip was to the famed Wimbledon Lawn Tennis and Croquet Club, just a few miles down the road from the TI offices. The road to Wimbledon was packed with cars and busses, but Marley deftly drove off the main roadway and onto a side road, bypassing it all.

It made sense, given that Marley was the security director of the Club and, as such, would know his way around thoroughly.

With my case still weighing on my mind, I still readily agreed when he asked if I'd like a little tour of the place. At this point I needed a good distraction, since I felt like I was treading water on my case. Walking onto the immaculately groomed grounds was a thrill. Alice and I had recently taken up tennis, even though I teased her that it wasn't a real sport, because it didn't involve bodily contact.

Once inside, Marley introduced me to everyone

we encountered, as if I was a special guest from the States. He outfitted me with a pass, which seemed a bit above a visitor badge.

"Wear this around your neck," he said, "and stick close by me. They are wrapping up two weeks of tennis on the courts and the finals will be upon us this weekend."

What I thought would be just a walkabout, turned into a two hour, behind-the-scenes walkthrough that included players locker rooms, physical therapy rooms, the under-building delivery areas for tons of food and paper products, for waste management and access by employees. All the services were carried out like clockwork, by very dedicated staff, who were dutifully watched by hundreds of security personnel.

"This building contains Centre court and the members only areas. Centre Court is used only two weeks out of the year, and you are here for them." Marley explained.

"I'm actually fourth down the line in hierarchy in the security program and we are rotating duties this week and next. This evening, I will work until the last match is completed, which could be at ten o'clock or two a.m., depending on how many games are played. He could tell by the look on my face that I was not properly impressed. "Follow me," he said.

We walked up three flights of richly carpeted interior stairs to an unlabeled, locked door. His badge unlocked it and we entered what seemed to be a control room with dozens and dozens of security cameras, staffed by what seemed to be a combination of soldiers, private security and police officers.

That was exactly what the mix was. "This is *The Championships* week," he said. It was then I got it. Wimbledon is the site of one of four major tennis tournaments in the world and this week, the United Kingdom was hosting what was believed to be the granddaddy of them all. And I had been completely unaware.

Marley pointed out all the camera views from the courts to the stands, to the grounds, to the lounge for the players and their family, to the infrastructure. And the views went all the way out to Wimbledon Golf Club and Lake on the outskirts of the property.

Cameras covered all views of the driveways, parking areas and walking paths. Over three hundred and fifty thousand people were expected to attend through the fortnight, including Prince William and Princess Diana, and other members of the Royal Family on the last days, Saturday and Sunday.

"How can you afford to spend any time with me?" I asked. "This is huge!"

"As I said," Marley replied, "It is so huge and so many operational hours are assigned, that none of us can be here all the time. So, we have to break it up into chunks. Right now, I'm free on days. Last week, I was working nights."

The tour was fascinating. I developed a larger appreciation for the history of the sport and the town of Wimbledon's role in it. And within it, even Wimbledon had its own history, as evidenced by a tradition that was as popular as Mint Juleps during the Kentucky Derby.

Marley pointed to several vendor trucks in the queue below, waiting to enter the underground cargo loading area. "Each year, attendees ritually partake of strawberries and cream, which were served as a treat at the first Wimbledon in 1877. In fact, these strawberries are harvested nightly on local farms, and brought in on pallets by the truckload. Here they are cleaned and packaged, on premises, for sale to the crowd the following day," he revealed. We were so close, I could smell the fresh strawberries.

Being somewhat of an analytic, I enjoyed Marley's historical explanations of how people, supplies and equipment, and vehicles moved along a roadway, which, though only two lanes, had been converted to one-way streets all around the Club, and created heavy, counter-clockwise traffic through a town the size of a small village. The entire process of coordinating all the elements safely and successfully worked like a well-oiled machine. There were thousands of support staff, all of whom had to be badged, and gotten onto the premises and off again, every day for the entire two weeks.

An army of workers and vendors bringing in fresh food, beverages, and souvenirs, also replenished the supplies nightly. They brought in things I would have never thought of, but which made perfect sense, such as toilet paper and napkins, plastic utensils, and for the upper crust in the VIP lounges, the detergents for managing the cleaning of cutlery and stemware and newly laundered linens.

And of course, there was the waste of nearly a third of a million people that had to be removed from the premises. Bathrooms and drinking fountains were cleaned regularly throughout the day, and sanitized nightly. Trashcans were emptied all day long into large dumpsters, while full ones were replaced with empty ones. A constant caravan of queued rubbish-removal trucks hauled the separate dumpsters of garbage and recyclables away on an ongoing basis. "Imagine," Marley said, "your Super Bowl being done all day long, fourteen days in a row. Then throw in two stadiums and fourteen tennis courts along the way."

It was truly a logistics marvel, and I was disappointed when the tour ended. It was fascinating to be among the crowd, and although I never got to see one ball served, I felt that I had received more entertainment value than many would ever know. But it was now time to get back to Marley's station.

On our way out, Marley walked us past the Wimbledon gift shop, grabbed a couple Wimbledon logo tennis towels, had them put them on "his chit" as he called it, and handed them to me. "Toss these in your suitcase, as souvenirs," he said.

As we waited in his Jag for a garbage truck as it pulled alongside the stadium, he pointed to my towels and said, "By the end of the week, these will be sold out, and street hawkers will be selling them for two or three hundred U.S. dollars each. "Hang on to them." Then he navigated us off the one-way Church road, took us through some back roads and returned us to Putney.

■ ■ ■ ■ ■

WITH THE GREATEST OF CAUTION, the young man finished loading his backpack and looked around the shop. The burners were turned off, and the raw chemicals and compounds were stored in the locked steel cabinet. The larger bags on the wooden skids were covered with a tarp.

Hoisting his own bags over each shoulder, he took one last look and locked the door behind him as he left, walking south toward University College London. Just before the Psychological Services building, he hopped the Euston bus and headed west. He was on a mission.

■ ■ ■ ■ ■

BACK IN HIS PUTNEY CONSTABULARY, Marley sat at his military-grey desk and pressed the power button on his computer. The screen glowed green. I was wondering about the efficiency of a British database. When I was a cop in Detroit, the FBI *National Crime Information System* and the Michigan State Police *Law Enforcement Information Network* were the best, when it came to fast retrieval of criminal histories and outstanding arrest warrants. I wasn't so sure about the British system, given the country's strict rules on personal

101

privacy. And besides, much of what I was looking for involved simple things, but items that weren't usually found in a criminal history database.

Marley entered the identifiers for Clare, and Nidal and Ahmad Halima and said, "Okay, now we wait."

Then he loosened his tie, inviting me to do the same, which I did. "So, tell me, Michael," he asked, "What was it like being a Detroit copper?"

There was that question again. I don't know if it was the Detroit Police Department that had such a name for itself, or if it was the fact that because of crime in Detroit, in the seventies, the City was known world-wide as such a hell-hole.

I smiled, unsure how to answer him. "To be honest with you David, it was the right job for a young guy like me, who liked to get paid to drive fast, fight in the street and carry a gun. And every day, I got to go play with some of my best friends for life. It was great."

I stayed away from the part where we were hated by many of the very people we served, or how difficult it really was to have to shoot someone, or watch someone die in your arms. In a country that still didn't let most of their officers carry guns, I wasn't sure if I'd have any credibility left if I talked about that.

Much faster than I expected, an alert flashed across Marley's screen, then another, and finally a third.

"Let's see what we have here." Marley said.

He tabbed through the information without commenting, and then hit what must have been the print-key, causing a steady stream of paper to spill into the tray of his dot matrix printer.

He read through the papers one more time before commenting to me. "The address Clare gave you seems to be a good one. If you want, we can take a drive by there and we'll likely find her home. She has no car and her only sibling lives in the north country. It is unlikely she has yet gone home, packed, purchased a ticket and found a route that will get her out there, given the brief amount of time since she left her office. Frankly, there is nothing of interest in her file.

"But as to Nidal and Ahmad, on the other hand, look what have we here."

I moved around to the side of his desk so I could read the papers over his shoulder. I still didn't know what I was looking at. Rather than a narrative, there were just dozens of lines of raw data. Obviously he had seen reports like these many times before, so he interpreted them for me.

"Firstly," he said, "We're going to have a problem. If their address is a good one, it is in the heart of a Muslim enclave where we are not likely to gain admission, without causing a disturbance."

I had heard of such places in London. Refugees started out by densely settling in a particular zone. Then they bought the local businesses and changed the signage to Arabic, so as to omit shoppers who could not read the signs. Then they spoke only Arabic with customers. And soon, some severe form of sharia law was imposed on the Muslim locals. In time, the police were not called anymore, or on the rare occasions when they were, they encountered hostile crowds that forced them out of the area. I found it unbelievable that the police or the local government had allowed this to happen. I raised my eyebrows in disbelief to

103

Marley.

"I know," he said. "It happened very slowly, and before long, it became politically incorrect to discuss this as a dilemma. The conventional wisdom evolved into letting them solve their own problems. About the only services they will accept are trash removal and fire protection. They will not even let an ambulance in.

"We do not have a reliable, accurate census count anymore. They establish a local government and soon one of their members runs for larger public position, the community votes en mass and the official is elected."

Marley continued, "But that situation is not our biggest problem. Right now, every constable, every detective, and every member of our domestic intelligence force is focusing on the IRA. So as long as the Muslim community remains quiet, we can do our work elsewhere, which is trying to identify the network responsible for these bombings."

And there it was again. I recalled the warning from Herb Lawrence at the State Department.

"And what about you, David. Aren't you running flat out on the bombings too?" I asked.

"Well, yes and no. Because I am working Wimbledon for the next two weeks, they are cutting me some slack. And the most I can contribute right now, by way of investigations, is to keep my team's informants out on the street. It is all any of us can do. But truth be told, there is barely any chance anything will come of it.

"The IRA is a tight clan and they are segmented and decentralized as to activity and to leadership. So, even if someone knows something of value, we are unlikely to hear of it, since the penalty for squealing is death. It is mostly our federal resources who are gathering the intelligence, and you do not want to know how that is happening."

No. I thought to myself, *I sure don't.*

I wanted to redirect our thoughts back to my case.

"What about the checks? Who presented them and who cashed them? Can we find that out, and where they were cashed?"

Marley reached for his Rolodex on his desk, flipped through some business cards, then grabbed the phone and dialed. After a mere introduction by phone, he explained what he wanted. It was obvious that he had been put on hold. But within a moment, he was reconnected. "Yes. Got it. Yes. Okay, Thanks." He said.

"That was a friend at Barclays. The same person, a local merchant with a numbered account there, presented all the checks to the same Wandsworth branch. They are faxing over the details for me now."

Again, I was amazed at how well the British system worked and how easily the police could access information. Before Marley could even give me the address to the branch, the fax machine rang two desks away.

Marley waited as the thick, pale, yellow paper squeaked its way out of the thermal printer. He tore off the duplicate sheets and walked them back to his desk, handing me a set.

"The man's name is Eli Schiff. His business was used to pass the checks, hence his choice of a numbered account. The business is simply enough called *Schiff's Jewelers and Rare Coins* on Wandsworth High Street. It's really not too far from here, if you want to talk with the merchant."

I certainly did want to talk with the owner. I was hoping he could give me a description of the guy or girl who presented the checks to him, and to find out what jewelry they bought for a half million dollars. "Let's go." I agreed.

■ ■ ■ ■ ■

WANDSWORTH WAS LESS THAN FIVE miles from Marley's office and the ride in his Jag was smooth and quiet. He took the time to expand on his findings on the brothers.

"There were a couple more anomalies that surfaced when we dove into the boys backgrounds. The first is that they are in our country on expired work visas, which termed about two years ago. They were admitted because of their electrical engineering backgrounds. However, looking over their resumes, the prior employers do not include any companies that normally would hire any electrical engineers."

"But the job they were doing for us didn't require an engineering degree. A high school diploma would suffice," I reminded him.

"Their employment background confirms they have been employed mostly in simple jobs, like your call center, nothing requiring technical skills degree. But don't count on a detention and deportation retainer being put out on them, as long as there have been no other crimes committed. Our

Immigration folks wouldn't dare take a run after them."

The brothers were beginning to sound more and more interesting to me. I was ready to take a run at the previous employers and see if they had any similar experiences. But Marley interrupted that plan.

"There's more, Michael. Going back to the resumes you provided me, I have yet to see one company that I recognize from the local towns they claim in their work history. And I was assigned to one of their specific locales for several years. I could be missing something, but it is worth checking on when you talk with the boys. Meanwhile, I'll do some more checking on this tomorrow."

This time, I wasn't letting them off the hook until they gave me specific answers. They were either going to tell me the truth, or they were going to be fired for lying. Better yet, I might be able to box them into a corner and have them give me that admission I needed. And since I was playing by the Queen's Rules, if I got an admission, I was turning it over to Marley right away.

Marley nodded as we turned onto Wandsworth High Street. "That's the place, third shop off the corner."

I read the sign, *Schiff Jewelers - We buy gold and silver.*

■ ■ ■ ■ ■

THE YOUNG MAN STROLLED SLOWLY through the Oxford Street shopping district, browsed some of the windows, and occasionally entered one of the quaint alleys that offered exclusive menswear and accessories. Based on his attire, it would seem that most of the shops' items would be priced above his income level.

He appeared to be merely a university student, toting his heavy backpack and book bag over his shoulders. He tugged his black ball cap down over his eyes and continued west toward the Marble Arch, in the late afternoon sun.

The Arch was a major attraction and a stop on the bus routes and Underground system, in and out of the northeast corner of Hyde Park. It would soon be crowded with locals and tourists from all over the world, and with employees heading home from the areas shops and embassies. All of that served his purpose perfectly.

A few blocks east of the Arch was the US Embassy, and at the far west end of Hyde Park were the Russian, Iranian and Lebanese Embassies. They were far enough away to be safe, yet close enough to take notice of his work. It would take him only twenty minutes to walk almost across Hyde Park, from one side to the other. That would put him at the Bayswater Tube Station, where he would easily board and ride out of the area, hidden away among the mass of riders heading out of town. He had walked the venue a dozen times and knew exactly where he was going and how he was getting out of there.

■ ■ ■ ■ ■

Schiff's jewelry store was small by many of our standards back in the States. It was more of a store-front shop than a retail store. But it was neatly laid out with spotless, wood and glass display-cases, arranged in a logical order. Larger art pieces were displayed in brightly lit alcoves along the left wall, and running all the way to the back of the store. The right side of the shop seemed to be a jewelry cleaning and repair area with a steam cleaner and a small work shelf with tools expertly arranged, as if on display themselves.

Lining each side of the carpeted center aisle were display cases of all the items I would have expected. On the left side were earrings, necklaces, bracelets and finger rings for men and women. There was a brilliant display of engagement and wedding rings. Almost every piece seemed custom made, with exquisite stone settings. Yellow-gold items and diamonds were in abundance.

On the right side were two six-foot long cases, containing displays of rare antique and vintage coins. Most were shown in velvet lined display boxes, along with their certificates of authenticity, and many were in paperboard and plastic coin holders. But dozens more were merely piled into shallow boxes, as if to say, *I have so many of these, they aren't worth much to me in trade.*

Schiff's shop may have been small, but the value of his stock was dazzling. And given the excessive markups that jewelers use, there must have been a fortune in inventory. His was no pawnshop that bought junk jewelry for resale. It was all first-class merchandise and one would assume the same about his customers.

What also caught my eye were the certificates hanging on the wall over the one-way glass, leading to Schiff's back office.

London Bullion Market Association, LBMA Affiliate Member, LBMA Authorized Wholesaler, and LBMA Authorized Jewelry Manufacturer.

Marley saw me scanning the wall and said, "The LBMA is the leading association that sets the standard for gold buying and selling throughout the Kingdom. Only refiners approved by them can refine gold, the same for jewelry manufacturers and sellers. If one wants to convey a sense of credibility in the world of gold buying and selling, these are the certificates required to do so. Schiff's business seems legitimate."

Schiff may have been a legitimate merchandiser in the gold business, but he still cashed corporate business checks given to him by someone without proper credentials. He was high on my list of suspects.

An older woman, in a tailored skirt and matching jacket, walked toward us, and stood behind the jewelry counter. Her eyes gave us the once over. She surely didn't figure us for customers. In a very proper accent, that I thought was Jewish, she said,

"May I help you gentlemen?"

Marley produced his Metropolitan Police Identification and introduced us, not mentioning that I was a private citizen of another country. She blanched to the point I thought she was going to pass out.

"Oh, my God," she said. "What has he done?"

■ ■ ■ ■ ■

ADELE SCHIFF HAD PLACED HER hands on the glass counter for stability, unaware of her damp fingerprints staining the shining surface.

Marley seized on the moment, "What do you mean, *what has he done*? What makes you think he has done something?"

She began wringing her hands as if to wash some invisible dirt off them.

"Two men came in here just moments ago and they began arguing with Eli. He ran upstairs to our flat and within minutes he came back down with a travel bag, and left. All he said was not to worry and that he'd be back soon. Then they all left together."

"Who were these men? What did they say to your husband?" Marley asked.

"I do not know them. They are gold customers, but I do not know their names. And all I could hear was the sound of their voices. I could not make out what they were saying, but their tone scared me. What has he done?" She repeated.

111

Marley was playing it perfectly. He wasn't answering her questions, but was keeping her in the answering mode. "Your husband may not have done anything wrong, Mrs. Schiff. But the two men gave him stolen and forged checks. That may have been what they were arguing about. If your husband was going somewhere quickly, where might he have gone?"

Adele Schiff thought a moment because it was obvious this behavior was unusual for him. "We have a small home in Basingstoke," she replied. "We use it when we go on holiday. It is possible he has gone there, but that does not explain why he did not tell me where he was going, or why he took a travel bag. We have clothing there."

It sure seemed to me that Schiff was taking it on the lam and fleeing somewhere. Basingstoke may have been an option, but I doubted that, especially since he was with two other men.

"These two guys your husband was with, what did they look like?" I asked.

Mrs. Schiff noticed my American accent right away and looked questioningly at Marley, who smoothly said, "He's from the States and we are working a joint investigation."

She turned from me and answered my question to Marley, "They are Arab boys. I thought they were nice men, but they seemed very dangerous today."

"Yes," I persisted. "But what did they look like?"

"Well," she said facing Marley. "They are dark complexioned with black hair." As she paused to refresh her memory, I thought, *well you have narrowed it down to a few million.*

"Oh, yes," she said. "They are twins. Identical twins."

112

Marley and I exchanged confirming glances as he said, "Mrs. Schiff, I'd like to see your transaction records for these men."

She replied, "Well, I don't know what to look for. Eli always dealt with them."

"You told us they were gold customers. Let's start there with your gold transactions."

She nodded her agreement and agreed to get her ledgers. She paused as the three of us heard thunder off in the distance. "I don't believe the forecast called for rain today," she said as she went into the back room and was gone for quite a while. I shrugged it off as Marley passed the time by looking at the displays. In the States, one of us would have accompanied her to the back room to make sure she didn't come out with a gun. In a matter of a few minutes, she returned with two large ledger books that she laid out on top of the display case.

She leafed through several pages, then began shifting back and forth between them, while she muttered to herself, *That old fool. Now what has he done?*

"Here," she said. "This is the first of their purchases."

I interrupted her. "Do you mind if I ask what the price of gold is?"

"Well, it depends," she began. "It is fixed twice a day and it depends on the purity of the gold. The purer, the higher the cost.

"Let us look at the transactions," she said.

And she pointed out the date of the first transaction as we followed with her fingertip along the line of the purchase details. I saw it right away. There was our Transeget Industries name and our check number as the method of payment, and there also followed Nidal Halima's name.

"So, they bought gold on this day for three-hundred ninety, point eight British pounds, per troy ounce," she said.

Marley looked at me and said, "The exchange rate is about one dollar and sixty-three cents U.S. per British Pound."

I was again trying to do the math in my head when Adele interrupted, produced a small calculator, and said, "That comes to about six hundred thirty-seven US dollars an ounce."

I read down the line and saw that the purchase amount was eighty thousand pounds. Those bastards had written a TI check for eighty thousand and Schiff had honored it. That was about one hundred thirty thousand US dollars and there were four checks like that.

"Does he sell them gold jewelry or ingots?" I asked.

"Oh, no," she replied. "Ingots are for the refiners and the manufacturers. We sell gold bars of different weights, and we provide the certificates that validate the bar's source, purity and weight."

Looking in her book, I could see another of our checks a few lines down for the same amount. Marley caught that too.

"Mrs. Schiff, let me look through that ledger." And he smoothly reached over and swung it his way. At the same time, he reached into his jacket pocket, pulled out his pen and a detective note pad, and began copying the information for the transactions.

"Mrs. Schiff," I said. "Their transactions represent a lot of money, especially when I look at the others. How much gold did these guys buy, and do you keep that many gold bars on hand in here?" And with that I gestured at the small size of the shop.

Adele smiled condescendingly. "No, of course not. We might have a bar or two on hand, but we can get any amount of gold that we need, usually within twenty-four hours. But these purchases were different." And with that she opened the second book.

"These are the *Vault* sales," she said. "What that means is the gold never physically changed hands." She must have seen the confusion on our faces. *Why would someone buy all this gold and never own it?* I wondered.

"You will note," she continued, "that each purchase in the sale book is marked with a "V". That means we issued a certificate of ownership and quality. But that means the boys wanted us to store their gold at our bullion bank. In effect, it never leaves the vault, but the ownership was registered to the boys."

I still didn't understand why they didn't want the gold, so I asked.

"Oh, they wanted it alright. Gold transactions are untraceable, but it seems they wanted another layer of secrecy. So, we bought the gold back from them the next day and recovered the certificates."

That didn't clear it up for me either, but I waited for her to continue.

"In this manner, we are not acting like a bank, to cash a check for someone. We are not licensed to do that. But we can sell gold and we can buy it. So, when we buy the gold back, we pay the seller in cash. And before you ask, no, we do not keep that kind of cash on hand, but our bank is just around the corner, Barclays." Marley nodded his agreement with that. That is where the numbered account would be.

"Eli takes a margin of profit on the gold sale, takes a margin on the vaulting fee, and takes a margin on the buy-back."

"So, in effect you are laundering stolen money for a profit, under the pretext of conducting a legitimate business?" I accused.

Marley, seeing how this could go sideways, added, "Your husband seems to have gotten himself involved in a serious matter, Mrs. Schiff. I am going to have to confiscate these journals. We will make copies of them and return them to you as soon as possible."

I was impressed with how easily he managed a seizure of evidence without a search warrant, when he added, "If that is alright with you?"

To which Adele Schiff replied, "That old fool will ruin us. Yes, but please get them back to us soon. They are our only record and we will need them for an audit by the LBMA."

I wondered if the LBMA even cared about how simple it was to launder money, using this system. I guessed they fully understood, and knew full well that this process was used worldwide.

■ ■ ■ ■ ■

SHE SLOWLY EASED HER CAR down the

quiet, tree-lined residential street and stopped at the corner. Soft new leaves on established boughs fluttered in the breeze, and she could hear them rustling through her open window. She refused to be taken in by the false sense of tranquility, and maintained her focus. At one time, it was a lovely and desirable area for people to move into their starter homes.

Over the decades the occupancy had changed, as housing pressure increased to accommodate a surge in immigration. The ethnically mixed neighborhood was evolving, and there was an equal sense of competitive anxiety in the faces of people who walked the sidewalks.

She looked at the first vertical row of corner bricks on the building that housed the apothecary store. No marks. She would check it this afternoon on her way home.

■ ■ ■ ■ ■

THE MESSENGER THOUGHT ABOUT THE fresh chalk mark, on the base of the light post outside the entrance to Queen Mary's Gardens. He despised having to work with a woman, much less a demanding one, who now wanted to see him. The fact that she was physically appealing to him angered him even more. She was a distraction.

The Gardens were less than a mile from his warehouse, but she had no way of knowing that.

He took great care to arrange his meetings with

her at different places far away from his safe houses, his warehouse or his apartment. Both of them needed the assurance they were not being followed, so each initial meeting place was a waypoint that contained a code as to the true location of the meeting. It allowed each of them the opportunity to ensure that no one was monitoring them, with a crew that got there first.

By using a dark pink chalk, she let him know it was urgent. With her, when she wanted to meet, everything was urgent. All he had to do was make a responding, coded chalk mark on a brick of a corner store, to let her know when and at which location.

He was wise to keep his personal phone numbers from her. This allowed him to set the details of their rendezvous, making it harder for her to trap him. She was smart, and he knew she was trying to milk him for information. But when she tired of him, or no longer found him useful to her needs, she would kill him.

The information she wanted seemed simple enough on its face. She wanted the location, and any other information he could gather, on two men. He knew exactly who she was talking about. But this time, he wasn't going to pass along the information. It was better if she believed he could do some things and not others. And in this case, it was much better not to give her this information.

The Messenger was smarter and was manipulating her for his own purposes. Information was, after all, a two-way street. When his mission was complete, he would take great pleasure in killing her slowly. For the moment, however, she would have to wait. He had his own agenda, and right now, it didn't include meeting with her.

His thoughts turned to the devices in his bags. The timers were set on a delay of thirty minutes, and set to detonate within ten minutes of each other. The first would be placed in the hedgerows on the north side of the park, at the Arch. The second would be placed in a parked, rented delivery van that was already in place for him, at the corner of N. Row and Park Lane, just across from the Park. Besides extensive injuries, the first explosive charge would cause enormous property damage, at least that was what he planned for. But this exercise was designed to test something else with his precisely measured loads.

His first device would cause multiple injuries and mayhem for at least two blocks around, and would blow a devastating shockwave southward through the open park grounds. Those in close proximity would have their insides emulsified, rather than be killed by shrapnel. Nevertheless, the fragments of metal would blast through clothing, skin, bone and construction material with equal ease, inside the close-in blast radius, especially along the north. Those structures would be first devastated by the outward force of the explosion, occurring within a split second of detonation, blowing glass and concrete deep into the building interior space. But the negative pressure behind the shock wave would cause even greater destruction. In essence it would create an enormous vacuum that would pull the already weakened building materials back out into the street with great force. And that would all occur in an instant. The structural damage would be severe enough to destroy most buildings for thirty to forty feet inside, and several stories high.

The second device was loaded with shrapnel, and timed to exert maximum casualties on the good Samaritans and emergency responders as they converged to render aid. He could not help but smile, when he thought about what the scene would look like.

It was a flawless, well-researched plan that would be cleanly executed. And of course, he would disappear, leaving a recognizable signature on the remnants of his devices.

■ ■ ■ ■ ■

AT THIS TIME OF DAY, there were plenty of seats on the Bayswater route eastward from Hyde Park. Most travelers were still at work or making their way to where he had just come from. He knew these things from the surveillance phase of his target planning. It was partially why he had chosen this route.

The Messenger didn't merely throw a pin at a map and decide where to strike next, or how to successfully flee the area. His process was intensely more complicated than that, following his methodology exactly the way he had been trained.

He had identified several targets, based on impact, proximity, likely reaction, and damage likelihood. But more than merely guessing at those outcomes, he studied them.

His surveillance began with obtaining a simple tourist map and then marking it up, for each possible location. He obtained prints or diagrams when he could, or made his own drawings if he had to. He marked important sites on his maps, such as blast radii, impediments, exit routes, and access points.

Then he spent days at each location, monitoring routine but repetitive traffic patterns. He marked the times and directions of foot and motorized police patrols, pedestrian surges, maintenance worker schedules, bus and train tables, and even the way shadows were created at various times of the day.

Then he would randomly walk those sites to gage the reaction of regulars to his presence there. And he would do that until he became an anonymous pedestrian again. Mindful of surveillance cameras, he would enter buildings and walk the public and private corridors as a test of security and to identify locked or unlocked exit and office doors, and maintenance closets. And he would use what he learned to fill in his map and drawings as to architectural failure points for blast damage projections.

And once he selected his target, he would make several dry runs to test both his timing and his access to the areas he would need.

No, none of what the Messenger did was guesswork. He was a trained professional whose goal was to live to fight another battle. He tested and retested every element of his attacks, including which railcar he would stand in when he left the scene.

This time, the young man in the hooded shirt preferred to stand by the rear doors and face outward to the east. No matter what the chaos was, less than a mile away above ground, this underground train wouldn't stop again until he was well clear of it. He could do his damage assessment based on the news reporting. He knew better than to remain at the scene to see for himself.

■ ■ ■ ■ ■

MARLEY AND I DECIDED TO walk the short distance to the Barclays branch, where the Schiff's had their numbered accounts. The setting sun was at our backs and cast a golden hue on these historic buildings as we walked. Marley's radio chirped. "I've got to get this," he said.

I tried not to eavesdrop, but I could hear enough to know that something important had happened.

Marley turned back towards the car. "I've got to get you back to your hotel," he said. "There's been another bombing and the trains are going to be either shut down soon, or overcrowded."

"Do you have to respond?" I asked.

"No," he said, "but there is bedlam, right now. This is the second time the bomber did not call ahead where civilian casualties could be high, and they were. But this time, there was a second device that went off just about the time our police, fire and emergency units arrived and the casualties are very high. My station is on stand-by alert, so I've got to get you back right now. We can come back to Barclays and finish our other interviews, hopefully tomorrow. And don't worry, I'll see to it that we get some time to finish."

I knew Marley wanted to be with his fellow officers in a time of grief. I'd been in his shoes several times, and knew that his instinct was to get to a hospital, as a show of support, where the officers would be conveyed. I knew he was giving me special treatment.

"Look, David," I said. "Go ahead. I know you need to be with your fellow officers. I'll make my way back to my office in Putney, and I can arrange transportation from there."

"No," he said. "You'll never be able to get back to your hotel without some help. The bombing was at Hyde Park, just a few blocks from your hotel. There is massive damage, roads are closed and the inbound and outbound roads are being held for emergency vehicles only. You'll ride with me."

I was beginning to believe I'd be safer on the streets of Detroit.

Marley began by driving south, and away from my hotel. "All the roads will be backed up," he explained. "It will take a while, but we'll make it faster this way."

It did take a while. And had it not been for his emergency rooftop light, and knowledge of the road system, we would have been locked up in traffic for hours.

As we pulled up in front of the Grosvenor, with Marley's blue light still flashing, I could hear the constant wail of sirens entering and leaving the area. "Right now," he said, "the only tube stations running will be the out bounds. You might as well sit tight for the entire evening. Even if you got out somewhere for a dinner, you might not be able to get back into this area, later. Consider ordering your food in tonight. We can do sightseeing another time. I've got to run," he said. "I'll call you tomorrow."

As I exited, the doorman held open the car door for me. I could see he was trying to decide if I was a good guy or a bad guy, being dropped off by a constable. Marley's smile and wave, answered his question.

I walked the few stairs to the main floor of the lobby and sat in an armchair, gathering my thoughts as well as reviewing Marley's faxed notes.

Going through the reports, I saw Clare's address. I asked the desk clerk where that was and how far it was from the hotel. He told me it wasn't too far, but it was not within an *easy jaunt* either, as he described it.

I gathered my things and went back out the front door and asked the doorman if it would be possible to get a cab. He majestically lifted his arm and signaled a black cab just down the street. "They are assigned to us, otherwise, I'm sure he would be booked already, given the disturbance." I marveled at how he used his language to understate there had just been a catastrophic bombing a few blocks away.

■ ■ ■ ■ ■

ABOUT THIRTY-FIVE MINUTES LATER, we pulled up in front of Clare's apartment building. Dusk had set on the modest three-story, Georgian, brick structure with its clean white Palladian windows. I entered the unlocked front entry and walked to the second floor unit, and stood in front of her door. It was slightly ajar.

Rapping lightly on the door, I called out, "Clare?" No answer.

I backed from the door and looked up and down the halls, but all the other doors were closed. I knocked again, "Clare, it's Michael Christian," I repeated, as I pushed the door in gently and looked inside.

The small room appeared to be empty. There were signs that the room was normally tidy and neat. But there were also signs that this was not a normal day. There was a spilt teacup on its side on the kitchen table and there were cookies on the floor. I stepped inside the room and immediately saw that there was no need to call out to Clare again.

The first I saw of her was a nylon stocking-clad leg, sticking out on the floor at the foot of her bed. One shoe was firmly on, but the other had a broken strap and was barely on her foot. As I approached her, I noticed the top of her bare thigh, with her skirt pulled up over it. The back of her pretty cream sweater was now saturated in blood. Her eyes were open, staring sightlessly into some future place. There was no need to check for a pulse.

My first thought was to look about quickly to make sure no one else was in the room. But that was a wasted gesture. I could see the entire room from where I stood. My instincts kicked in and I stood cautiously, backed to the door and touched nothing as I carefully exited the room.

I knew that my mere presence in the room had

already contaminated the crime scene. And I came to another conclusion. The brothers had already reached out to Schiff and warned him off, and I wondered if their warning to Clare hadn't perhaps gone sideways. Maybe they had no intention of warning her and this was their goal all along.

Out in the hall, while I was pondering what to do next, I heard footsteps running down the upstairs hall towards the opposite end of the hallway. Old habits took over, and I raced toward that exit on the far end of the second floor.

Through the wire-crossed, glazed glass of the security door, I saw the shape of two figures running down the stairs ahead of me. I grabbed the knob, twisted it, slammed into the door as hard as I could, and ran smack into it.

This old building was grandfathered in, before the fire codes required public doors to exit outwards. The impact almost knocked me down. I gathered my footing and yanked the door open, hearing as I did so, the sound of the downstairs door, slamming open at the street level.

I knew I had lost them.

By now, other doors on the floor were opening and people were looking out into the hall at me. "Call the police," I shouted, knowing that my briefcase was still in her apartment, and I was now the prime suspect in the murder of Clare Bennett.

■ ■ ■ ■ ■

IT DIDN'T TAKE LONG FOR the police to arrive. Apparently, we were far enough away from Hyde Park for them to not have to respond there. They were understandably surly as they briefed me on my rights, before they unceremoniously hauled me down to Scotland Yard. Even though I wasn't handcuffed, I was embarrassingly led in through a prisoner entrance. On the other hand, I was placed in an office and not in a cell.

I knew enough to keep my answers to a minimum, but I wanted to establish whatever credibility I had as quickly as possible, and to that end, I continued to drop Marley's name generously.

In short order, the detective, who appeared to be in charge of the investigation took a call. I could tell it was from Marley, because he respectfully called the party on the other end, *Sir* several times.

"Well," he said, "Marley vouches for you, and says the two of you were working a case that involved Ms. Bennett as a possible suspect. That doesn't clear you, I'm afraid. So, for the time being, until Marley gets here, you're still a suspect, but we'll dispense with the formalities of an interview, for now."

I felt only a bit relieved and asked if I could have my briefcase back. If they said *No* I knew I was in deeper than I wanted to be.

"As soon as we are through going over its contents and making copies, we might be able to do that. But we'll wait for Marley. Things are busy

127

enough around here as it is."

I knew he was talking about the bombing and the likely deaths of many police officers, and indeed there seemed to be quite a commotion of activity, but I pushed on. "There's some information I want to share with you," I said. "And it's in the briefcase."

"You mean the copies of our police files that happen to be in your briefcase? Is that what you are talking about?"

Now I was hoping that I hadn't gotten Marley into a tight spot with him sharing that information with a civilian, and one from another country.

"Well, sort of," I continued. "David and I had developed a lead and I think the sooner you move on it, the more likely you are to solving Clare's murder." I intentionally used Marley's first name to establish a sense of familiarity that we might share, while at the same time trying not to sound like I was diverting their attention away from me, even if I was.

"We'll wait for Marley," was all he said.

Almost two hours passed before Marley finally arrived. During that time, I had been either ignored or stared at with mixes of curiosity or animosity.

I wasn't sure what to expect from Marley. We had known each other for only a day, yet we seemed to get along pretty well. On the other hand, I was a murder suspect and he had nothing to gain by going out on a limb for me.

He nodded to me and to the detective before beginning. "Sorry it took me so long," he said. "I had to get back to the station, then make some calls before I could turn around and get back here. Things are still in disarray at the scene." He said.

I was sure there was still some form of chaos at the bombing scene, but there was that gift of understatement again. Since I couldn't tell if Marley was apologizing to me, or to the Constable, I just nodded.

He turned from me and said to the detective, "Might I have a word with you?" I knew he meant out of my earshot.

At first I could only see them huddled down the hall. After several minutes, I heard the detective exclaim loudly, "Really," as he looked over his shoulder at me.

They continued their private conversation a while before I heard the next words, "Are you sure?" The detective asked loudly. Marley must have answered him, because they straightened up and walked back towards me.

"You may go," The detective said, as he refilled my briefcase and returned it to me. He turned to Marley and said, "This is still my case Inspector and I have to close it. If you intend to come visiting through my district, I would hope you would do me the courtesy to include me going forward, Sir."

He used the word *sir* as some form of afterthought, demonstrating he was both polite and offended.

Marley assured him of our cooperation and motioned me toward the exit.

Back in his car, I asked Marley how he made that happen, and why.

"Those calls I made were to check up on you, Christian. It seems you are highly regarded. I started with the State Department and got Herb Lawrence. Not only was he confident of you, but he gave me some leads to follow up with in the States, which I did.

"It's still business hours there and I was able to reach Special Agent Maniaci, the head of the FBI office in your New Jersey. He speaks very highly of you. He offered me several other names as references for you, but given their titles and roles around the world, I felt that it was unnecessary. Why didn't you tell me these things about you when I asked about your background?"

I was guessing he was talking about other law enforcement agencies I had worked with around the world. Bragging about one's credentials just isn't something one does. "I don't know, David. It just never occurred to me," was all I could reply.

I realized we weren't heading back to the Grosvenor and said so. Marley said, "Since I can't trust you to keep your nose clean, I thought we would take a drive by the brothers' house. They live together and it is only about twenty minutes from here. We will drive through to see what we can see, but we won't be taking any chances in there without a uniformed backup, at least not tonight."

■ ■ ■ ■ ■

THE TWINS WALKED QUIETLY FROM the mosque toward their small flat.

"That did not go well at all," Ahmad said. "I was expecting some greater form of support, especially given what just happened. And I am not at all pleased that our Imam feels he has to tell the

130

Messenger of these developments. We have taken great pains to remain distant from that end of the business. I am beginning to doubt his intentions with us."

Nidal walked in silence a bit before responding. "We must maintain control of our own destiny at this point, Ahmad. We have spent years in preparation for our calling and this is not the time to lose it all. I think it is time to cover all our tracks and return home, or maybe disappear into Germany or the United States.

"I know we had no choice but to report this up to the Imam, but I did not expect him to seek advice or input from the Messenger either. We should also believe that the Messenger has the same reaction we are having, and that he too will begin to clean up his loose ends. And at this point, Ahmad, we should believe that would include us."

"But surely they will see that we are doing our part," Ahmad offered. "Silencing Clare must surely be seen as redemption for being exposed. The Imam will carry the message of our service and our loyalty to the Messenger.

Nidal tried to calm his brother. "I do not think we should panic at this point, my brother. I do not want to have to start all over somewhere else either, but I am also afraid it is not wise to remain here any longer."

Nidal thought back on how just a few hours ago they had silenced Clare. It seemed such a waste. She had provided a practically untraceable source of funds, so much money for them. And she had been a perfect sex partner. It was a real shame to kill her, necessary, but a shame nevertheless.

And the same with Schiff. The old fool actually

131

thought he could rely on them for a quick escape. It would be only a matter of hours before the police showed up with that security investigator. Taking him out was the only expedient thing to do. The wife knew nothing, but she had seen their faces. They might have to go back.

Yes, they had cleaned up behind themselves and there was no need to report further to the Messenger. That thought caused Nidal to shudder. They had only two true loose ends at the moment, that constable from Putney and the Transeget investigator from the States. A plan began to form in his mind. They must prove that any risk to the Messenger had been eliminated, and that they were the ones who had taken care of it. Otherwise he would take care of them.

He turned to his brother and said, "Tomorrow, we must call the investigator and tell him we want to meet with him. That will put him right where we want him."

"What if he brings the constable with him?" Ahmad asked.

"Then we must kill them both," was all his brother replied.

■ ■ ■ ■ ■

"THERE IT IS, THE FOURTH doorway up there on the right," Marley said.

I couldn't get over how close to the sidewalk the houses were built. But of course, these buildings predated the sidewalks and were constructed alongside cobblestone roads meant for horse drawn carts and wagons. It was a testament to their craftsmanship.

We parked in the darkness and waited. I wasn't sure what Marley had in mind by being here, if we couldn't get out and interrogate these guys. Men walked by in groups of two or three, looking into our windows, but we were in enough shadow that they couldn't be sure who we were or what we were doing there.

"Pretty soon, we will be confronted. The people here know that we are not regulars and neither of us can pass for Muslims," Marley observed. "Tell me what you see," he said.

There was indeed something out of the ordinary, and I knew exactly what it was.

"The people walking on the sidewalks are all males. There are no bars or sidewalk cafes, like in all other parts of the City. And there are no entertainment venues on the streets," I replied. "Is that what you mean?"

"Exactly," Marley replied. "This was once a busy nightlife scene, now it is a ghost town in that regard. And although no one is sure, the population is thought to have doubled here in recent years."

I was getting a lesson in civic mismanagement during urban resettlement. "The fact that we cannot operate safely in here is problematic, especially when a crime is committed outside the area, by someone who lives within the area," Marley continued. "It forms a pseudo sanctuary-zone for them."

Two men walked by the car, peering inside as they passed. About ten feet past us, they looked back, then ran up the street.

"Was that?" Marley exclaimed.

"Yes, the twins!" I shouted as I bolted from the car, crossed the street and ran after them.

Marley wasn't far behind me, but he kept calling, "Christian, stop! Stop!"

I wasn't gaining on the two, but I quickly realized that I wasn't going to catch them either, not in my dress shoes. Marley's words began to make sense, but I had to admit to being disappointed that I wasn't better prepared for this. And was Marley yelling the word *Christian* out loud in a Muslim neighborhood?

As I pulled up, he ran alongside me. "Man, I love your instincts," he said. "But what in bloody hell were you thinking? What would you have done if you had caught up with them, or if they had let you catch up with them in an alley? They are suspects in a gruesome murder, and may be armed. Are you?"

It was at times like these when I realized what a challenge my career choices had been for me. Over the years, I had become less and less of a capable cop, and more and more of a corporate manager and white-collar crimes investigator. I had all the right instincts, but lacked some of the tools. I'm in great physical shape and train in hand to hand combat. But I was unarmed.

While having a gun would have been ideal, this was the United Kingdom and there was none of that, not even for the coppers. Just what would I have done? I had no clue.

I turned to Marley to apologize and wipe some of the embarrassment off my face, before he had to. What I saw surprised me. Marley was holstering a nine-millimeter pistol.

"What?" was all I could get out. I'm sure he saw the look of surprise on my face.

"Don't look so surprised," he said. "Officers are not armed under normal circumstances, but we can make a request to be, and I am trained and certified as an armed response officer and licensed to carry. That's just what I did, given what you saw at Clare's, and the fact you likely chased an armed killer this evening at her apartment, and the fact that they seem to be quickly covering their tracks. I'm not taking any chances with these two and I'm not taking any chances with you."

I was hoping he meant that he was going to protect me, not worry about me getting us killed.

The foot chase hadn't attracted any attention. "So now what? Maybe we should just go knock on their door and see what happens? I'm up for it if you are." I recommended.

Marley didn't even hesitate. "No," he said. "These two won't likely be back at their place. And if they were to go there, they surely will not be opening their door to us knocking on it. I'm taking you back to your hotel, but first we are stopping on the way for dinner. Do you like Indian food?"

■ ■ ■ ■ ■

WE WERE HEADED BACK TOWARD the area of the Grosvenor when Marley made a wide swing to the south of Hyde Park. "Let's see what's going on here, first," he said.

The area was still a scene of feverous activity. Sirens were no longer wailing in the night and most ambulances had turned off their emergency lights as they sat, waiting for the last bodies or body parts to be loaded in to them.

Photographers were still taking thousands of pictures amidst working task lights that were being set up on scaffolds. Camera flashes appeared across the park nearly non-stop. The entire east area of Hyde Park was lit up as if it was day.

Marley handed me the blue roof light again, had me fasten it to the top of the car above my seat, and activate it. He then headed back east along South Carriage Drive and bypassed all the emergency vehicles parked there. He had to flash his credentials only once at a checkpoint before we entered the roundabout near the Grosvenor.

I had seen a lot of sights in my travels, but this one was depressing. The fronts of five and six story buildings lay as rubble in the streets. You could look right into the rooms of the apartments and offices they once held. And workers on the sidewalks beneath them constantly looked up, afraid that debris might tumble onto them, as they photographed the scene and hunted for evidence and body remains.

The shredding of human flesh could only be imagined, and this beautiful park's trees and shrubs had been shredded as well. Responders worked somberly in the knowledge they would likely find the foliage draped with strips of skin and organs. Recovery would take a long time for all involved, physically as well as emotionally.

By the time Marley pulled into the rear of a

nearby Indian restaurant, my thoughts were a jumbled mess. I tried to focus on my case, but kept seeing the photographers' lights flashing, knowing they were capturing the remnants of someone's family member on the ground, on street signs and on the building surfaces. I had pretty much lost my appetite and really wasn't too sure about Indian food, but I sure could use a drink.

Marley's knock on the back door soon brought a response. When the door opened, a white-shirted, very large man wrapped his arms around him and gave him a big hug. "David Marley, how good to see you. We were all concerned that you might have been part of the second explosion." Everyone seemed to grasp that the second device was meant to target responders.

"I am fine, Suresh, just fine. I was nowhere near here when this happened." Marley replied. "This is my good friend Michael Christian. He's visiting from the States and we are working a case together."

I noticed how Marley had again upped me to being his friend and it felt good, as I shook Suresh's big hand.

As we entered the restaurant I was surrounded by the smells coming from a large cylindrical tandoor oven, baking fresh breads along its interior walls, and of skewers of seasoned lamb and chicken hanging inside while they roasted. I realized I was famished.

And in the next moment, I noticed the main dining area was empty, and so did Marley.

Suresh said, "We are closed, but we are making meals to bring over to the emergency workers. My whole team showed up when they heard." I was impressed again with the civic mindedness of this culture, and I had seen similar in the States.

"Sit, sit," Suresh said. "I will bring you dinner."

In short order, he reappeared with two bottles of ice-cold Kingfisher beers without glasses. Marley raised his towards me and said, "Cheers." We clinked bottles and gulped heartily. Soon food began appearing at the table, warm, soft, fresh-baked bread, a ginger-based rice dish I didn't recognize that was absolutely delicious, and a chic-pea cold salad with mint and coriander. My taste buds were exploding in pleasure. We were both eating with our fingers, using the bread as our utensils, when Suresh said, "Pace yourselves. I am making lamb for you."

Any misgivings I had about Indian food were long gone and I was looking forward to the main course.

And that was when Marley received a radio call.

He rose from the table and stepped away. I could only hear snippets, but I did hear him ask, "Are you sure? Where is he now?" Then he closed with, "Okay, we're on our way over there." There was a pause then he continued, "Christian. Yes, the security guy from the States. I'm bringing him with me. This is his case too, and he has good instincts."

I was already up and grabbing my jacket. If they had found Schiff, I wanted to talk with him, but I was getting the impression our trip was for a different purpose.

Marley apologized to Suresh while we made our way to the door, and the owner asked if we wanted our food to go. Marley declined.

"Schiff?" I asked.

Marley nodded as we entered his Jag. Once we

got seated, he pulled out of the alley and onto the street. "He's dead," was all he said.

I had a million questions but it was obvious he didn't have any answers yet, so we drove in silence for a while.

It was just as well. I needed to figure out just how far I was going to continue with this case, given that two of my suspects were dead already, and I was likely still a suspect in one of those murders. And I had to wonder if Marley was keeping me near him for that very reason. Obviously he didn't think I was a threat to him.

The hell with it, I thought. The only way I could surely clear my name was to solve the case. If Marley was trying to solve it too, so much the better.

We had been traveling for about twenty minutes and I realized, in the warmth of the car, that I was becoming drowsy. Thinking back, it occurred to me I had been awake over twenty-four hours, and I was fading. It seemed we were headed back towards Wandsworth, and soon my hunch was borne out, when we crossed the Wandsworth Bridge over the Thames.

This far down the river from the London City Center, the river had lost its charm. Only the glow in the sky from lights of Westminster Abbey and Big Ben could be seen around its bend, and the small enclaves along its banks offered no additional light. This was one of the world's most historic rivers, yet tonight, it just seemed black and lifeless.

As we crossed to the south side of the bridge, I could see we were practically back at Schiff's shop. "Where are we going?" I asked.

"Just down the road past Schiff's," Marley said.

"His body was found in an alley behind the Silver Saber Pub, on the corner."

■ ■ ■ ■ ■

THE IMAM LOOKED BACK AND wondered how he had managed to get himself involved in an undertaking, where his own violent death now loomed as a real possibility.

As an older man and a respected spiritual leader who had spent his years in prayer and in leading others to pray, he should be looking back on a life filled with accomplishment and redemption. Instead, he was a link in what he believed was a terrorist plot.

Over the years, he had observed without complaint, while the Great Prophet's message of peace had been corrupted and co-opted into a mantra of hate and divisiveness, even between fellow Muslims. Then he gradually accepted his role of advancing that interpretation. He watched as the poor, the jobless and the disaffected gained a sense of belonging and entitlement in the new movement.

He watched the recent transformation, as it raced across the Middle East. And in this awareness, he recognized the history of violent extremism repeating itself, as it had for centuries.

It was bad enough that Muslims were driving peaceful people, of their own faith, out of their own lands. But when people chose to flee, by the millions, it created one of the largest re-settlements in history. It is how he ended up in London, to find peace and make a new living as a man of Allah.

But now this jihad had followed him here as well, demanding that everyone must either *embrace and submit to Muslim authority, or die.*

For centuries, Muslims had taken up jihad to force the world to follow the Prophet. But the leaders of those global conflicts had turned the Prophet's words to their own desires. And somewhere, Ramzi Ayyad, the Imam of Al-Irschad, had ended up on the side of hate and became an enabler in the war of a thousand cuts.

His decision was now filled with deadly complications.

His instructions were very specific: Identify local resources for untraceable cash. Provide the money to the Messenger. Receive money from Iran and redistribute it to the Messenger. Create barriers at each point of contact so nothing would ever be traceable to the Messenger, back to Iran, or to Hezbollah. And keep a low profile, so as not to alert the faithful of the mosque, or the authorities to their activities.

Instead of a smooth and secret operation, the brothers had put it all at risk. The police were involved and were suspicious of them. And there was an American conducting an investigation that might lead directly to the twins. Someone had already been killed. And the brothers were insisting that the Messenger must not be notified. But there were two other problems, much larger ones.

As the brothers came up with these large amounts of cash, the Imam had been setting some of that money aside for himself. It was his intention to be able to flee someday. He didn't know where, but he knew he could not stay trapped in a web of his own making.

At first he rationalized that the money was for the mosque. There was so much good that he could do with it. But soon, the money ended up in the hands of a killer, or in private accounts that he had set up for himself.

And that was the first problem. If the brothers and the Messenger ever got together to discuss these complications, the true amounts of money would be discovered and they would both realize the shortages were at the Imam's end. He needed holy guidance on how to proceed. But he knew where this would take him. He had to eliminate either the brothers or the Messenger.

The second problem was much more difficult.

His orders came from Hezbollah and there was no margin for error. None.

The Messenger was a Hezbollah proxy warrior, and he operated as an independent cell, financed through the Imam. It was Ayyad's job to keep the cash flowing and the Messenger anonymous. Even he did not specifically know what the Messenger's business was, but he had a good inkling and it was an ugly reality. The Messenger, therefore, would certainly be the most dangerous risk to manage.

The Imam had recruited the brothers from the membership of the mosque. The two traveled to Syria and then to Afghanistan, received their training and returned to London.

Hezbollah provided their identities and their resumes to establish their credibility. And they moved them from employer to employer, around London. Once there, they stole corporate money any way they could, and they had proven quite adept at it.

But the brothers were soft, completely unlike the Messenger. They were merely fundraisers who now had to learn how to kill. If they were captured, though, Ayyad did not feel they could be trusted to remain silent. Yes, they were a problem, and yet, perhaps the easiest to address.

He had no choice but to help Hezbollah. One is not given a choice. He was chosen and then ordered to identify disaffected young men from the mosque for radicalization and training. Ayyad was not of Hezbollah, so they would not close ranks to protect him.

He wondered whom he feared more, Hezbollah, the Messenger, or his possible exposure to the British authorities by the brothers. As he considered his options for saving himself, the easiest path became more obvious. He wasn't trained to be deceptive, but he could be if necessary. That wasn't the problem. The problem was that he wasn't trained to be a murder. His dilemma was about protecting his life from people who had already killed, which could very possibly happen to him too, unless he eliminated his first level of risk. His path forward became clear.

The way to permanently remove the brothers was by using the Messenger as his weapon. He merely had to get an explanation to him before the brothers did.

His fingers moved over the beads of his *Misbaha*, as he prayed quietly, thanking Allah for the budding idea, and requesting further spiritual enlightenment.

■ ■ ■ ■ ■

THE SILVER SABRE WAS A neighborhood watering hole and hotel combined, and it had occupied that same corner for over one hundred years. One of its unique features included an outdoor garden in the rear. You got to it from inside the pub, or from a narrow sidewalk around the corner. It was the kind of place where everyone knew everyone, for better or worse. Like *Cheers* only with a British accent. I was coming to respect how the British revered their neighborhood history and kept so many of their architectural reminders fully functional.

Uniformed constables had cordoned off the entire side of the building, and the hedge-trimmed walkway that accessed the courtyard. There, in that little aisle laid the body of a man I presumed was Eli Schiff. Jacketless, he was on his stomach, with his face flat in the dirt. Even though he hadn't been, with his arms and legs stretched out, he looked as if he had been crucified to the ground. His white shirt was drenched in a pattern of blood that showed multiple penetrations to the back and neck.

Given the amount of blood oozing from the body and onto the sidewalk, I surmised that at least one artery had been severed somewhere, but not until several of the other stab wounds had also caused significant internal bleeding from critical organs. One of his loafer-shoes was hanging off his right foot and the other was missing.

144

"Hi Marley," said a woman bending over the body.

Marley ignored the greeting. "What have we got?"

"Nice to see you too," the woman replied, knowing she had been snubbed.

"Well, Cheri, what have we got?"

The woman appeared to have taken over the scene, but she didn't look like a detective. She had on a black zip up jacket and a pair of black dress-slacks that looked out of place, with her kneeling on the ground. Her black, mesh tennis shoes seemed more practical for the type of work she was doing.

"We won't know for certain until I get the body on a table," Cheri replied. "But from the looks of this, I'd say there was a violent, but short struggle that began over there." With that she pointed her light deeper into the courtyard.

"It looks like they fought there briefly, because that's where his other shoe is. But he was also stabbed over there at least four times, given the different directional spatters we have identified. I'll have a better count when we get some floodlights on the scene. Most of them are being used at Hyde Park right now."

Cheri continued examining Schiff's lower torso as she filled us in. "It looks like he managed to crawl here, where the final cuts occurred. I total eleven on his back, and one in his left buttock, as if he was trying to move away when that thrust occurred. One of the wounds is a slice that occurred when the victim was falling to the ground, while the blade was being used to support his weight. There will certainly be some damage to the intestines with that one.

145

There do not appear to be any fatal head or facial wounds, but there are defensive wounds on the hands. One particularly deep one seems to be from when he grabbed the blade of a sharp weapon. His right little finger is barely attached. From the numerous stab wounds, I'd say the killer or killers were in a state of frenzy at this point. Any five or six of the back wounds could have been the fatal puncture, and a few on the front could have been as well. Death wasn't instantaneous, but it didn't take long.

I won't know how long it took, or which was the fatal blow, until I open him up and examine the order of the exsanguination. There is a high possibility that at least his descending aorta has been cut, by several of these wounds, either on purpose or by accident. Regardless, he bled out in a hurry, right here. So, for the moment, *what you have* Detective Inspector Marley, is death by stabbing."

She struck me as competent and succinct, capable of clear communications, and obviously a forensic expert. Her tone also let Marley know that whatever the problem was between them, she was capable of disciplined analytic skills.

Marley apparently wasn't through with her yet. He was being blunt, if not curtly impolite. "How many assailants?" He asked.

I knew where he was going with that.

Not rising to the bait, she leaned back on her haunches and looked at Marley for the first time while answering, "It could have been just one person with two knives, but he would have to be very, very proficient with bladed weapons, very strong, and nearly ambidextrous, given the placement and deep penetration of the thrusts on both sides of the torso."

"So, you're saying it was one person, with two knives?" Marley asked.

"No, that's not what I am saying, Marley," she replied. "What I'm saying is that it was more than likely two persons, but you know I don't like to guess. Either way, since there seem to have been two weapons, I will rule out a crime of passion. I'm ruling out robbery too, since he still has his wallet, money and credit cards. And check this out."

With that, Cheri aimed her flashlight beneath one of the shrubs that ran between the sidewalk and the building wall.

In the darkness it would have been nearly impossible to see, but with her lantern, the area was better illuminated. She, or someone on her team, had been quite thorough in investigating the entire crime scene, including the less conspicuous areas. There I saw a well-worn, black, leather travel satchel with a brass-handled, pull open top, sitting upright under the bush.

"Look inside," Cheri told Marley. "That's another reason I don't think this was a robbery. But use a pencil." With that she handed him one from her jacket.

I knew what she meant. The crime scene guys hadn't dusted it yet for prints and a pencil was a means of prying open a closed lid, without smudging any evidence.

Marley ignored her offer and slipped his expensive pen from his jacket and began fiddling with the lid of the bag, but it was too firmly closed. I offered him my thick-barreled Bettoni pen and with those two tools, he was able to ease it open.

147

Marley let out a slow whistle and motioned me over. Even in the dark, a small brick-shaped object was catching enough light to reflect off its surface. Sitting on top of a once neatly pile of clothes, was a solid gold bar.

"Hold these," he said and handed me the pens. Marley reached into his pocket and while I held the case open, he shined a pocket penlight into the bag.

Clearly stamped, on the brightly reflective bar, were the words *The Royal Mint Refinery, 1000g 999.9, Fine Gold,* with an apparent serial number below that. *Definitely not a robbery.*

From my Detroit Police days, when bulk street heroin was sold in kilograms, I knew there were two point two pounds in a thousand grams, or a kilogram. I was trying to do the math out loud and convert English measure to U.S., and pounds to dollars again, when Marley said, "It's about 35 ounces, and about twenty-two thousand dollars." Marley continued to impress me.

"So, he wasn't robbed, or at least the killers didn't know he had gold in his bag," I ventured.

Cheri turned sharply to me and said sternly to Marley, "And who might this yank be Marley? He sure as bloody hell isn't a constable, and he is mucking up my death scene."

Marley didn't reply to the question. He merely said, "He was never here and neither was I. We don't go in your report, either, Cheri. Just make sure I get a copy."

And with that we left.

As we turned the corner out onto the street, I asked, "What the hell was that all about David? What's up with you and Cheri?"

His gaze seemed distant as he reflected on *what was up* with her. "Ah, Ms. Cheri," he replied.

"We had a go at it a while back and I was actually falling for her. You know, Christian. Dinner, candlelight, wine in the garden, operas, quiet walks, slow kissing, maybe more. That sort of thing. As you can see, she is quite a looker and smart as a whip.

"Whenever we had common time off, I'd ask her to join me on holiday retreats. But she was always off to the Isle of Man, doing a scuba dive with her friends. She's a bit of an amateur photographer. Well, maybe more than a bit. She sells her art to magazines, like National Geographic.

"Anyway, I didn't take it very well when I learned she was seeing another copper and a doctor at the same time."

"Were you guys going steady or anything like that?" I asked.

"We aren't high school kids, Michael. She and I weren't exclusive or anything like that. At least she wasn't. I realized she was playing the entire field, and I just didn't want to compete for her attention any longer.

"When I found out I wasn't as important to her as she was to me, it bothered me a lot. I didn't have any reason to be, but I was actually hurt, angry. You know? So, eventually I stopped calling her. Whenever we bumped into each other, I made it a point to walk away. She tried calling, but I wouldn't pick up her calls or return them."

"So you broke it off with her, or maybe just eased your way out of it," I concluded.

"More or less," he said. "As you can see, I just don't manage our meetings on the street very well."

149

As we got in his Jag, I asked, "She obviously meant a lot to you. Did you ever tell her how you feel?" I asked.

"Skip it," was all he said. He closed the door without slamming it.

I thought about having another go at Mrs. Schiff, just up the street, to see if her husband's murder jogged her memory any. But this wasn't the time and I didn't know what additional value it would bring. I also wondered if she was in danger, but I thought she would be able to figure that out for herself.

At this stage of my investigation, other than the twins and Barclays, there weren't too many leads left for me to follow. I didn't see where the boys would be very forthcoming, and if they were good for the murders, then they had more to hide than just stolen checks. Whether they believed the police suspected them or not, finding them might be hard enough, much less questioning them.

Barclays could wait until tomorrow. I'd try first thing in the morning to get an appointment with them. It was becoming less a matter of urgency for me to get the money back, than it was for Flannery. I thought about the General Counsel and the fact that I was here only because he wanted to stick it to Barclays, and it doubled my resolve to give it my best shot.

The thought occurred to me that, given the time zone difference, I could call and update him. My seemingly simple larceny case had turned into one where the suspects were dying off at an alarming rate. Flannery and I both knew that as much as I liked finding out who committed the crimes, and getting signed admissions, solving murders for the local police was way out of my bailiwick. Been there, done that.

Common sense and fatigue were telling me to drop the *who done it* of the murders, and focus on getting our money back.

If I could get off Marley's suspect list, I would make a casual day of tomorrow, visit Barclays, and maybe do some sightseeing and shopping for Alice.

"David," I said. "I'm exhausted. Can you take me back to the hotel?"

"Of course," he replied. "It's been a long one for both of us."

Twenty-five minutes later I was in front of the hotel, watching him pull away. The last thing he said when he left was, "This time, don't go anywhere without checking with me first."

At least he didn't pull my passport.

As I entered the lobby, to retrieve my key, the desk clerk handed me an envelope. Inside was a message written on linen card stock. It was a phone message from Nidal Halima.

In expert penmanship, the desk clerk had written a local phone number, and the words, *Mr. Halima requests the favour of a call to him in the morning.*

■ ■ ■ ■ ■

I HAD A HARD TIME getting to sleep, even though I was exhausted. The day's events played over and over in my mind, as I thought about poor Clare's bloody body. I had seen her young face when she was alive, and could tell that she had a lifetime of opportunity in front of her. She was bright and full of youthful energy. Seeing her dead, and murdered in such a gruesome manner, was disheartening.

Based on my interviews that day, I had my suspicions as to who it was that killed her. I wondered if Marley agreed with them, even though we never got around to airing them to each other. I was hoping I wasn't high on Marley's suspect list any more, and that kept me up a while too.

I replayed the visit to Schiff's store. It was an eye opener to learn about laundering money through gold purchases. But finding the old man killed in nearly the same way as Clare, but so much more savagely attacked, tightened my focus as to who might have done it. I figured it was only a matter of time before Marley picked up the two brothers, at least for questioning.

Finally there was the chase in the Muslim sector of the two guys I recognized as the twins from Transeget. Now Nidal wanted me to call him in the morning. There was something very wrong about the brothers being involved in nearly my entire day yesterday. About the only time I didn't bump into them was with Marley at Wimbledon.

And the fundamental question still had to do with motive. Why steal so much money and run the risk over and over? Why buy gold? Why kill Clare and Schiff? And if they did just steal and forge the checks, why didn't they just disappear? It seemed easy to do with a half million dollars.

Things were getting interesting and I decided I

was going to follow my hunches. I was going to solve my case, either with or without Marley. And if it turned out that my thieves were also murders, so much the better. I just had to make sure not to end up at the end of Ms. Cheri's flashlight beam somewhere.

And with those questions tossing about in my head, I finally fell asleep. I dreamed fitfully of Schiff and Clare's corpses, drenched in bloodstained clothes, driving a huge truck and chasing me down a narrow street where I couldn't outrun them. They were both waving bloody swords out their windows as they closed in on me.

■ ■ ■ ■ ■

MY ALARM JOSTLED ME AWAKE and it took a while for me to get my bearings in the room. The first thing I wanted to do was call home, but it was only about midnight in New Jersey. I tossed on my sweats and ran about five miles on the fitness center treadmill, and added some heavy dumbbell exercises.

I was missing my daily one-hour workout with my martial arts trainer, but I'd be back on track in a few days. So, I wrapped up my workout practicing kicks with a half-dozen chagi maneuvers, instead of running again on the treadmill.

I showered, had breakfast in my room, made up my case notes from yesterday, then waited for businesses to open in London before I called

Barclays.

My call to them went easier than I thought. Although I only spoke with the secretary, she was most agreeable to adding me to the bank vice president's schedule that morning at ten o'clock. I was about to ask for extra time, but she anticipated that as well, "Mr. Finch will only be able to meet with you for fifteen minutes tops. You see, he has a full calendar as it is."

Well, if that was the way he was playing it, I would have to make my point clearly and concisely. And that would be where my carte blanche came in.

I reviewed my notes from the meeting with Flannery to be sure I knew how much was at risk with Barclays. And then I called Nidal Halima.

He answered on the first ring and when I introduced myself, he demandingly said, "I told you to call me right away."

I wasn't about to be pushed around by a suspect. "You said to call in the morning. It's morning. What do you want?"

"Why were you watching us last night at our home?" he asked.

"What makes you think we were watching you? And why did you run? What are you afraid of?" I responded. I was getting ready to hang up on him, but we both knew I would wait for an answer, so we could proceed to the reason for his call.

"We are afraid of nothing," he replied. "We thought you were robbers and were coming after us."

"Cut the crap, Halima," I said. "Tell me why you wanted me to call."

He said, "My brother and I know that you think

we stole the company's checks. We did not, but we might know who did."

This was about the weakest attempt at a set up I had ever seen, but the only way I was going to find out what he was up to was to play along.

"Meet me at my hotel," I suggested, knowing they would never agree.

"No," he replied. "Meet us at the Transeget office, at twelve-thirty."

I was actually pleasantly surprised about that, so I agreed. It would surely be safe to meet them there, and although it seemed unlikely, maybe they actually did have something to offer. But first I had to head over to Barclays and get our money back.

Using the information in Flannery's report from our finance department, made me feel like I was bringing a blackjack to a bare knuckles fight.

I was ready.

■ ■ ■ ■ ■

THE BARCLAYS BUSINESS OFFICE WAS not a retail branch for the average customer. It was located in a courtyard inside a fortress-like building, with a driveway that passed through an attended gate. My credentials must have been in order, because I was admitted based on my name and that of the vice president, Peter Finch.

The entry door, at address 936b, opened as I approached it, and an attractive woman in a grey business dress invited me in.

"Thank you for being punctual, Mr. Christian. Mr. Finch will be with you promptly." With that she seated me in a comfortable but small outer office, and disappeared from view. I began looking over my note highlights, but within moments I was greeted.

"Mr. Christian, I'm Peter Finch. How do you do?"

"I'm well, Mr. Finch. A pleasure." I replied just as formally as his greeting.

"Come this way," was all he said, as he guided me to his office, without offering me a handshake or his business card. I pocketed mine.

He motioned me to a chair and, rather than join me in discussion there, returned to sit behind his desk. The battle lines were drawn and I figured I had about fourteen minutes left.

"Mr. Finch, I know you're busy, so I'll keep this short," I began. "We want our money deposited back into our account, all of it, with interest."

Finch was about to object, but I pushed through. "Your Wandsworth branch accepted a Transeget Industries corporate check in an amount over retail branch transaction levels. The check was signed twice, with neither person presenting any of our corporate credentials, and neither name appearing on record as an authorized signor. In fact the first-line maker's signature is illegible."

Finch was about to object again, but I had one more quick point to make.

"We both know that it is the bank's responsibility to properly identify the presenter, even in a simple retail transaction, and that was not done."

I then paused for effect, as much as to solicit a response from Finch.

He seemed bored and was looking at his watch,

so I continued.

"As fair warning to you, I want to make you aware that you have a very short window within which to attempt to recover your loss from Eli Schiff's numbered account at the Jewelry shop."

That got his attention and sat him up in his chair.

"How did you come by this knowledge?" Finch asked.

"It really doesn't matter, Mr. Finch. But you and I know full well that you are on very thin ice here, and I'm sure your legal counsel has advised you of the same. Your only recourse is against Schiff. And his assets are likely to be frozen within the next twelve hours, if they haven't been already."

"What do you mean?" Finch asked. He now seemed edgy and I had his full attention.

"Schiff was murdered last night." And I let that sink in.

Finch seemed confused. "Murdered? What do you mean, *murdered*?" he asked.

"What part of murdered don't you understand? Someone killed him last night, stabbed him over and over until he was dead. Murdered."

Finch was no longer safe in his elegant office, away from the fray, making decisions worth millions of dollars, while remaining once or twice removed from the effect of his actions. Someone had killed a customer of his that he was trying to protect from my prying eyes, and to keep us from recovering our money.

And now here I was in his office with more information than I could have possibly been aware of, unless I was close to it in some way. I was letting that hang out there for him. If he thought that perhaps I had come across the Atlantic pond to kill

157

someone involved in a forgery of our checks, then that was fine with me.

A new, thin film of moisture glistened on his forehead and upper lip.

"I believe I have only about ten minutes left, Mr. Finch. So, if you don't mind, I'll continue.

"As I said, we want our money deposited back into our account.

"I'm sure you have checked on my authority, but let me confirm that for you." With that I handed him Flannery's tersely worded letter, giving me full authority to speak for him and the company. He read it while I kept on talking.

"We both also know that Barclays is in the same position as the other members of your "Big Four" British banks. Your retail sales are diving and the industry average is showing a loss of about twenty percent, in the ten years from nineteen-eighty to nineteen-ninety. I expect you fit right into that average."

Finch was listening in disbelief to every word I said, and must have been wondering how a security guy would be on top of a British financial institution's track record.

"You're like the others, experiencing downward pressure on your margins, so every penny of your deposits is critical. And I'm sure your own personal performance is measured by deposit growth and customer retention. Those metrics probably factor into calculations for your year-end bonus."

"Barclays is solid," Finch replied. We're having one of our strongest growth periods ever," he huffed. "I believe it is time for you to leave."

I wasn't through with him yet, but I could see he was backing against the ropes. I was going to mess with him a bit more.

"Actually, we both know that's not true, Finch. Barclays' growth rate, in particular, has plummeted by thirty-five percent in the last year alone, so the competition must be eating away at you." Finch seemed stunned.

I knew these very same facts must have been keeping him up at night. Now was the time to bring out the blackjack.

"So, let me cut to the chase, Finch. Transeget Industries has about six million U.S. dollars deposited with Barclays in accounts that you manage. We have enjoyed our relationship with you, but you seem to view our financial friendship as a one-way street." With that, I produced the blank check that Clare had given me and waved it slowly in front of his face. "Pretend for a moment, Mr. Finch, that this is a withdrawal slip.

"If I do not see every dollar of those forgeries back in our account by four o'clock this afternoon, with interest, compounded daily from the date of the first illegal withdrawal, then I will have our manager prepare a certified money order at our local Putney branch, in the entire amount remaining in all our accounts with you.

"That is over six million in U.S. dollars, Finch. Tomorrow morning, I'll withdraw it from your accounts and within the hour, I'll deposit it all into a single new account at Lloyds Bank, your chief competitor. You know I have the authority, and I think you know I have the mindset."

Finch looked like he was somewhere between passing out and vomiting.

With that I rose. "And I would be more than willing to set up a press conference announcing our

159

new partnership with Lloyds.

"Now, sir. I believe my time is up. Do you have any questions?"

Finch was pale. He rose but did not move from behind his desk. He looked at his desk and fiddled with a single sheet of paper. I could see *Transeget Industries* written at the top and I could see the four checks listed and their amounts. I guessed he was doing a calculation, trying to decide whether sticking to his original refusal to return our half million dollars was worth losing six.

"Would you be open to negotiating some settlement less than the whole amount?" he countered. "Don't forget, your security was weak over protecting the blank financial instruments," His voice carried no sense of confidence.

"No," I answered firmly. "Our security meets all acceptable business standards, and Transeget Industries was not negligent in that regard. Our protocols were criminally breached. We will accept no compromise."

Finch hadn't given up yet, but he was done and he knew it. He said, "I'm sure we can come to some kind of agreement, Mr. Christian. Let me have our attorneys draw something up."

"The time for that was earlier, Finch, when you had a chance with Mr. Flannery. Instead you played tough guy. You basically said, if we didn't like it we could sue you. Mr. Flannery might consider that an option, but I'm afraid I am not that much of a gentleman," I stood in front of his desk and put both my fists down on it.

"I want it all back, by four o'clock local time today. And I want you to send a confirming email to Mr. Flannery, with a copy to me, well before then.

Here's my card. I'll see myself out."

And with that I left without looking back. He pissed me off, acting a financial bully in his fancy bespoke suit and tiny fingers.

I had a real threat to deal with next, and now I felt ready to take it on.

■ ■ ■ ■ ■

THE MESSENGER KEPT THE TELEVISION news channel on low volume as he read in detail the morning's stories from the Times, The Guardian, The Daily Mail and The Sun. The bombing had been covered on television and in all the papers, but he only had time for these. He was trying to obtain an accurate damage assessment in terms of dead, injured, and critically injured, and trying to separate those from the first explosion compared with the damage and death of the second one. The data was very important to him as he planned his coup de gras.

He was particularly interested in the blast dispersion effect. How far did the kill circle go and how much structural damage was caused to the buildings both on the northern and eastern streets? These facts would help him shape his next explosive load requirements. The Messenger was methodical and cautious.

He was irritated when his phone rang, because very few people had his number. He let it ring a while before he picked it up.

"Yes," Was all he said.

The Imam began with a short blessing then got right to the heart of the matter, "Your funding source may have been compromised. We need to talk. Where are you?" Ayyad knew they could not have an open conversation of this nature over the phone, even if there was little likelihood of eavesdropping. But more importantly, he wanted to learn where the Messenger could be found, if necessary.

The Messenger looked at his watch, mentally reorganized his day and said, "I can be at the mosque in an hour." Then he hung up.

The Imam stared at the phone, knowing he had been hung up on without a goodbye salutation. And the Messenger had deftly established the meeting location to avoid being discovered.

The Messenger was dealing with troublesome problems on both sides, but he was not incapable of managing them. He was quite ready, based on his damage assessment, to build the next device. All he had to do was escalate the timeline by one day and he could still deliver a historic moment to his enemies. One they would never forget.

Rather than be precise with the explosive composition of multiple devices, now he would go for maximum effect with just one. And he had an idea on just how he would do that. Allah willing, this plan might work out even better.

He packed up every piece of personal property he had in his apartment. It was time to shut it down. He would bleach the entire room before he left. Except for one, he put all the research on his next optional target sites into a metal pot. He spritzed acetone onto the papers and lit them. The flame lifted high into the room before it settled down. Within minutes the entire packet was ash. He picked up the remaining notes and slipped them into his satchel.

Once he had what he needed from his warehouse, he would clean and abandon it as well. In a few days, he would be a ghost, living and operating in another country.

■ ■ ■ ■ ■

I WAS FEELING GOOD ABOUT my meeting with Finch but it was too early to call Flannery in the States and update him. Instead, I dashed him off a summary email.

Around ten thirty, I decided it was time to call Marley from my hotel to see if he had any new information on Clare and Schiff's murders, but he called me first.

"It's Marley," was all he said, when I picked up. "Where have you been Christian?"

There was no courteous greeting, no first name basis. I wondered if I was higher on the suspect list than I would like.

I decided to play it straight with him. He had been up front with me all along, or so it seemed.

"I'm not sure what timeframe you are talking about, but I worked out this morning downstairs and then I was at Barclays getting our money back."

"How did that go?" He inquired.

"The workout or the Barclays visit?"

"You being funny, this morning, Christian? I meant the Barclay's visit."

"I gave the guy until later this afternoon and left him with a lot to think about. So, I won't know until then."

"They're pretty tough Christian, they are one of the big boys on the block," Marley said, as if he was trying to soften the blow of a refusal.

I continued as if I hadn't heard him, "I hope you don't mind, but I let him know about Schiff and used his surprise and anxiety to my advantage."

It seemed a while before he could frame his reply, as if he was struggling with different responses. Then he said. "It will be all over the tabloids today, if it isn't already. But that is not why I called."

I knew Marley wasn't calling out of courtesy, and I noticed that he had reverted to using my last name again.

"I've been thinking about coincidences of time and place," he said. "I don't like random events that come together too neatly. And I don't, frankly, much believe in them."

Neither do I, I thought.

Marley continued, "I want to go over my ideas with you, since you are a common factor of the equation that is present in all of them."

I was getting uncomfortable with the direction this was going in. "Where are you now?" he asked.

I couldn't tell if it was a good or bad thing that I was part of his unlikeable coincidence. With almost two hours before I was to meet Halima, perhaps it would be better if I had more information from him, before I met with Marley. I needed to buy some time. "I'm at the Grosvenor, Marley. But I'm supposed to meet someone at twelve-thirty. Can we talk later?"

Marley said, "I'm outside your door now. Open it." It sounded more like a demand than a request.

■ ■ ■ ■ ■

AHMAD HAD FINISHED DRESSING AND was waiting for his brother to do so as well.

"You realize once we do this, we cannot go back to work and we cannot go home?" He hated change and uncertainty, probably because he was not the logical thinker that Nidal was. Ahmad enjoyed the prompt gratification he received from responding to his emotional instincts.

Thinking things through was boring and frustrating, because there were always so many alternatives. He always got bogged down when too many variables influenced the choices he would have to make. Although he appreciated his brother's more analytic approach, he never really understood his reasoning. Nidal, was always, therefore, the leader, even over life altering decisions. And that left Ahmad in a constant state of timid anxiety.

Nidal replied, "We both knew this day could have happened at any time, *habibi*. The only thing we didn't plan for was having to do so much cleanup before we left. We have money, many passports, and we have other places we can go.

165

Are you unable to go through with this? Tell me now if I cannot count on you."

Nidal had just referred to him as habibi, a term of male endearment, and now, the tone that came from his brother was the most threatening Ahmad could recall since they were children, when they argued about skipping *salat,* prayers. And ever since Nidal decided to seduce Clare, they had been missing their midday *Dhuhr,* because they were with Clare. Nidal's warning frightened him and made him wonder about the bond of their brotherhood.

Ahmad resented that Nidal drove that wedge between them. Nidal used the tactic every time Ahmad disagreed with him. He made it seem like he was being disloyal to their blood relationship.

"Of course you can trust me. I am your brother," Ahmad replied, begrudgingly. "We are in this together, until the end."

"Then let us pray that our resolve carries *both* of us to success. Check your dharia again."

Ahmad slipped his right hand across his stomach to the front, left side of his waistband. Secured into his belt was a tooled, leather sheath containing the long-bladed knife. Normally worn across the waist by horse-warriors in the dessert, he had his dropped alongside his leg for concealment.

More of a short-curved sword than a knife, the weapon was a gift from his father. His brother possessed its twin. His father had presented the babies with the knives at birth and Ahmad wondered if his father might have known then, how they would be used. "It is good," he told his brother, as he steeled his courage for the upcoming meeting with the American investigator.

■ ■ ■ ■ ■

THE IMAM'S NEWS WAS WORSE than he expected, but not surprising. The Messenger knew that when working with others, who are less committed or who do not understand the full implications of the mission, you must always expect a degree of effort below your own. You must expect time-lines to be missed.

But one cannot tolerate intentional abuse, deception and self-serving actions. He began framing the rationale for his next move, thinking, *they steal from me and they are sinners against the teachings of the Quran. They should not have had sex before marriage, and certainly not with an infidel woman.* Had she not already been dead, I would kill her too.

They suggested that because they had eliminated any ties to the operation, that they had proven their loyalty and trustworthiness. Maybe the Imam bought into that, but not the Messenger. Beyond mere retribution and punishment, the Messenger knew that it was time to eliminate the risk they brought upon him and his mission. He had never met them and they did not know who he was, but it didn't matter. He knew who they were. The connection was there and it was time to sever the brothers from it.

■ ■ ■ ■ ■

AS I OPENED MY HOTEL room door, Marley walked straight in without a greeting and was followed into the room by a tall attractive woman. I couldn't place her age, but she appeared to be in her early thirties. I was relieved he wasn't in the company of a couple uniformed constables. That would have meant my arrest for sure.

"This is Miriam Bishara. She's now working this case." There was no further introduction and before I could offer a greeting, Marley turned to me and said, "Hear me out all the way before you interrupt me, Michael." I sensed a demanding tone in his voice and subconsciously, braced myself for the worse.

I shifted my body weight into a balanced defensive position, with my hands loosely at my sides. Bishara must have caught it, because she circled to my right and slightly behind me, while Marley walked to the center of the room and began, "You came to me, just yesterday, and when you introduced yourself, you told me you would be conducting a criminal investigation on British soil."

I was about to object, because I expressly told Marley that I was only conducting an internal investigation, but he plowed on. "I asked you to wait until I finished," he said.

"But the reality is you are conducting an investigation into a crime committed and reported in my jurisdiction. It's on my books. And that is why

I *volunteered* to join you yesterday." Marley held up his hand as if to say, *I'm not done yet.* So, I kept quiet.

"Then the first witness you and I interviewed ended up dead," He continued. "Not only did she die in her apartment, but you were the only one who could be identified at the scene.

"Then we interviewed your second witness. And the second suspect you and I talked with, ended up dead too.

"And finally, you were there when we staked out the twins and you let them get away in an ill-advised chase.

"So, I ask myself, *who or what is the common denominator.* And you know what I come up with?"

I knew the answer and I gave it to him, "Me," I said.

Marley looked at me strangely. "You?" he asked.

"No. You were with me all the time, after we left Schiff, so you couldn't have murdered him. And the witnesses, who live on the same floor at Clare's apartment building, agreed with your story that they heard footsteps running along the upstairs hall, as you ran down their hallway. And although I can't be sure, I am betting that Cheri will let us know that the time of death precedes you discovering her.

"No one saw you as you ran away from Clare's room, but many heard you and then saw you return and ask them to call for the police. If you could have made good your escape, why would you have returned?

"No, its not you, Christian. It's the money. Isn't that what you Yanks always say about your bank robbers? *Follow the money?*" With that question hanging out there, he paused, as if finally giving me permission to speak.

I wanted to remind Marley that one of the reasons I returned was to grab my briefcase from inside Clare's room, but this wasn't the time.

"Well, if I'm not a suspect, let me take your reasoning one step further," I said.

"There's one more common denominator," I said, "and we both know what that is. It's the brothers, themselves. And I agree the money is the link. If these are really the guys who stole the checks, they should be living way above their means, yet don't seem to be. So, the question is, what did they do with the cash?"

"To answer your question about the money," Marley said, "we've checked. They only have one bank account, with both their names on it. It's a savings account only, with only moderate cash in it. Not even two thousand dollars. They seem to be living paycheck to paycheck. So, yes, where is the money?"

"Exactly," I concurred. "And where are the Halima brothers?"

"As for Nidal and Ahmad, we're trying to locate them right now. As soon as we find them we are going to bring them in for questioning," Marley replied.

I could see where this was going to get complicated, so I opened up to Marley.

"I received a message from Nidal last night, after we saw them in their neighborhood. He wanted me to call him this morning. I spoke with him this morning by phone and he wants to meet with me. We set up a meeting at the Transeget office in Putney, for twelve-thirty this afternoon."

Marley looked at Bishara and asked me, "You

know why they want to meet you?"

"He didn't say, but I'm guessing either to see where we are in our investigation, or to feed me some bad information to throw us both off the trail," I replied.

"Possibly," Marley said. "But there could be another reason."

I knew where he was going with this, because I had the same sense.

"Maybe they want to eliminate you too."

I would have been lying to say the thought hadn't crossed my mind. But to hear Marley explain it so simply, put a new edge on my resolve and upped my caution level.

"I'm not too worried about that," I replied. "Have you seen these two? They look pretty soft. And even if they were responsible for killing Clare and Schiff, that would make them knife guys. I'm not too worried about that."

I had faced plenty of people with knives before and had been in Tae Kwan Do training for years. I could handle a guy with a knife.

Marley tried to curb my false enthusiasm. "Let me tell you what Cheri passed on to me this morning, from her preliminary autopsy reports on Clare and Schiff.

"Both were stabbed with two different, but similar weapons, and she confirms two assailants, both right-handed. In both cases, one assailant was in front and to the victim's right, while the other was slightly behind and to the victim's left, based on the entry angles of the blades.

"There's an interesting twist, and a new one for me. Based on penetration, Cheri described the blades as longer than a traditional knife, and they

171

have a dramatic upward curve to them. Skin and organ damage also show that both weapons seemed to have a seam down both sides of the center of the blade.

"And although several of the stab wounds were blunted as they struck bone, the majority were completely through and through. These are very sharp, very long-bladed knives, Christian.

"So, do you still think it's a good idea to meet with Nidal? And what would you do if Ahmad showed up as well?"

Marley was making a good point. I was capable for sure, but I wasn't so certain how successful I might be if both of them were armed with long-blades, or whether I could even get to one of them, before getting killed by the other.

"Do you think you could let me borrow one of your guns?" I asked.

"I'm afraid I could never do that, Michael. But I could secretly accompany you to even up the odds, so to speak." And with that Marley finally turned toward Bishara. "I believe it's time to tell him," he said to her.

Having been given her opening, Miriam Bishara turned the most beautiful pair of brown eyes on me that I had ever seen. They were flaked with gold speckles that flashed in the light. It was as if this was the first time I had noticed her.

Her facial features were flawless and slightly angular, not Asian, but definitely Middle Eastern. She was lean, yet appeared muscular, not skinny. Although she wasn't wearing any makeup, it looked as if she was ready for a photo-shoot. Miriam Bishara knew she was beautiful, and she knew I was taking it in. She calmly met my gaze straight on.

"Christian," Marley barked. "Pay attention."

I merely nodded to Marley, unable to turn away.

Bishara reached into the small purse hanging from her shoulder, opened a wallet containing her credentials and presented them to me with a smile. "Miriam Bishara, MI5. How do you do, Mr. Christian?"

Her fingers and short nails were perfectly formed, but I noticed callouses along the ridges on the underside edges of her palms. Bishara was not just a pretty face. She was a fighter.

Without waiting for a reply from me, she continued, as she put away her ID.

"When Marley entered the query on your brothers, into the PNC, it triggered an alert in our tracking system. These fellows are on my watch list and I was notified."

Marley saw me hesitate. "Police National Computer," he clarified. "It's an interagency database, shared throughout the Kingdom."

Bishara continued, "Most of MI5 is watching the Irish, as am I. But my specialty is Muslim radicalization. We believe your boys are up to no good, but I had no evidentiary cause to put an active surveillance on their activities.

"It is not only politically unpopular to be perceived as watching Muslims, it is considered to be xenophobic by all levels of our government. So, unless there is solid intelligence, such surveillances are procedurally forbidden, even for MI5. Until now, we could not watch the Halimas. Marley's alert was the first crack I've had on these guys in a while."

For the next five minutes, Bishara continued updating me with general background information on the two, demonstrating she had memorized every detail of her investigation. It was the way all good detectives operated. But Bishara was no regular detective constable. If she was an MI5 officer, she got there because she had some special intelligence gathering experience and talents. I listened, but didn't seem to be learning anything Marley hadn't already told me. Then she began describing what she believed to be the motive for the thefts.

"The boys belong to the Al-Irschad Mosque. We have developed our own intelligence, and we have received solid confirming information from MI6 and from our friends abroad, that young men from the mosque are making regular trips back to Syria, Somalia and Afghanistan to be further radicalized and trained.

"They then travel to Canada or South America, where they assimilate into the Muslim communities there, or slip into the United States through your southern border. They also return to London and back to Al-Irschad, as a safe haven from which they can further disappear into Great Britain. These are our future terrorists.

"Your boys came to the United Kingdom with very good identification and personal resumes that we have now identified as fraudulent. They then walked into a relatively safe place at the mosque and your Transeget office, until now.

"We are also most curious as to what they are doing with the money, since it doesn't seem to show up anywhere in their spending or saving habits. Couple all that with the murders of your suspects in your case, and we believe we have something worth pursuing. I believe they are financing the travel for this future crop of terrorists or they are involved in an upcoming operation."

I was impressed with her summary and with the intelligence she was sharing. "I appreciate your confidence," I said.

"You, yourself, have quite an interesting file with Interpol, and even your CIA and FBI seem to regard you favorably," she said. "Welcome to my team, Mr. Christian."

I looked over at Marley, as if asking *what the hell?* He merely shrugged his shoulders. Not only was Bishara a capable constable, she was now the team leader, and I was on it without being asked.

"Let us prepare you to meet with Nidal," she said.

With that, she walked to the door, opened it and admitted two men in plainclothes. They seemed fully aware of my meeting Halima, and it appeared that my cooperation had been already predetermined. So much for personal privacy safeguards in the UK, not to mention tromping on those of a US citizen in their country.

The metal briefcase one of them was carrying looked familiar. My suspicions were confirmed when one of them set it on the desk and opened it.

Inside were a miniaturized audio transmitter, along with its small antenna wire, a long length of wire attached to a very small microphone fastened to a tiny clip, and several loose batteries in a clear plastic bag. The microphone had a small half-shield around it to prevent the fabric of one's clothing from brushing against it, thereby muting or creating a fuzzy sound during recording. The case also held a receiving and recording unit with audio controls, and a roll of your everyday, toolbox-brand, adhesive tape. I had wired up plenty of other witnesses, and had been wired up myself, when going undercover on many occasions, but those were *my* investigations. Now, I was merely someone else's confidential informant.

"Take off your shirt," one of the techs instructed me, as the other slipped fresh batteries into the unit.

Bishara said, "I'll take it from here," as she took the transmitter, the microphone wire, and the tape from him. She walked across the room, until her back was to everyone else. She looped the microphone wire around her fingers a few times. "Turn around," she said.

I turned until my bare back was facing her. She reached under my arms with hers and handed me the microphone. "Hold this right here," she said, centering it to my chest with both her hands. If Bishara's goal was to make me uncomfortable, she was succeeding. She drew the microphone wire back under my arm, held it in place with one hand, tore a strip of tape with her teeth and secured the wire along my right side. It was obvious she had done this once or twice before. The extra coils of wire would allow her to properly position it and yet give me some flexibility of movement, if I needed it.

She then plugged the microphone wire into the transmitter, which she slipped into my waistband at the small of my lower back, and held it in place, while she asked, "How does that feel?"

My first thought was *fantastic*, but I figured she meant *is it comfortable and is it secure*? "It's fine," I said.

She then inserted the antenna wire and taped it, along with the excess microphone wire, across my waist then upward, and under my left arm, where it was taped again. If I were to be patted down across the back, the wires would be completely unnoticeable.

Bishara lifted my shirt off the chair and gently draped it over my shoulders. Her fingertips felt like hot irons. "Get dressed," she said.

I turned in time to see Marley managing a wry smile.

One of the techs had turned on the machine. "Give us a test there, Mr. Christian."

"Keep calm and carry on," I said, quoting a famous World War Two British rallying cry during the German bombing runs. There were no smiles of acknowledgement. The tech said to Bishara, "Everything's working fine."

Bishara then instructed me in how to turn the thing on and off from outside my shirt. And although I had done it dozens of times before, I appreciated her attention to detail, and in taking nothing for granted. "We'll keep it off until you leave our car to meet the boys. Then we'll give it one more test. That will save the batteries," she said.

"If you get a chance, try to get some admission from them, anything that allows us to continue the investigation beyond today." I was not impressed with the British way of prohibiting the police to investigate fully, given the probable cause we had.

I nodded that I understood.

"Now we wait," Bishara said.

■ ■ ■ ■ ■

NIDAL AND AHMAD WAITED IN the bookstore across the street from their workplace. They had been browsing amongst the books for over half an hour, but hadn't read a word. They were watching across the street at the front of the Transeget office. From their vantage point, they could see their own entry, as well as the door fronts to either side. They would see Christian before he could see them.

"It is very busy out there. We will be seen for sure," Ahmad said.

"It doesn't matter habibi, when it is done, we will disappear," his brother replied. "We will escort him into the stairway, with you in front and me behind. I will strike the first blow, but we must finish him together, quickly. No one will see us there with everyone still out to lunch. And leaving him at work will be a fitting end to him." Nidal reasoned.

Ahmad was, again, not calmed by his brother's rationale. He knew that workers could return from lunch at any time, but his brother seemed determined. Although no one had yet come back to the office, it would be a bad thing if anyone from work stumbled upon them. He knew very well that any witnesses would have to be killed too.

Regardless of what Nidal said, Ahmad knew he wouldn't feel at ease until they had walked away from the area and had made good their escape. He reached over to his side to make sure again the dharia was secure. It was, and he felt comforted by the gift from his father, may Allah rest his soul.

■ ■ ■ ■ ■

THE MORE THE IMAM THOUGHT about it, the less he liked his odds of surviving the exposure the brothers had brought upon him. From their end, there was the possibility that they could inadvertently reveal the role of the Imam. Worse, if the police picked them up, they might try to cut a deal by offering up the Imam as a more publicly known figure. That just wouldn't end well for him.

Then there was the one they called the Messenger.

The Messenger was a different type of person altogether. He was intelligent, deliberate, very well trained and highly unlikely to leave himself vulnerable. The Imam knew the Messenger would see him as a liability. And that would certainly mean his death.

From this point on, he would have to be very aware of who was around him. He considered the possibility of using one of the newly returned candidates for protection. But then he opted away from that. He would merely be extending the list of people to whom he was susceptible. This situation was very worrisome indeed.

He had already put into movement a plan to eliminate the brothers in an effort to ingratiate himself with the Messenger. But now he had to go further. He had to figure out a way to eliminate the Messenger, without tipping off Hezbollah that he was involved in any way with it. He needed time to think.

■ ■ ■ ■ ■

THE BRITS PULLED UP IN front of the stairway that led down to the Tube station, and parked in the no standing zone with their emergency flashers on.

"Give us another test, there, Mr. Christian," the tech guy said.

I flicked on the transmitter and was going with another trite British phrase, when I thought better of it. I was about to meet a couple guys who might very well try to kill me. "Make sure my wife gets my wallet," I said.

"It's working," he said to Bishara.

Bishara leaned over to me and said quietly, "Don't get yourself killed over this. There's nothing shameful about running away if they come at you with knives or swords, or whatever they have. If that's what it comes down to, run away and let us handle them."

For some reason, having someone as sexy as Bishara tell me to run away seemed emasculating. I was looking for something to say that showed her I could handle myself, but realized it wouldn't matter. She was right. If it came down to it, letting the armed backup deal with armed assailants made the most sense.

"Right," was all I could think of.

I exited their car and walked the next two blocks to our office alone. Standing in front of the building, I knew better than to look around to see if I could spot them, or how close the MI5 team might be if trouble broke loose.

One thing was certain. They weren't visible ahead of me. All I could rely on now was that the transmitter continued to function.

Trying to look like I was meeting someone, which I was, I stood in front of the office and casually scanned the area immediately around me, to see if I could spot Nidal before he spotted me.

■ ■ ■ ■ ■

THE MESSENGER SAT BEHIND THE rooftop balustrade and waited for his moment. This action was extraneous to his primary objective. It wasn't as if he cared one way or another about killing someone individually. It was just that each time represented an unnecessary exposure, which brought with it, risk of identification. And that was not allowable.

It wasn't as if people didn't know who he was. He had several jobs, and even though he kept to himself and did not make friends, people recognized him and knew his face, but not in this context. No one knew him in the context of his calling. He would have to be sure to remain out of sight until it was absolutely necessary to finish the task. He could not be discovered before his final mission in London.

It was his plan to wait here for the brothers in case they showed up at work. It was the only other lead he had, besides their house. He had watched their home all night and they did not return there. As he waited, they surprised him by walking straight towards him and into the shop below him. If they had not returned to work, his task would have been tougher. He might have had to change direction and protect himself from the Imam. He just might do so anyway.

A tall man in a suit had walked up to the building entrance, but did not enter. He had no information on the American investigator, and wondered if this was merely a business customer or one of his targets.

This one would have to wait, but that would not be a problem. The Messenger was a patient and deliberate man. Besides, his two primary targets were sitting in the bookstore downstairs. These two had to be eliminated to ensure the line back to him stopped with them. Nothing could get in the way of that plan.

He also had another motive. They had cheated and betrayed him and he wanted vengeance. Eventually the brothers would move out and head back to their office and he would kill them, right there on the sidewalk.

As patient as he was, he was becoming irritated. The longer he waited, the closer he came to missing his midday call to prayers. He was almost out of time, and he was facing north, not east. Since they were not yet out of the bookstore, the

Messenger opted to pray until they came out. He turned slightly to the right.

■ ■ ■ ■ ■

Ahmad's glance moved across the street, and that is when he saw Michael Christian walking slowly toward the office doorway. He was alone. Instinctively, Ahmad's hand again moved to his dharia, hoping to bolster his courage as he followed his brother from the store.

■ ■ ■ ■ ■

I WAS ABOUT TO GIVE THE technical guys another radio test when I saw both brothers emerge from a shop across the street. They had obviously been watching for me. As they hurriedly side by side, they kept their arms outside their long jackets. They didn't appear to be holding weapons, yet. That was a good sign.

Their greeting was brief.

"Mr. Christian, regardless of what you may think, my brother and I are innocent, and we have something for you that we believe you will find most interesting. Frankly, we hope it will persuade you to finally leave us alone, and more importantly, it might help you solve your case." Nidal said.

As he spoke, the brothers casually surrounded me, one on each side, with Ahmad slightly behind me and to my left. I actually had to turn my head to keep him in my peripheral vision. Was it their intention to try something right out here, on the sidewalk, in broad daylight?

I wasn't having any of that. I moved so they were both on my left side, giving me a better line of sight and some swing and thrust room, if I needed it.

"I'm listening," I replied.

"Let us go upstairs, where we can talk."

Having the meeting upstairs seemed logical and innocent enough. I felt better about going back to our offices than having them ask me to join them in a car somewhere. And if Bishara and her crew lost us in traffic, I'd be on my own with these guys and I was less comfortable with that. By the same token, being in a narrow hallway might be disadvantageous. I decided the odds were more in my favor in narrower confines though. I nodded my agreement, and with that, Nidal pulled opened the entry door. Ahmad quickly entered ahead of me, with Nidal following close behind.

■ ■ ■ ■ ■

THE MESSENGER HAD CLOSED HIS eyes to pray, and through his eyelids, he could still see the glare of the sun at its apex. He tried to focus, but after a couple minutes, the bright redness worked its way into his optical nerve, distracted him from prayer and brought him back to his mission. He turned his head and in that moment, saw the twins enter the building across the street with the man he had seen earlier.

He had missed his moment by praying. He would not make that mistake again. Now he must wait until they exited the building. He repositioned his rifle and waited, splayed out in the prone position, his eyes trained on his iron sites and the door across the street.

■ ■ ■ ■ ■

I SENSED IT WHEN I first saw them walking across the street. Not only was Ahmad acting more stressed than the situation called for, he hadn't said a word, and seemed almost distracted by other thoughts. I really didn't like the way this was starting to play out and put my senses on a higher level of threat awareness. Nidal was walking so close behind me that if I stopped, he would likely run right in to me.

I again had one of them ahead of me, and one behind me, much like it must have been for Clare and Schiff. In a few seconds, none of Bishara's team would be able to see me. I hoped to hell the transmitter was working. I ignored where I was, relative to the top of the landing, and focused on the rhythm of our paces on the stairs, measuring the time each of their steps each was taking and their pace.

There were a dozen and a half stairs to the top of the landing, and we were about mid-way up when I saw something firm protruding under the hem of Ahmad's knee-length jacket, every time his left foot stepped up. Glancing back, I could sense, more than see Nidal pulling open his jacket with his left hand and confirmed it with a slight backwards glance.

I wasn't going to wait for Nidal to pull a damn blade on me. I reached up and grabbed Ahmad's right ankle as he lifted it to climb the step, and with my other hand, I grabbed the collar of his coat. With my right foot braced against the riser of the step, I executed a pivot turn and dragged him off-balance and backwards, pulling him by me and propelling him into his brother behind me. Nidal had begun drawing a sword-like weapon from a leather scabbard on his left side.

The impact of his brother slamming into him, caught him off balance and pushed both of them tumbling down the stairs. They crashed into the doorframe below, shattering the jamb that held the ancient mortise lock and pulled the door off its hinges. They both spilled onto the sidewalk.

I rushed down the stairs, grabbed Ahmad, who was closest to me, and executed a solid roundhouse punch to his jaw, just below his temple, knocking him unconscious. But as I turned toward Nidal, two rifle shots rang out in quick succession from across the street, with bullets striking him somewhere on his torso. His body jolted off the pavement in two, quick spasms. Then he was still.

From my crouch, I looked up to see where the

police were firing from and saw Marley and Bishara running toward me. Neither of them had a long gun, and the shots seemed to have been coming from across the street and upward.

Highlighted by the sun, I spotted someone on the roof of the two-story building on the other side of the road. The shooter and I were close enough to make face-to-face eye contact, and we both stopped for a moment of recognition. Then without hesitation, he leaned into his rifle stock and rushed off a third shot sending splinters of concrete spattering in front of Ahmad and me, and embedding itself just inches above the concrete beside me.

Instinctively, I grabbed Ahmad's collar again, dragging him inside the doorway and up a few stairs. Another shot rang out, but it didn't enter the stairway.

Hopefully we were both out of range in there. The angle seemed safe enough, but I couldn't be sure. I shouted into my concealed microphone, "Be careful. He's on the roof across the street!"

I heard a few more shots, but they seemed to be an exchange of pistols and a rifle.

I had no idea where a backdoor would exit from, in case I had to worry about a second gunman. But if the first gunman came through that front doorway, we were both finished if we stayed on the stairs. I got my footing and dragged Ahmad a few stairs further up.

As I pulled him upward, I heard a distinct thump on the stairs. It was the sword. Quickly, I jerked back Ahmad's jacket and drew the blade from its sheath. The handle actually fit perfectly in my hand and the heft was well balanced. I knew I could do some serious harm with it under normal circumstances. But in this case, I really didn't think a cutting instrument gave me any advantage. It wasn't made for throwing, and if an armed man burst through that doorway, I'd have barely a split second of surprise on my side. *Never bring a knife to a gunfight* echoed in a corner of my mind.

I pulled Ahmad up another stair and ran back down to the landing, sneaking a glimpse across the street at the roof. There was no one up there. If he came through that doorway, I wanted to be close enough to strike. But I knew if he approached that door from directly across the street, he'd have me in plain view, and I'd have to run back upstairs.

"Christian!" Marley shouted.

"In here!" I yelled back.

Marley and Bishara came running through the door. They were both carrying pistols.

"Are you hit?" Bishara asked. Marley was staring at the sword.

"I'm not, but I'm not sure about him," I said, as they rolled Ahmad over on his back. He was starting to regain consciousness, and didn't appear to be bleeding from anywhere, other than on the back of his head where my punch slammed it into the concrete.

Bishara's radio crackled. It was one of her team. "We saw the shooter, and followed him into the underground station. He's one train ahead of us."

Bishara ordered, "Pass along his description and place officers at every exit. Have the cars boarded and searched heading in every direction."

"That has been broadcast, but he may still be armed. He concealed the rifle on a sling under his jacket," the officer replied. "And we have only his clothing description."

"I saw him," I said quickly.

Bishara said, "Describe him for me."

I knew what I had didn't amount to much, and I sure as hell didn't want to spend the next three days looking at MI5 mug shots of possible terrorist suspects.

"I don't have much," I replied. "But I'd say mid-to late thirties, dark complexioned, definitely Middle Eastern. He's wearing a black ball cap under a grey hooded sweatshirt. There's a red logo on the hat, and he appeared to be right handed, given the way he held the rifle. So, he's likely to have the gun slung under the right side of his jacket. I'd say the rifle was a semi-automatic, given the two rapid shots. So, he's got plenty of firepower."

Bishara passed the information along to her crew and I knew that it was going out to hundreds of Constables throughout Metropolitan London. I wished I had more to offer.

"If you saw him again, do you think you could recognize him?" She asked.

There it was. An honest answer to that question could keep me bound up there for days, but I had no choice. "Possibly," I said. "He and I actually had a moment where we stared right at each other, just before he took his third shot."

"That settles it then. You're with us," She said. "Marley, its your lead from here. I'll gather the Intel, and you start knocking on doors. But first, we're going to have a go at Mr. Halima, here."

I was relieved to know that I was still part of the team and not reconciled to a desk. MI5 could have just as easily pulled my passport until they were through with me.

I looked at Marley and asked, "What about Nidal?"

Marley, the man of few words spoke even fewer this time. He merely shook his head, and that amounted to an entire sentence. Nidal Halima was dead.

Marley bent down and placed handcuffs on Ahmad, who was only semi-conscious, and walked him around his brother, who was lying on the sidewalk. He bundled the remaining twin into a marked police car that had pulled onto the scene. Take him to the Putney Station," Marley said.

From inside the car, I saw Ahmad twisting in his seat to get a good look at his brother and I could hear him screaming, "What about my brother? He needs medical attention."

"No," Bishara countermanded. "Take him to MI5. We'll have more privacy there, and other resources."

"I wish to go to a hospital. Call an ambulance for my brother!" Ahmad shouted. "I want a solicitor."

Bishara stared him down. "You are not a suspect in a criminal case, Halima," she said. "I'm holding you under the Security Service Act. You only get what I give you. And you are getting neither a solicitor nor medical treatment until I say so." And with that, Bishara slammed the door and pounded on the hood of the police car. She had just sent a very clear message to Ahmad Halima, who stared back at her with his mouth moving silently as they drove away.

Marley bent over the still warm body of what had been Nidal Halima, half a twin. He pulled back Nidal's jacket and examined the sheathed sword's handle, then looked at the one I was still holding.

"These engravings are beautiful," he observed. "And the tooling on the leatherwork is superb."

Then he looked up at me and said, "I'm going to have to take that one from you, Michael. It too is evidence in at least two homicides."

I looked more closely at the fighting sword and appreciated it for its artwork, but more so as a killing tool. I would have loved to own it as a souvenir.

"After you turn that stuff over to your uniforms, Marley, meet me at my office," Bishara said, and drove off separately with her crew.

Marley turned to one of the uniformed officers who were gathering and securing the scene, and handed him Halima's sword. "Mark it as evidence, taken by me from Ahmad Halima and take the other one with you and secure it as my evidence also."

I knew what Marley was doing. If the evidence was marked as taken off Ahmad by me, I would have to appear at every court case in the proceedings against Ahmad. If I failed to come back across the pond for any one of them, the defense would move to strike Ahmad's evidence and the case against him would dissolve. The same held true for Ahmad being complicit in my assault in the stairway. Marley had walked the path of making a case before.

He continued with his instructions to the officer, "Then I want you to call the forensic coroner's office and get someone over here – ask for Cheri Monahan. She's working the two murders these were used on. If she bitches about coming, tell her Marley said to button it and get over here. Tell her we have her murder weapons and a suspect."

191

Then he and I hopped into his Jag.

"We heard you on your transmitter, Michael," Marley said in the car. "Otherwise, we would have run right into his line of fire. Good thinking. Thanks."

"Do you think there's a chance we'll find him?" I asked.

"There's a chance," he said. "But I'm hoping it's by guys from our Armed Response Units. Otherwise, we might end up with casualties, if this guy doesn't get rid of his weapon first."

"What did Bishara mean when she said she'd *handle Intel and you knock on doors*?" I asked. "Are you relegated to something else now?"

Marley responded, "No. She basically said that as a handoff of duties to me, as well as for your instruction.

"Law enforcement and domestic intelligence against foreign threats are part of the same fraternity, but with distinct functions. It is somewhat like your FBI and your local police, except that, even though many MI5 officers come from the local police, they do not have arrest powers. We do. It is our division of authority.

"And the distinction between MI5 and MI6 is similar to the separation between your FBI and your CIA. Your CIA handles foreign intelligence and your FBI handles domestic. When we work with MI5, we handle evidence, arrests, warrants and things like that. If they get good intelligence, then they will share it with vetted officers from the Metropolitan Police for disposition.

"And apparently, Michael, she thinks you are vetted enough to hear all these things. I'm really not familiar with a civilian being brought in this close on an MI5 case before. So, if you are in the least bit uncomfortable with all this, tell me now, and I'll get you back to your private life right away."

I was already in deeper than I had ever expected to be. My case was merely a corporate financial crime that had spun out of control. There were three deaths now, and a shooting attack that could have been an attempt on my life.

On too many levels, this had become an investigation best left to the British authorities. My ego had already been stroked enough by the mere invitation to join the investigative team, especially with Bishara on it. And my adrenalin was pumping at the thought of being back in the chase again. But my common sense told me it was time to get our money back and go home.

I listened to the words roll off my lips, hardly aware that I had said them. "I'm in," I told Marley.

"Glad to have you," was all he said. I couldn't tell if Marley was disappointed that I'd still be tagging along, or if he was just a man of few words. *The hell with it* I thought. Bishara wanted me on the team and that was good enough.

■ ■ ■ ■ ■

I DIDN'T KNOW WHAT I was expecting of MI5 headquarters, but to be driven to a contemporary architecture building on Gower Street, near a train terminal, didn't fit in with my image of where British domestic intelligence services would be hosted.

193

I guess I was expecting some staid, non-descript building, constructed a hundred years or so ago, with no numbers on the front, and only accessible through a myriad of underground tunnels. I should have known better.

I was probably influenced by the James Bond movies of my youth, where Moneypenny guarded the access to M's private lair, all properly ensconced in burnished wood panels, with antique furniture and quietly carpeted floors.

This was more like the FBI headquarters, or *J. Edgar Hoover* building, as it was known, on Pennsylvania Avenue, in Washington, DC. That too was in a boxy, concrete, corporate-looking building.

In contrast, the Central Intelligence Agency's offices were in a modern complex, on beautifully landscaped grounds in Langley, Virginia. Armed soldiers stood at the gate and seriously checked the ID of everyone entering, even known faces. MI5 was no Langley.

As Marley and I entered the main entrance of the building, from the parking garage, it seemed even more functional than impressive. I was a bit let down.

By the time Marley and I got there, Ahmad Halima was already in isolation in an interrogation room. He sat handcuffed with a short chain around his waist that linked through his manacles and fastened him securely to the center of a steel table. His back was secured to a steel chair, to the point he could hardly move. His ankles were tightly strapped to its legs, which were bolted to the floor in the same manner as the table.

He wasn't going anywhere and he wasn't about to commit suicide on MI5's watch, at least not until they were through with him. He had not yet received even simple first aid. Bishara wasn't kidding. Halima belonged to them body and soul now.

"Michael, are you sure you're not hurt?" Bishara asked.

It wasn't lost on me that she had shifted to my first name. Marley's slight smile indicated it wasn't lost on him either.

I figured it was the noble thing to do, so I reciprocated in a manner of professional friendship, "No, Miriam, I'm fine. Thanks. Where do we go from here?" I asked, indicating I was ready to do what it took to find out where the money was, and what the brothers had planned for it.

"We're going to interview Halima and you're going to watch. Marley and I are going to play your American version of good guy - bad guy. I'll be the bad guy."

With that, she grabbed what I presumed was Halima's intelligence file, and walked down the hall to the interrogation room, with Marley and I in tow.

"Can I ask you something?" I posed the question to Marley. "Back in Putney, I saw that Bishara was carrying a gun. I thought that MI5 types didn't carry, that they just gathered intelligence, and that you guys did the arresting and scuffling."

"Most MI5 officers will never carry a gun," he replied. "But Bishara came from our ranks at the Metropolitan and she is a trained *Authorized Firearms Officer*, or AFO as we call them. When we decided to go after the Halima twins, I offered her a gun and she accepted.

However, giving her one of my weapons is not on the books, Michael. In her current assignment, she could be demoted or fired if it gets about that she's carrying, so let's keep mum about that, shall we? The MI5 boys on her technical team know, but they are her handpicks. Your knowledge makes you the odd man out."

I thought to myself, *well she picked me too*, but I merely nodded in agreement that her secret was safe with me.

He and I stood outside the room and watched through the one-way glass, and listened, as Bishara walked in.

■ ■ ■ ■ ■

THE MESSENGER WAS SWEATING PROFUSELY.

He had barely escaped the armed pursuing officers, and his rifle, banging against his side as he ran, made it difficult to get a solid lead on them. He caught a break when the alley he had chosen opened onto a street with a fork in the road. He decided to take the left fork and hoped that the team wouldn't see him. That would force them to split up. If they didn't, he still stood a fifty-fifty chance that they might take the wrong fork.

He knew he couldn't trust that it would be that simple, so he ducked into the first alley he came across and headed back the way he came. He was a mere three blocks from the entrance to the Underground and although they were watching all the exits, it was unlikely that the cops would have the entrance covered yet. His plan was to get on the train and head east. He'd ride just a few stops then grab a black cab. His goal was to get to the Tottenham Street Metro station, just west of his warehouse and walk. He could blend in easily there.

The Messenger knew he couldn't go home, but that was no longer a concern. His apartment was empty and he had almost cleaned out the warehouse. But he did have to go back there and get his truck. Then he could return to his safe house and park it in the barn. He really only had one more point of exposure and that was getting off the train and into the crowd at the London College campus.

No one seemed to be closing in on him on the train, but he knew he could be under surveillance at any exit. He couldn't take off his jacket to disguise his appearance without revealing his rifle. He probably should have dumped it before he got on the train, but there was no time.

He'd have to take his chances topside, and it would be better to be armed, since the police were not likely to be, unless the armed coppers got there first. He got off at Tottenham Court, as planned and disposed of the rifle and his jacket in a trash bin, in the restroom.

As he walked up Hampton Road toward the warehouse, the Messenger was unaware of two things.

The first was that he had been spotted and was being followed by the police.

And the second was that he was only one block from MI5 headquarters, where his second target sat, in a locked room, ignorantly safe from his would-be assassin.

■ ■ ■ ■ ■

AS BISHARA ENTERED THE ROOM, her prisoner glared at her defiantly. She walked slowly, closing the few paces between them, her eyes never leaving him. Then she settled herself softly in a chair opposite Halima without addressing him, and set her folder in front of her.

She slowly leafed through the intelligence file, making a show of displaying the folder cover to Halima, so he could clearly see his own name officially printed on it, along with the Crest of the British Security Service. Even from outside the room, I was impressed. But it must have devastated Halima to realize his activities had not been anonymous.

Every now and then Bishara would look up from her notes to stare at him unwaveringly. She interspersed her reading with simple utterances, like, *false passport, fraudulent resume, theft, fake ID, bank fraud, forgery, money laundering, illegal entry* and *murder.*

She was taking her time, while Halima's anxiety built. And the more time that passed, the more difficult it was for him, sitting locked in his manacled state, as he came to realize this was no simple arrest.

Finally, he said, "I want to see my solicitor."

Bishara looked up, "No," was all she said. Then

she looked down at her notes.

When she turned the last page of the file, she closed it, cover side up and placed it to the side of her desk.

"I believe you are aware," she said, looking directly into Halima's eyes. "But I need to be certain you know this. Nidal is dead," she said. Then she paused to watch his reaction.

Ahmad was unable to form his words. He started to speak several times but couldn't turn his jumbled thoughts into words. His beloved brother was dead. But he was also free from Nidal directing every aspect of his life. And yet, he needed Nidal desperately at this moment to help him think. He didn't know which emotion to respond to. Confusion was all he had.

His brother had always been the thinker, had given them direction, even when he disagreed with his brother.

Nidal had told him, that after they killed Christian, they would leave the country. But the details were locked in his dead brother's head. Nidal never let Ahmad handle any finances, and he didn't even know how to get their money from the bank, or where their passports were kept. Should he be released, he had nowhere to go, had very little money, and no travel papers. Ahmad felt lost and abandoned. For the first time ever, he contemplated suicide.

Ahmad had seen Nidal on the sidewalk as the police were stuffing him into their car, but he had fervently hoped Nidal was merely unconscious, like he himself had been. The fact that he was dead was horrible news. Not only did he lose a brother he loved, his *habibi*, but his death left Ahmad to get out of this mess on his own.

A side of him resisted being of any help to these infidels. Yet another side wondered if he would be better off giving them tidbits of information to buy him some time. What he didn't know was if he had anything of value to bargain with. The only other person who could help him was an accomplice.

He needed help. If his father were alive, he would ask him. But he had been killed in a border skirmish with the Syrians, when Ahmad was just a boy. He must speak to the Imam. The holy one would tell him what to do.

"I wish to speak to my Imam," Halima said.

Bishara's response was matter of fact. "No. You speak only with me.

"You have only this one chance to tell me what you did with the money, why you killed Clare and Schiff, and why you were trying to kill the American."

"I do not know what you are talking about," Halima replied. "I want to talk with my Imam." And in a state of newly found courage he said, "You are an infidel bitch and I have nothing more to say to you."

In many interrogations, the officer will not let a denial be completed. The interrogator will interrupt the suspect to keep that from happening. Once the denial is made, the suspect is forced to defend it, making a confession that much harder to obtain. I wondered if Bishara knew that.

Calmly, Bishara rose from her seat and walked toward Ahmad. Standing behind him, she opened her hand wide and locked it, and then she arched her arm stiffly in a powerful blow that struck Halima fully on the side of his face and ear. Much like I had done earlier. It must have hurt like hell.

Had he been standing, he would have been driven to the ground by her follow-through. Securely bound to his chair, his head took the full force of the punch, which rendered him nearly unconscious. His eyes watered instantly and a ringing sound blared in his ear, as his shocked body spasmed for air.

When Halima finally straightened in his chair, he tried to muster a response, but Bishara repeated the punch from the other side, her rigidly locked hand landing fully on the side of his head.

Ahmad began weakly struggling and futilely trying to free himself from the chair.

Bishara leaned in close and whispered at a level just below a shout, "Bitch? You are my bitch now Halima. And this will go on for days until you tell me what I want to know." And with that, Bishara hit him again.

Watching from outside the room, Marley waited for that last clout to Ahmad's head, then he calmly said, "Now." He threw the door wide open and entered the interrogation room.

"Stop it! What do you think you're doing?" he shouted to Bishara, who was nodding from behind Halima. "Get away from him," he yelled.

Marley rushed over to Halima and placed his hands on each side of a face that was bruising dark red already. He looked him in the eyes and sincerely asked, "Are you ok? Ahmad, can you hear me?" He gently shook Halima's head back and forth trying to clear the cobwebs.

When it appeared that Ahmad had recovered enough to see, Bishara walked to the door and said, "I'll be back, you little son of a bitch. Your ass belongs to me, and I may work that over next." With that she exited the room and slammed the door behind her.

She joined me at the one-way glass and calmly asked, "Well, what do you think?"

I had to admit, I was impressed. "I've been involved in some pretty intense good guy-bad guy interrogations in my time," I said. "But I've got to tell you Miriam, this one ranks right at the top with some of the best."

She smiled, "So, Michael. Then I'm not just another pretty face?"

"Indeed, you are not," I replied.

She feigned surprise. "I'm not?" She asked.

"No. I mean, yes. I mean …"

She had manipulated me without breaking a sweat. I wasn't used to being uncertain and it felt uncomfortable, in a strangely good way.

Bishara smiled, leaned in, and gave me a soft, too-friendly, shoulder-bump. "I'm just messing with you, Michael," she said.

Indeed, she was, and I liked it. I could smell a vague hint of Dior Dune on her, and this close to me, she smelled like warm vanilla, citrus and amber.

Comfortable now, I was thinking up an appropriate response, when I had a thought of Alice at home, thousands of miles away, and felt a flashing trace of well-deserved guilt. I turned back to the one-way glass.

"Let's see how Marley handles him now," I said, completely the professional again.

■ ■ ■ ■ ■

INSIDE THE ROOM, MARLEY ASKED, "Can I get you some water?" But Halima shook his head without answering, blinking back tears of pain.

"She can get pretty emotional at times," Marley said. "She's the agent in charge, and I must also warn you, she will be back. She will be worse every time you fail to give her what she wants. Eventually, I will be removed and two members of her team will join her. They are specialists in extreme means of interrogation. Do you know what I mean?"

Halima's eyes widened and he looked straight into the mirrored glass, as if trying to see if Bishara was watching.

Without waiting for an answer, Marley continued, "You will tell her what she wants, but to be honest, I think she is hoping you will hold back. She likes hurting people who resist. And because she *always* gets the answers, she has never been disciplined." Marley paused to let that sink in.

Then he switched direction. "That investigator from America, why did you want to kill him? He's not one of us."

For a moment, it almost looked like Halima was going to answer. Then he tightened his lips, as if to keep the sounds from coming out.

Marley looked up at the glass, almost as if he was looking at me.

"Let me talk with him," I said to Bishara. It seemed she was thinking it over, but was leaning

203

away from the idea.

"We have nothing to lose," I offered, trying to push her toward a *yes* answer.

"You're right," she said. "We have nothing to lose at this point. Eventually, he will tell me what I want."

When I walked into the room, Marley rose from the opposite side of the table, to give me control, but I strode past him and sat on the edge of the table, practically knee to knee, with Halima.

"Ahmad," I started. "When we met on the sidewalk, I could tell that you were very uncomfortable with the meeting. And as it turned out, I think I know why. It wasn't your idea to kill me. It was your brother's, wasn't it?"

With that, Ahmad began to frame an answer, but I cut him off.

"And I'm guessing that you didn't want to kill Clare either." Again, I paused just long enough for him to begin thinking of a way to deny it.

"And I've met your brother, which leads me to believe that your brother decided that as well."

With that I leaned in close to him, with our knees almost touching and my face just inches from him. I locked my eyes on his, waiting for him to stare into mine, before I continued, "I can tell, Ahmad, that you actually cared for Clare and didn't want to even hurt her, much less kill her. Am I right?"

"Yes," he whispered.

As close as I was to him, I could barely hear him. Knowing the conversations were being recorded, I asked him, "What did you say, Ahmad?"

"Yes," he said, quietly. "I did care for Clare.

"She was sincerely good to me and we liked each other very much. It did not matter to her that we were Muslim or Middle Eastern. She just liked me for who I was. Our plan was for her to desire to marry one of us. That would solidify our standing here, and serve as a stronger cover. But I actually began to care for her, and hoped she would seek me out."

I interrupted him, not wanting him to begin taking a shred of truth and spinning a lie into its fabric. "You cared for her? How did that happen? Did you just fall in love?"

He was quiet as he thought about Clare. "Our relationship started out as just sex, really free and open sex, just the three of us." He caught me off guard with that, and I wondered what Marley was thinking. We had both met Clare and that would have been the farthest thing from our minds.

Ahmad kept going, "But soon I came to realize that Clare was a good person and I became attracted to her more for that."

"So, did you make her stop seeing Nidal? Is that why he wanted to kill her?"

"No. Not at all," he answered. "She liked having sex with both of us. Often, she was the aggressor. But we still had something special, Clare and me. I cared for her and she did for me. It was Nidal's idea to eliminate anyone who might suspect us. And that included Clare and you."

"Why didn't you talk him out of it? You had feelings for her. Didn't you try to save her?"

Halima looked forlorn and began wringing his hands, trying to wash the guilt of a terrible deed off them.

"I could not control Nidal," he said. "He was always in charge and could be terribly abusive, if I ever disagreed with him. He made up his mind that we were in danger because of Clare suspecting we likely stole her key. Nidal said we had to eliminate her. She was too much of a risk, if you got her to talk."

Halima was positioning himself to shift the blame away from himself and his brother and onto me. I stopped him cold.

"What about Schiff," I asked.

"Yes, especially Schiff. That was Nidal's decision too. I am not a murderer," he lamely claimed. "But Schiff was the only one who knew about cashing the checks for gold.

"Again Nidal convinced me that we had to first test him to see if he could be quiet. But when we met with him, Schiff became enraged that he and his business might have been exposed.

"That night we met him, Nidal challenged him to keep silent, but Schiff began screaming, *I should have known better. A Jew working with a couple fucking Arabs*, is what Schiff said. It was then that Nidal stabbed him. When Schiff began to struggle so fiercely, I was caught up in fear and I grabbed him."

"And you stabbed him too," I filled in.

Halima lowered his head. "Yes. My brother insisted that I participate to prove my own worth to him. It is why I hesitated when we met with you. I didn't agree that we had to add another killing. I begged him to just leave the country with me. But he insisted again that I prove my loyalty to him. This is what he has done our entire life."

"Well," Marley interjected, "You won't have to worry about that any longer."

Halima seemed ready to cry. It didn't matter to me why, but I knew from my training in neurolinguistic programming, and behavioral symptom analysis, that once we had him talking, any break in the rhythm of the interrogation would be a setback. I didn't even let him get his first sob out.

"You took all those risks for your brother, and you knew he was just using you," I continued, "What did he do with the money, Ahmad? Obviously, he didn't allow you to spend it on good living."

Halima began an answer, and then stopped. His eyes shifted from recall, to recognition. Then his entire demeanor changed.

"I want to talk with my Imam," was all he said. Then he stiffened up in the chair, as much as he could, hardening his resolve against any further conversation.

I was aware we had lost the moment. *What caused him to make that shift* I wondered? I did a quick reflection on the moments immediately before. Marley was preparing to take back the interrogation, when it came to me.

We were talking about the money, when Halima did a fast shift to the Imam. He was no longer asking for his solicitor. He wanted the Imam, and at that moment, so did I. I stopped Marley from interrupting.

"What is your Imam's name, Ahmad?" I asked.

"Ramzi Ayyad," he replied. "I insist on speaking with him."

I set him up for the psychological punch, the blackjack effect, "Why, Ahmad, do you want to speak with the man who wants you dead?"

The effect was exactly what I was going for. Halima looked sharply up at me in surprise. "What are you talking about? My Imam is my spiritual leader. I want to pray with him," he weakly replied. "He would not want to kill me. He is a man of Allah. He will help me get out of here."

I looked over to Marley and directed my next comment to him. "Perhaps we should release Ahmad to the Imam."

Then I turned back to Halima, leaned in close again and asked, "How many people remain alive, who know that you have stolen the money, Ahmad?" I quietly asked. "Clare is dead, and she didn't even know for sure. Schiff is dead, because you killed him. And you were trying to kill me. And your brother is dead. There is likely only one other person who knows about the money, Ahmad, and that is your Imam."

I was on thin ice here. If I was wrong about this, the interview was over. Screw it I thought. It would be over anyway, given Ahmad's resistance at this point. I decide to forge ahead, when another thought occurred to me.

"Think about that. Your Imam knows, because you were stealing the money and giving it to him," I guessed.

"You told him, didn't you, that I was at your office, conducting an investigation. You told him and now he knows he is at risk, either from you, from me, or from someone upwards of him. Your holy Imam doesn't give a rat's ass about you. He wants you dead, Ahmad. That is how he has chosen to protect himself. It is he who hired the man on the rooftop to kill your brother and to try to kill you.

"The only reason you are alive right now is because I saved you, and you know it. And now you have figured out, without your brother having to tell you, that your holy Imam turned you over to a killer. He gave up your life and killed your brother to save his own."

I stood and repeated to Marley, "Maybe we should just turn him over to his Imam?"

Before Marley could respond, the door to the interrogation room burst open and Bishara came striding in with her two technicians in tow.

■ ■ ■ ■ ■

"SCREW THAT," SHE SAID. "I want more from him and I intend to get it."

With that she turned to her men, "Set it up here," she said, pointing to the edge of the table where I was sitting. "You," she said to me. "Out of the way."

One of her crew opened a wooden box. He extracted a power cord that he handed to the other man, who plugged it into a wall socket behind Halima.

The device was by no means a polygraph machine. It had red and black cable clamps, and looked much more like what you'd use to jump-start a car with a dead battery. In fact, that was exactly what it was, but on steroids! The juice would come right out of the wall outlet.

As the first tech turned it on, the dials all swept across their meters and back to their set modes. The machine began to hum and the sound became a small whine, each time the tech amped up the power dial.

209

Bishara moved to the mirror and pressed a button on the side of the frame, lowering a full window blind.

Meanwhile, one of the techs had yanked off Halima's shoes and sox and placed his feet in a tray, into which he poured a pint bottle of water. The other had unbuttoned Halima's shirt, yanking it down over his shoulders, exposing his bare chest. "Bite on this," he then said, and placed a rawhide twist near Halima's mouth.

Standing across the room, Bishara said, "I know your Imam, Halima. And I know what is going on from within your *dar al-'Amn*, your house of safety, inside the mosque's walls. I know that Iran, Syria and Hezbollah are using it to recruit and train its proxy warriors."

"That is not true," Halima blurted out, his eyes never leaving the two cable clamps, now being held by one of the techs.

Bishara continued, unfazed by Halima's denials. "I have been watching it for a long time, and now I know that you are involved in financing it. I am wagering, also, that the Imam has you involved in something bigger than you know about, and that is why it was necessary for him to have you killed.

"I am not giving you a martyr's way out, Ahmad. I intend to keep you alive for a long time, not kill you. But you will soon wish, over and over, that I did."

With that, Bishara nodded to the tech managing the box. He turned the dial slightly to what appeared, from my vantage point, to be a low setting. "Clear," he said.

With that, Marley, Bishara, and the other tech backed away from the table. It didn't take long for

210

me to realize they meant for me to follow suit.

Ahmad Halima began to writhe in his chair as he emitted a low wail, "Nooooooo."

The tech took the red lead and clamped it to the steel table leg. He quickly tapped the black clamp on the table and sent a jolt of electricity into the table and across the chains onto Halima's wrists.

His entire body arched against his restraints as the current shocked through him for a moment. I was getting a bit worried. I didn't want to be a witness to torture or a murder, regardless of what MI5 was trying to extract from this guy. He had already admitted to the murders. I wondered what else Bishara was going for here.

As if on cue, Marley and I moved further to a corner of the room, giving Bishara center stage. I'd read about such techniques, but had never been present during such an interrogation. I was riveted to the process, and I was mesmerized by it. It was like watching a train wreck about to occur. I couldn't take my eyes off of it.

"Hook him up," she said.

Ahmad's eyes never left the device from the moment they opened it, but I thought they would pop out of his head, when Bishara said that. Halima was by no means an independent thinker, but he was even much less a hero.

He turned to me and screamed, "I didn't want to kill anyone! I had to. My brother made me. I don't know anything, please don't let them do this to me."

Somehow, I had become the good-guy, instead of Marley.

"I don't know anything. Please don't let them do this! Tell me what you want me to do," he begged.

Bishara must have been waiting for this

moment, because she took control. "Look at me," she shouted to Halima, "You talk only to me!

"I barely gave you a shock, Halima. It was set at the lowest setting. But that dial turns up a long way.

"You and I both know that you were brought to our country for a purpose and it was not merely to praise Allah.

"You may not know what was going on with the money. Perhaps only your brother knew, but your Imam made sure we didn't get to ask him. You two were paying that money upwards to your Imam, and I intend to find out what he is up to."

"Look at me!" She shouted again to Halima, grabbing his hair and turning his face toward her.

"I think we both know that once he finds out that you are alive, he will want to make sure you are dead. And that sniper, for certain, will want you dead.

"Right now, Ahmad, we are your only hope of staying alive. I want you to think about that." With that, Bishara turned to her technicians and said, "Everybody outside a minute," and herded us all to the door.

"What about my solicitor?" Halima whispered, with his head down on his chest.

Bishara looked back at him. "Solicitor? You're not under arrest. Unless I say so, Halima, you no longer exist." On that note, we left the room.

■ ■ ■ ■ ■

OUT IN THE HALL, AND before I could even muster up a complaint or praise for what I saw, Bishara turned to me and said, "Christian, I've been at this too long to believe they were stealing large-sums of money merely for donations to their mosque, for the greater good of Allah. Something is about to occur that is worth a half million U.S. dollars and is worth killing for. I want to know what it is.

"I want you to go back in there and see if you can get him to arrange a meeting with the Imam, under our supervision. If he agrees, all is well and we'll take it from there. But if he doesn't, I'm going to give him a few more volts to let him know we aren't kidding.

"One way or another, we're going to set up this Imam for a confession, or I'll put him on the box too, if I have to. We're going to find out who that sniper is, and find out what else is going on."

Bishara had my full attention. She obviously had no regard for individual rights, or else the government gave MI5 a lot of latitude in intelligence gathering. She hadn't really put serious current to Halima, so maybe she was bluffing. Or perhaps she was just trying to make sure I gave it my all. Or maybe, like Marley had said, she had a mean streak in her that was both awesome and frightening at the same time. Fortunately, I wasn't going to get the chance to find out.

Another MI5 officer came running down the hall toward us. "They've located the sniper and followed him to a warehouse," he blurted out. With that he turned back the way he had come, and continued to update Bishara as we all jogged behind him, leaving Halima chained to a table to stare at that box and ponder his navel.

The MI5 officer added as we ran, "We have additional marked units on the way, with Authorized Firearms Officers responding, and at least one armored response vehicle is joining them. If we leave right now, we might even get there before the AFOs arrive," he said.

With that, Marley and Bishara broke into a full run down the hallway to the parking garage. Lacking any order to stay behind, I piled into the back seat of Bishara's car as it squealed down the exit ramp. "We're only about five blocks away," she said.

■ ■ ■ ■ ■

THEY WERE RIGHT, THE WAREHOUSE on Cardington Street was merely blocks away. A steady evening rain had stopped and the cobblestone driveway and yard were puddled and wet. The grounds had only minimal exterior lighting, hardly enough to create a reflection on the shiny pavement. There was a bare bulb over the pedestrian door, and a similar light about midway from there to the end of the building. Otherwise, the building was dark.

A uniformed sergeant approached us.

"We caught a break at the Tottenham Court Station, a few blocks away," he reported. "He was spotted by one of our officers as he exited the tube station. He dumped his coat and the rifle in a trash bin, and we have recovered both.

"The officers followed him here, and radioed it in. We now have the building surrounded, but we haven't gotten a good look inside yet because the windows have been painted over. I've called for some AFOs and they should be here momentarily."

Since this was a police activity now, Marley took over. "Do you have at least two officers at all the exits?" he asked. "There is no reason to believe he is unarmed, just because he dumped the rifle."

"We will have them doubled up soon," the sergeant replied. "It took a while for us to assemble enough officers just to cover all the sides and the back, but none of them are armed, so we could not force an entry."

Before long, the AFOs arrived with their firearms and ballistic protection, and prepared to breach the building.

Marley said, "Michael, you wait here. I'll call for you once the scene is secure." He left me standing there with other unarmed officers, as he joined the group preparing to enter through the front. Another team had been deployed to the back.

One thing I liked was that there was no chitchat about negotiating the sniper out of there. They were breaching the place. *Pretty ballsy*, I thought to myself. *Not very tactical, but ballsy nonetheless.*

It was over in a matter of a few minutes. There had been no shots fired and no loud exchanges from inside. Soon, an armed police officer came up to me and said, "Inspector Marley would like you to join him inside."

As I entered the doorway, several officers turned their weapons on me. "He's with me!" Marley shouted. "Get a good look at him and for God's sake, don't shoot him." That was reassuring.

Someone had found the power switch and turned on all the lights in the place. It appeared to be empty except for a few tables, wooden pallets, and some empty plastic sacks and jugs.

I read the labels. "Holy mother of God!" I exclaimed.

"What?" Marley said. "It looks like a chemical drug lab."

"These empty bags," I replied. "The plastic jugs. I know what these are used for and its not drugs. Someone was in here making a bomb!"

Bishara shouted, "No one move! Check the area for trip wires and don't move anything!"

Suddenly, flashlights were aimed at floor level. These guys knew what they were doing because gradually, as the beams swept along the floor, the lights shone about waist high, then chest high. One of the officers called for a demolition team to control the area and search it further.

"How can you be sure?" Bishara asked.

"I've seen this process before," I replied. "The jugs and empty bags tell me plenty. They're the individual components of a high-explosive bomb, even more so when under pressure. Three parts Hydrogen peroxide, three parts Acetone and ammonium nitrate. The TATP is the igniter or detonator. The ammonium nitrate will be highly explosive under pressure or when mixed with an accelerant."

"Fertilizer," Marley said.

"This can't be," Bishara said. That's the IRA's signature cocktail and each of those engineers is dead."

"Well," I said. "Either he's alive, or a student of

216

his is cooking this stuff."

Bishara followed, "But we are following Middle Easterners here, not the IRA."

"That would explain why there was no intelligence about the IRA right in the heart of London," Marley said. "They're not here. And the latest bombings were likely not set by the IRA.

"The IRA, or someone they taught, must have trained these guys."

"And that would explain why there has been no claim by the IRA of the last three," Bishara said.

I was browsing around while the two of them were validating what already seemed obvious to me. Some of that stolen money had been going into bomb making materials, and maybe into training the guy who built them. The sniper, it would seem, was also a bomber, likely a one-man cell with multiple locations to use as hideouts.

I was looking at the empty pallets, trying to calculate just how much material could have been set here in the planning phases.

"Marley," I called out. "Take a look over here."

Marley came over. "Take a look at the pallets and tell me what you see."

He shined his lantern onto the wooden skids. "What am I looking for?" he asked. "I don't see anything."

"Where have we seen this before?" I asked, as I knelt down and directed his light at the dark purple and red stains on the skids.

It was taking too long for him to put it together.

"At Wimbledon," I reminded him. "You showed me the flats of strawberries being brought in every morning for the berries and cream. That's where."

Marley looked up at me in agreement, and his

217

face began to show a look of worried disbelief, not wanting to put into words where these clues might be leading us.

While Marley explained to Bishara about our tour of Wimbledon, I walked to the rear overhead door area. I was in my element now. Industrial theft had placed me inside all sorts of warehouses, all over the world. I felt right at home, and was looking to see if all the furniture was in order.

I wasn't sure what I was looking for, maybe the one thing out of place, or one thing missing from its place that would give me a clue. To what, I didn't know, but right now, any clue would be helpful. I was taking it all in, bit by bit, as I walked, though. As I walked to the rear of the building, I saw something.

"Marley, Bishara, come here," I shouted. It was coming together too fast and I didn't like what I was seeing, or smelling.

I pointed to the floor as they arrived. "The closed garage door has been recently lifted. There is still fresh rain just inside the doorsill." I pointed out. "And here's a hydraulic lift."

Bishara said, "I can see that we just missed him. But what's the significance of the lift?" She asked.

"First, tell me what you smell," I answered.

They both stood still and sniffed the air around them. Bishara said, "I smell something but can't place it."

Marley said, "Fuel oil."

"Yes, diesel fuel, to be precise," I confirmed. "If the handcart had been further in the building, I'd say that the last items it hauled were dropped off deeper inside the building. But being right here near the rear overhead doorway, and about the

218

length of a heavy-duty truck from the door itself, my guess is that the last time it was used, was to put something into the rear of a truck. I say truck, because those pallets weren't loaded into a car. And the smell of diesel could merely be from the truck. But given what else was in this building, I would say that the fuel oil is an accelerant for the ammonium nitrate.

"I'll leave it to you to confirm that or not, and to figure out what he might have loaded in that last cargo he took out of here. But I am betting that it's a bomb, and its somehow connected to the Strawberry delivery trucks."

Bishara and Marley waited, knowing I had more to add. "And I am thinking that he's going to detonate it at Wimbledon."

Bishara spoke first. "Stop right there, Michael. Before we jump to any conclusions of that magnitude, we'll need to be sure. I'll need to order a rush-test to confirm those stains. And I will want to swab all those tables and see what chemical residue, if any, can confirm your hunches.

"I want to look around and see if perhaps that handcart could have been used to load something off the truck onto a rolling table or other type of conveyance to bring something into the building.

"Even if you are right about a bomb-making lab being here, and strawberry stains on wooden skids, that doesn't lead to a proper conclusion that Wimbledon is the target.

"I cannot possibly ask my boss to wake the Home Secretary about a plot we do not even know exists, or to ask him to add more security to the Championships, if that is even possible. And the Secretary would surely ask my boss, or me, if I thought it necessary to notify the Queen, or to cancel the match, given the added risk."

"What added risk?" I asked.

Marley fielded that one, "Princess Diana will be in attendance with her son tomorrow, at the women's final match," he answered.

"I need to get on those tests," Bishara said. She turned and headed for the front door with us close behind. She was on her radio the entire way.

■ ■ ■ ■ ■

WHEN WE PULLED INTO THE parking garage at 140 Gower Street, the place was buzzing with officers and trucks pulling out. I guessed they were the technical crews heading over to the warehouse.

As we exited Bishara's car, Marley said, "Come with me." And he started for his car. "I think your hunch is good Michael and I have to get out to Wimbledon and I want you with me. You have the best visual of him than anyone else right now."

"Not so fast," Bishara said to us. "First I want the Director to meet you, Christian, and let him ask you any questions he may have directly. Then you can go."

Marley shrugged his shoulders, grabbed his radio and began speaking as he walked with us.

Bishara marched me into an upper-floor office with the décor I would have expected at Barclays. In here, the walls actually were solid-wood paneled, and military awards, ribbons and memorabilia adorned the polished veneers. The MI5 crest was beautifully mounted on a large wooden plaque centered behind his desk.

James Fairweather was a tall, thin man and meticulously groomed. There seemed to be an air of nobility and quiet power about him. I couldn't tell if it was real or feigned, but he wore it comfortably. And if all those campaign ribbons were real, he had quite a distinguished combat record. One didn't have to be cut like John Wayne to be a real hero.

"Mr. Fairweather," Bishara began, "This is Michael Christian. Michael, Director James Fairweather. He minds things around here."

I was impressed. Fairweather being the *minder* of MI5 things, was the equivalent of being told J. Edgar Hoover emptied the waste cans at the FBI.

"Mr. Fairweather. It is a pleasure sir. I'm honored," I replied.

The most senior officer in MI5 returned the greeting warmly. "Mr. Christian. I have heard nothing but good things about you."

With that he turned to Bishara. It was obvious the courtesies were over.

"What do you have?" he asked her.

Again, Bishara demonstrated that amazing recall and the ability to organize her thoughts and statements into terse, but complete concepts as she related the entire day to Fairweather. As she did, I began to realize what a long day it had been, and my mind drifted to Marley's plan of making it even longer.

"And what do you think, Mr. Christian?"

Fairweather caught me off guard, at a moment when my mind was elsewhere. He was sharp enough to recognize that and smoothly continued,

221

"About the reality of there being a bomb somewhere on its way to Wimbledon."

"I know that my assumptions are based only on partial information," I began. "And those facts may stack up to be something entirely different with the addition of more intelligence.

"I have been watching things unfold as my own investigation progressed. It moved from simple theft, to money laundering, to a couple of murders, to an attempt on my life. It was only when Officer Bishara, here, added the element of the mosque to the equation that the facts began to point to the thefts of our checks being more nefarious than a personal enrichment scheme.

"When Ramzi Ayyad, the Imam that Halima asked for, turned out to be a person of interest to you, the general concepts of a plot began to emerge for all of us. But when we got to the warehouse and I saw the packaging for chemical elements that are never used together, other than for bomb making, I drew my conclusion. It was pure luck, and at this point speculation, that the pallets are stained with the same stains as on those pallets making their way in and out of Wimbledon.

"So, if you are asking me, Director, if I think there is a plot to detonate a bomb at Wimbledon, as weak as it may seem, it is all I have right now.

"I would most certainly encourage you to increase security," I continued. "And heavily inspect every strawberry vehicle entering the facility. And if there are any already on the premises that are leaving, I would ask that they be checked again to see if our sniper is driving. I would do the inbounds quite a distance away from the compound, to avoid collateral damage, which might have just as serious an effect outside the perimeter as an attack inside the venue itself."

Marley interrupted, "And if our guy is leaving, driving an empty truck …"

I finished his sentence for him, "Then we can assume there might be a bomb planted somewhere on the grounds that he would have had access to."

"Yes, well thank you for that Christian," he replied. He nodded to Bishara, who escorted me to the door.

"One more thing, Christian," asked Fairweather. "Should I recommend to the Secretary that he cancel the Princess's appearance?"

I was flattered, but had no good answer for that one. It was a political hot potato no matter which recommendation he made. The lack of specific data would make him vulnerable to opposition, with any position he took.

"I'm sorry sir, I don't know the protective capabilities of Wimbledon or the Princess's security detail. I would think DC Marley would be better served to answer your question. He is one of the security directors at Wimbledon." It was all I had.

"Marley, yes," Fairweather said. "Well, thank you again Mr. Christian. It was a pleasure." With that he nodded dismissively to Bishara and Marley.

This time, as we walked to the door, the senior director of the British Security Service did not call me back.

As we walked, Bishara said, "Fairweather liked your assessment. And he probably agrees with it. But he has to be certain of his facts when he meets with the cabinet members. He lives in a very political world."

"I get it," I answered. "I'm familiar with corporate

politicians, and frankly, they are not much different than elected or appointed politicians. No matter what the right answer is, they'll always dilute it to a point designed to protect their careers."

"I'm turning you back over to Marley," Bishara said. "I have to lead the evidence mission, find out who rented that warehouse, and help draft the recommendations for Fairweather. I may try to grab that Imam too." Then she stopped walking and stepped in so close to me that I could feel her heat emanate from her.

"Listen, Michael," she whispered quietly. "I hope this gets resolved well. And maybe when it does, we can spend some time together, not chasing bad guys, but just getting acquainted on a personal level. I'd like to buy you dinner, while you're here."

I was being invited to dinner by a stunningly beautiful, and totally ruthless officer from British Domestic Intelligence, and my ego was throbbing with endorphins. *That would be wonderful* was forming on my lips, when Marley shouted down the hall, "Christian, let's go!"

I smiled with a look that said, *I'll get back to you on that*, and headed down the hall after Marley.

Soon Marley was speeding westward on the 501 to get me back to my hotel. His night was not yet over, but I couldn't add anything of value at this point. He was turned practically sideways in the front seat as he spoke to me.

"Listen, I'll come get you in the morning, early, say six o'clock. It's too late to try to set up new checkpoints outside the Wimbledon grounds. The berry trucks will be arriving at any time. One of our security coordinators is working with a consolidator on behalf of a half-dozen strawberry growers in the area, to see if any of their trucks are missing, or if they noticed anything unusual about their drivers. I've added armed officers at each checkpoint.

"But only one company will deliver all the berries there, and we are vetting them and their drivers as we speak. We'll check each driver's identification, as they arrive, and match them to employee lists we have been provided. And I'm going to have them verify the drivers again as they leave.

"My people are being as discrete as possible, but we are inquiring specifically about drivers of Middle Eastern descent. Once that gets out, there will be an uproar, of course, about our xenophobic investigative approach."

In the back of my mind, a nagging thought began to form. We were working under the assumption that because strawberry pallets were used in the warehouse, that a strawberry truck would be used to bring a bomb into Wimbledon.

"What if it's a different truck?" I asked. I hated to do it, but I had to broach the idea to Marley. He seemed crestfallen to hear me say out loud what he was already probably thinking. Suddenly I felt very tired.

■ ■ ■ ■ ■

THE FIRST THING I DID when I got back to my hotel room was to check my email. There were a couple dozen, but I scanned down the list of senders and found what I was looking for. There were two of interest, and one of them was from Barclays to Patrick Flannery, with me copied on it.

It started out with the usual formal greeting of a business correspondence and then got to the heart of the matter.

Dear Mr. Flannery,

After consultation with our law department, and in consideration of our long partnership with Transeget Industries, we have come to the conclusion that it would be in the best interests of both our organizations, if Barclays made good your loss.

This letter, and our actions in support of it, in no way constitute an admission of wrong-doing on the part of Barclays' Bank or of any of our agents or employees. Nor are we making any assumption about the standard of security of your financial instruments. Our gesture is made as a matter of goodwill.

Your account has been credited with £308,356.46.

Kind Regards,
James Finch
Vice President, Business Marketing
Barclays Bank, London

CC: Michael Christian

I wasn't going to try the math at this late hour, but I knew it was roughly the half-million we had lost. Flannery would be pleased, and he would likely never know what methods I used to get the results.

I opened the second email, which was from Flannery. It simply said, *You are indeed one bad ass. Well done.*

It had been a trying day and my body was aching for some sleep, but since it was only about nine in the evening back home, I could still talk a few minutes with Alice.

I wondered why she didn't pick up the call, as I ended up leaving a voicemail. Sleep overtook me mercifully, and I dreamed of lying on a cold, steel bed with Alice and Miriam embracing while looking at me through a one-way mirror. Suddenly the lights in the room began flashing and a warning claxon sounded over and over. The women's faces disappeared as a sense of anxiety swept over me.

I awoke to the phone ringing on my bedside end-table, in the familiar British double chirp. It was only four o'clock in the morning, and the caller was Marley.

"I'll be there in an hour," he said. "Wear a suit and tie." I had a plenty of questions for him, but he answered the critical one first, and without me asking.

"All the trucks cleared security and have left the premises. There was no dangerous cargo on any of them and the drivers all checked out."

There was a side of me that felt enormous relief. Then I thought about Fairweather and wondered if he had recommended cancelling the Princess's visit today.

"What did Bishara have to say about that?" I asked.

"Her lab team confirmed all your assumptions last night. We have every reason to believe there was bomb-making activity going on in there," he answered. "And one more thing, Christian. The warehouse was rented on a one-year lease by Ramzi Ayyad. We have a crew bringing him to Bishara at MI5 now. Look, I'll answer your other questions when I get there. Try to grab a bite to eat. It could be a long day." Marley concluded.

It seemed they were all long days, from the moment I got here.

■ ■ ■ ■ ■

MARLEY DROVE US TO MI5'S offices where Bishara greeted us by the garage elevator. She was wearing a dark blue business suit, nipped at the waist, over a cream-colored blouse open at the neck. It was obvious that she had cleavage, but none of it was showing. Very tasteful. It looked like she had gotten about ten hours sleep, a massage, and a fresh hairdo. There was no sign of fatigue on her at all.

"Fairweather wants to see you," she said to me, as she turned and escorted us through the building. "Put these on." She was all business. Although she kept up a pretty good pace, we weren't running through the halls this time.

Marley and I clipped our blue colored "Level 1-

Authorized Visitor" identification cards to the lapels of our suit jackets. "As long as you are escorted, you will not be challenged as to your presence. This just makes it easier for me," she said.

As we walked through the corridors people stopped what they were doing to stare at us. Again I wondered if I was about to be arrested for something.

Fairweather's secretary had us wait in his outer office. "He will be with you shortly," was all she said, before returning to the work on her desk.

Bishara said, "Check your piping."

That was a strange comment. Out of instinct, I checked my tie alignment to my shirt, jacket, belt buckle and zipper. All was in order. Marley was doing the same. Bishara was flicking imaginary lint off her jacket and slacks. Her piping looked amazing.

A buzz on the secretary's desk prompted her to action. She rose and said, "He will see you now," and escorted us to the door to Fairweather's inner office. "Sir," she said as we entered.

"Yes, thank you," Fairweather replied formally to her, as she shut the door behind us.

There was no invitation to sit, and there would have been no place to do so. Besides Fairweather, there were already three men seated in the room. Each was wearing a bespoke suit and tie, and each was as impeccably groomed as Fairweather. None of the three rose to greet us.

Fairweather remained standing and began, "Gentlemen, this is Detective Inspector Marley of the London County Putney Constabulary. And this is Michael Christian, the gentleman I told you about, and you all know Bishara, here."

He made no effort to introduce the others in the room to me.

He continued, "Marley is leading the initiative to isolate our suspect at the Championships and Bishara is handling the development of further intelligence in support of that initiative.

"It was Christian here who made the initial observations and developed the theory we are working off of at the moment. I'd like Bishara, here, to address the information she has come up with so far. Bishara." And with that he turned it over to her.

In the style I was coming to admire, she used a condensed version to bring them up to speed as of last night at the warehouse. Then she continued.

"This morning, my evidence tech teams established that the residue they found in the warehouse is dual-purpose. They have seemingly innocuous uses as everyday farming, gardening or industrial products. But taken together, they are also the raw materials used for bomb making." Again she paused, to let that set in before continuing.

"Worse, they also confirm the presence of compounded chemicals used as detonator substances, if you will, that would result from their proper mixture.

"And we have identified the presence of raw material explosive products in the building, specifically, ammonium nitrate and diesel fuel. Based on the number of pallets that tested positive and their arrangement in the warehouse, we conclude a significant number of explosives were previously present in the warehouse. That is fact. From that, we also assume that these materials may have been made into a bomb or bombs already.

Fairweather seemed unfazed, but the other three started fidgeting as they listened.

"The signatures of these explosives match those of Paddy Flood's engineers." Bishara stopped there to see if further explanation of Flood was needed. It was obvious they knew of him and his former role as the lead bomb-making engineer with the IRA, but they did seem surprised about linking the bomb to Flood. He, like nearly all members of his team had been killed, either by the police, or by their own leaders. She pushed on.

"We have also determined that the warehouse in question was leased by Ramzi Ayyad of the Al-Irschad Mosque. This mosque has been on our watch list for quite some time, and we believe Ayyad is providing a safe haven and recruiting center for Hezbollah initiatives. We hadn't made the connection between the mosque and the warehouse until late this morning."

With that revelation, the guests in the room stirred uncomfortably when Bishara connected the mosque to radical Muslims. Even though the facts were true, and they had been unofficially surmised for some time, the three guests couldn't even listen to such an intelligence report without seeing political implications, from being officially briefed.

I looked across at Fairweather, who seemed to read my thoughts, but gave no indication where he came down on them. Bishara continued.

"Lacking any direct evidence, and under the governing regulations, relative to investigating Muslims in our communities, we had to put further intelligence gathering on the back burner. Until now, that is." Again she paused, as if to make her point that this could have possibly been prevented had they been allowed to investigate earlier.

"We have Imam Ayyad, in an interrogation room, and I intend to have a little chat with him too," she said. And again, the strangers in the room seemed uncomfortable, as if their plausible deniability had just gone out the window, or perhaps they had heard about Bishara's *chatting* methods.

"Hopefully he'll shed some light on the nature, timing and location of an attack, if there really is one, in the immediate future." It was the first time, in her presentation, that I heard any backpedaling on the theory of an imminent attack. She was right, of course. But it was my theory that was being doubted, and my presence in the room began to make sense. I was the scapegoat.

With that, Bishara completed her presentation and turned to David. "Inspector Marley, would you like to take it from here?" she said.

Marley took a half step forward and started in without any hesitation. He quickly brought the guests in the room up to speed on the murders, and the search activities that took place overnight out at Wimbledon. He ended with the fact that our suspicion of a bomb, possibly being brought in by a strawberry delivery truck, had not panned out. Against the practical findings and the results gathered so far, my point-of-attack theory, and its timing, were looking weaker and weaker. I was pleased that I had no formal role in this. But that didn't last long.

"So, Christian," the Director said. "Tell us what led you to think we should be deploying our resources in this manner." It was obvious that he authorized the resources, to back my strategy last night, but had made it his decision. This morning, he was making it perfectly clear that I had some contribution to it. But it seemed like a lightweight move, for such a heavy hitter, in front of such an apparently austere audience.

I replied, with as much gravity as I could muster, "Sir, your team has pretty much explained how we got to where we are. And obviously, the method, time and place for a bombing were not correct."

"Obviously," he repeated. "Go on," he said.

I didn't think I had any more to offer about why we concluded what we did. But I did want to try to get myself out of there in relatively good graces.

"I do think, however," I continued, "that we can accurately conclude that a bombing attack is inevitable. The real questions still remain, *when, where, and how*?

"Looking back at your three prior attacks, two were at train stations and one was at Hyde Park, at the Arch. Each was increasingly more devastating. Yet your infrastructure has become so adept at recovery, that you are practically operating uninterrupted, as to everyday life, and as to your economy.

"I believe this is noteworthy, especially considering how destructive the last bombing was. So, the question is, why would the bomber want to stage another attack, and with what appears to be an enormous amount of explosives?

"I think the answer to that question will define the target. And the target might explain when we can expect the next attack. I still think it is going to be Wimbledon, given the Championship finals are today and tomorrow." The snappy dressers twisted uncomfortably in their chairs.

"Everyone knows there will be members of the royal family there," I continued. "People have come from all over the world to attend this event, including world famous athletes, wealthy patrons of the sport of tennis, government officials, and high visibility entertainment figures.

"And they are all presumed safe because you deploy your elite military and police forces for their protection at the event. I still believe *that* is the statement the bomber wants to make. That he was able to cause a disaster of horrible magnitude, and you were unable to stop him.

"If he can get in close enough, he *will* cause catastrophic injury and death, not to mention significant damage to one of England's most historic clubs. In one stroke, he will have singlehandedly undermined public confidence in your ability to keep your people safe, not to mention the Royals. And this message will resonate, not merely with the British people, but around the world." I stopped.

The silence in the room was palpable and continued until one of the un-introduced members spoke.

"So, what are you recommending, Christian? That we stop every man, woman and child entering the stadium and search them at gunpoint?"

I had seen that approach before, where a detractor, without a solution of his own, would minimize the value of a recommendation by taking it to the extreme, thus making it sound ridiculous. Having been put in that position many times before, I was ready for such an asshole, and prepared to deliver my response. *Let the U.S. Ambassador sort it out*, I thought.

Fairweather interjected, however, and saved me from a horrible diplomatic blunder.

"Mr. Christian, thank you for your contribution and your honest assessment.

"Bishara, would you see Mr. Christian and DI Marley out? Thank you." The three gentlemen did not rise as we left.

As we walked down the hall toward the interrogation room, Bishara said, "Well done Christian. You have just managed to tip over the Deputy Home Secretary, a Deputy Minister of the House of Lords and the Deputy Director of MI6."

"Tip them over?" I asked.

"Yes," she answered. "You have put them on notice of a possible attack on the Championships. If they take aggressive action, as appropriate to such an attack, and there is no assault, the criticism will ring for years and their careers may well be over within the month. If they take no additional action, and there is an attack, their careers, and likely those of their bosses, are over at the next emergency session of the Parliament.

"And while we are talking about careers," and Bishara looked at Marley, "ours are likely over as well, since it took a civilian, and a yank at that, to discover the plot."

I could see where she was going with this and she was right. It always rolled downhill and Marley and Bishara were smack at the bottom on this one. I was the only one without career risk, or so it seemed. And although it wasn't a mess of my doing, I was hip deep in someone else's muck.

"There is something we could do," I ventured.

Bishara said, "I think they'll not be allowing me to work with you any longer."

But Marley interjected, "He's pointed us in good directions throughout, Miriam. At least let's hear him out."

"What are you thinking?" he asked me.

"We can't just stop midstream and let this go to politicians to decide. We still have some stones unturned and I don't think that's the way you two operate. Let's have a crack at the Imam. See if you can break him into turning over the bomber. At the very least, get an artist's rendition of the bomber from him. It's something to work with, which is more than we have right now."

I was looking at Bishara, now. "You seem to have a way of twisting people around, Miriam," I said with a glint in my eye. "Why don't you go to work on him," I suggested.

"I'm going to go to work on you first," she said. She walked us over to one of her technical team members and told him, "Take him down to our photo group and have a forensic sketch artist work with him. He saw the shooter and we have every reason to believe that guy might be our bomber. Get me a drawing."

With that she turned and headed to the interrogation room.

■ ■ ■ ■ ■

THE FORENSIC ROOM WAS NOTHING like I expected. It was merely another bullpen of desks and officers poring over laboratory results and reports, and I couldn't see a single microscope. We were escorted to a drab desk.

"Bishara wants this guy to give you a description," was all he said.

The forensic artist was, above all else, an artist. His soft-spoken style was relaxed, and he lacked the intensity of a street investigator. I could see this was going to be a *process,* rather than a quick recollection of mine, that would ultimately turn into a pictorial rendering.

He started out comfortably enough, merely asking me to think about what I saw and to start anywhere with my recall.

I started with the eyes. "They seemed intense and focused, but were too far away for me to see their color."

The artist nodded, and merely made notes, rather than putting pencil to drawing paper. After a while, his notebook had begun to fill with half-page notes relative to spacing, width, shape, and brows. He added some type of numeric code to each of his notes.

From his verbal prompts I began to see the shooter's eyes relative to the bridge of his nose and was able to describe that as well. The tops of his cheekbones followed. I told him that the majority of his face appeared to be in a shadow, or perhaps it was a closely cropped beard or a couple days of growth. I watched as his pencil merely made more notes, never once touching the sketchpad on his desk.

After about an hour of this, he asked me to look at a series of photos of people's faces and told me to focus only on the eyes. Soon I saw a pair that looked similar. And as he worked, we refined his understanding of the eyes to match what he had helped me recreate from my memory.

Then we talked about the eyebrows. I told him that I couldn't really make out the brows because the guy's face was covered by a black baseball type hat, with a red crest or logo in the center. He pulled out another book and it didn't take long for me to point out what I thought might be a good match.

The process took a lot longer than I thought it would. My expectations were based on how quickly the sketch artists worked back in the Detroit Police Department, where they did thousands of renditions.

Before long, the artist began adding in the brows and the cheeks, working without any further input from me. When he stopped, I looked at the image and only barely recognized it from my description. The eyes weren't intense enough, but I didn't know how to characterize that. And the face seemed too full and needed to be sculpted along the hollows of the cheeks. So, he noted all that in his book and went back to work.

When he completed that second rendition, he turned the pad so I could see the sketch. And there, looking back at me were the eyes and the facial shape I thought I saw on the rooftop.

"Yes," I said. "That's really close." He then took back the pad and began drawing again for about ten more minutes. This time, in the lower right corner, he produced a nearly identical pencil drawing, but now the sniper was wearing the hat with the logo clearly visible. "That's it," I confirmed. "That's exactly it."

Marley leaned in to take a look. "Yes, I

recognize the logo – It belongs to the Gloucester rugby team. Are you sure this is a close match Michael?" he asked. "Because if it's that good, then I'll have a few hundred of these fliers printed up and sent out to all the stations, and of course they'll hit Wimbledon within the hour."

"That is him!" said a voice from behind us.

There was Bishara walking a man right up to us. If that was the Imam, from the looks of him, things hadn't gone well for him with Bishara in the interrogation room.

Bishara said, "Ayyad claims not to know who the building was occupied by, merely that he was told to rent it."

Ayyad persisted, pointing at the sketch, "That is the man we call *The Messenger*," he said. I do not know his name, but that is him. Where did you get that picture?" he asked while looking intently at the drawing.

"However, that is not his beard," the Imam corrected. "The beard is tailed at the bottom into a small twist, otherwise that is him."

The artist used a gum eraser on the sketch paper and went back to work, his fingers moving quickly. He turned the pad to the Ayyad, who said, "Yes, exactly. That is him."

We may not have known his name, but now we knew his face. Maybe we had a chance after all.

■ ■ ■ ■ ■

FROM THE MOMENT MIRIAM BISHARA looked in shock at the sketch, a sickening feeling gripped her stomach. She knew the face and she knew the Messenger's name, Rasul Elqisi. And she also realized she could never tell anyone.

Recovering her composure, she told the tech, "Send these out now to all our officers and get the word out on the street. I want that bloody son of a bitch. And send a set to our contact points at each of the branch stations throughout the Isles. I don't want him to have anywhere to hide. Then send a flash to MI6 and update them. Run off a hundred high-speed copies for Marley and make him a digital file, so he can print more."

The tech's fingers flashed over his keyboard and he said, "The print jobs are already in the queue, and I'm sending a broadcast email with a digital copy to his station houses now."

Bishara turned to Marley and said, "As soon as they are through printing, you need to get these out to all your checkpoints at Wimbledon and to your patrols. The digital copies will get there before you do, so you might want to a prepare briefing for the event's unit commanders, especially the military detachments, unless you want me to do that." Marley said, "No, I'm fine. They're my details, and I know their posts, so I'll handle the briefings."

"The gates will open soon," Bishara said, "So we can only hope we're not too late. Have the on-site security detail print as many extra copies as you need."

240

Marley said, "It's a big step, but I am calling there now to delay the opening of the gates until I arrive and can brief our security units."

Then she directed, "Right. Well, we'd better get you out there too, just in case you're right, Christian. You'll have the best recollection of this guy's face."

At that point, I wondered if I hadn't overstayed my luck. They were inviting me to join them at the scene of what could very well be a cataclysmic event, and I was following along, like I belonged there.

■ ■ ■ ■ ■

BISHARA STARED AT THEIR BACKS as Marley and Christian walked out of MI5 and into the predawn darkness. She ran to her desk and called the number Elqisi had given her as a contact phone, but she wasn't too positive about him answering. It wasn't merely the late hour. He never picked up her calls, but relied on coded messages to stay in touch. Given his plan, she doubted if he would ever contact her or respond to a meeting request from her again.

She reflected about the trajectory of her career going from that of a rising star, to that of a piece of detritus being washed down a sewer. Miriam didn't know if she should scream or cry. All she could do was what she had been trained for. She had to find Elqisi and interdict him from killing anyone else.

And given any chance at all, she had to kill him.

■ ■ ■ ■ ■

THE BIG ENGINE IDLED WITH a quiet, throaty rumble that was almost calming in the darkness of the cab of his truck. Soon the sun would crest the top of the stadium and the crowds would fill the grounds. Rasul Elqisi's fingers played idly over the big truck's pneumatic controls as he passed the time. He looked across the narrow, two lanes of Church Road from the designated parking lot for the service trucks. He almost didn't make it here at all, much less on time to be admitted with the others in his group.

His day had been long and filled with danger. Several times he had almost been caught, once when he entered the Underground station, and again when the police had raided his warehouse.

He had barely gotten out the back door before they posted the guards. And now he was exhausted, maybe from almost being shot while on the roof, by the two police responding on the sidewalk below. *How had they gotten there so soon? Were they protecting the Halima brothers, or the other man, who must have been the American?*

He had been right to anticipate having to escape in a hurry. And he was right in heading here immediately. His goal was to keep moving. As soon as he completed this mission, he would head to the North Country, where the geography lends itself to keeping a low profile. One cannot capture the stream while it is flowing.

His convoy had approached the Wimbledon security checkpoint while it was still dark outside. His ID card received a mere cursory inspection. The officer looked him right in the eyes with a look of familiarity, and politely asked him to wait, while another officer walked around his truck and screened beneath it with a mirror. There was no suspicion and there was no inspection of the interior of the truck. There hadn't been, actually, after the first couple days of him showing up in line with the ten other company drivers.

Now Elqisi sat in his truck, going over his escape plan. Once he completed his mission, he merely had to cross back north across the Putney Bridge over the Thames. The River had its own tide, otherwise, he thought it would be fitting to row across it, and climb its steps, carved by the Romans, thousands of years ago. Such a moment as today deserved such a fitting gesture. Once across, he would switch vehicles, and be lost on this large British Isle until it was safe to leave.

He had another option, but he didn't think he could ever again use her as his safeguard.

Rasul Elqisi, whom some called The Messenger, continued slowly rubbing the battery-operated razor across his now smooth, hairless face. While he did so, he prayed.

■ ■ ■ ■ ■

THE FIRST TIME MARLEY TOOK me to Wimbledon, the roads were merely crowded. Today they were jammed for miles. We had been on the road fifteen minutes already for a ride that normally took only ten, yet we were still out about a mile from the stadium complex when he drifted off onto a side road again. This time he had us approaching from the east. I couldn't believe the number of people walking miles to get to the stadium.

In the States, we were so accustomed to our automobile freedom, and intentionally oblivious to the economic and environmental cost of gasoline, that most of us would drive two miles to the grocery store without thinking anything of it.

"The auto traffic will be pretty intense from here on in," he said. "And the main inbound road will be clogged with pedestrians, service vehicles, buses and taxis. Not only will we be seeing tens of thousands of spectators both inside and outside the stadium, we have to search them and the thousands of support people who work here. There are over sixteen hundred catering personnel alone.

"A half mile more on the main roads, and it will be easier to walk than to be in the car." He was describing road names to me as if I knew them. We continued southbound through residential streets as uniformed officers at each intersection moved barricades for Marley's car.

Today, I recalled, was July 6th. Back in the States, we would still be celebrating our

Independence from the very British monarchy I was now trying to protect. Clean up crews would be removing fireworks debris and litter from the streets throughout the weekend.

I thought about the huge crowds who were gathering here to celebrate tennis, and I was reminded of New York City traffic, where I often hopped out of my cab and walked the last half-mile, getting to my destination before the cab would have.

Although it was very early in the morning, the tennis fans were in a festive mood. People everywhere were walking and smiling in excited anticipation to be attending one of the sporting world's biggest events, at one of the most renowned venues in the world, *The All England Lawn Tennis Club*. And they were oblivious of the fact that they may soon be either witnesses to or victims of a National tragedy.

At Revelstoke Road, Marley turned back west and drove us under the train tracks and onto a large open field, where hundreds of tents had been set up for vendors, near an adjacent VIP car park. "Short cut," he said as he swiped an access card through the barrier gate control.

I suppose it was. We were on more of a path, now, than a road, that ran alongside the eastern boundary of Wimbledon Park Lake. I could see the top of the stadium reflected on its still water. At this time of the morning, it was nearly mirror-like. At any other time, being here would have been idyllic.

"This is a beautiful pond, Marley."

"Actually, it really is a lake," he said. "It's almost sixty feet deep."

We drove onto Home Park Road where there

was no traffic at all. Not only was it blocked off to cars, but it was restricted to all but members of the Wimbledon Golf Club. As we drove along the underside of the course, I noticed that there were no golfers. "Closed for the Championships," Marley explained.

He knew right where we were going. Within minutes, Marley navigated us through a large encampment of service vehicles of all kinds, and right to gate number five. Rather than driving in, he waived off the admitting officer and parked on the sidewalk just outside the gate on the east side of Centre Court. We walked in from there, and soon we were underneath the main Clubhouse and in the lower-level security squad room. I was amazed at how cavernous the underground operation was. He referred to it as "the loading bay."

By the time we got to the briefing room, the area was filled with command officers from all the protection units and military details in attendance, including several off-duty members of the local fire brigades who had been impressed into security roles for the event. The room smelled of cigarette smoke and coffee. Everyone tamped out their butts and set down their paper cups, as Marley began the briefing.

He cut right to the chase, without going into extraneous details about how we got to this point. He just emphasized that the bomb-threat was credible, that authorities believed it was imminent, and that Wimbledon was the target, if not today, then tomorrow. Everyone in the room seemed to sense the gravity of the moment.

It was their responsibility to see to it that no one was injured or killed on their watch, especially any member of the Royal family. Unspoken was the thought that they too wanted to remain alive at the end of their watch. The room odor changed to that of sweat.

As Marley ensured that everyone had a clean copy of the artist's drawing of the Messenger, I expected a series of questions about the threat, or about the suspect. Interestingly, there were none. The command officers seemed to understand what was expected of them and were eager to pass the information along to their team members.

As the group began to break up, one of the Rapid Response Unit commanders said, "May we assume that the use of deadly force has been authorized?"

Looking up, to make sure the entire room got the message, Marley replied, "This man has already shot one person dead, including trying to kill this guy," as he nodded to me. "I want you all to presume our suspect is armed. If necessary, use deadly force with extreme prejudice. He would be very valuable, taken alive, but if it comes down to it, use force on him, before he uses it on you." Then he added, "And by the way, this bloke," and he gestured his thumb toward me, "is a Yank, and he's with me. Don't shoot him."

There it was again. Had there been some kind of friendly fire problem in the past? Just about everyone in the room was taking a long second look at me, as if they were taking Marley's recommendation seriously.

Marley exited the room with me in tow and said, "We're going to take a look inside. But before I can get you in, you're going to need an ID card." We walked down the tight concrete corridor to another room built into the right-hand side of the cement wall. The unarmed security officer, stationed outside, nodded to Marley as we entered.

Inside was a flurry of activity in front of banks of camera screens, attended to by private security personnel and overseen by uniformed police. Many of the views were panning across close-ups of thousands of faces in the queues outside, waiting to get in. A sergeant looked up and Marley stated to her, matter of factly, "Reenie, he needs an all-areas access badge. Be a dear, and see to that, would you?" And he wandered off with his wanted posters to a glass walled office, set slightly above the monitoring area. It seemed to be the control center for the entire room. In the back of my mind I was thinking, calling a woman *a dear* would likely bring a sexual harassment complaint in the States.

The sergeant led me to a smaller, much quieter room with a camera and an ID card maker, set on a typical, government-issue desk. There wasn't much else in the room. Within minutes, my photo had been taken and a copy was printed onto a durable plastic card that she efficiently slipped into a clear plastic folder. My photo was prominently displayed next to the Wimbledon logo, as was my last name in large letters, followed by my first and middle initials. "This will do you," the sergeant said. She fastened the badge sleeve to a green and purple cloth lanyard and instructed, "Slip that around your neck and wear it visibly, on the outside your jacket."

The green background color, along with various medallions in red, blue, and orange must have had all the significance they needed to get me anywhere on the property, not that I'd be going anywhere without Marley, anyway.

As we left the room, Reenie said, "So you're the Yank with Marley. I hear we're not supposed to shoot you." When I asked her what that was all about, she chuckled and said, "You Yanks all carry guns, and we're not armed."

Maybe Reenie wasn't, but there were plenty of soldiers, AFO's, and others I couldn't identify, in full tactical gear, and they *were* armed. I hoped they all got the message not to shoot me.

Marley came down from the control center office and escorted me back into the tunnel.

"This is probably the best time for you to see the stadium before it fills." We walked to the opposite end of the stadium then climbed the stairs that led to the lower level walkway, in the northeast corner of the stadium.

The top rows of seats were draped in shadows here, compared with the other side. Standing in the lower bowl made the stadium seats seem even closer to the court. In a matter of hours, over fifteen thousand people would be screened and seated in here for the Championships. He pointed out the Royal Box at the far south end of the court.

"We've been advised that if Princess Diana attends, she will bring one of her sons with her. Right now, it looks like little William will join his mum, if they come. The Duchess of Kent and her husband, the Duke of Kent will also be in attendance for sure. They are the event patrons. And the Ambassador of Argentina will attend to cheer on his fellow countrywoman, Gabriela Sabatini today. Her opponent, Steffi Graf is from Germany, but I have no information that the German ambassador will be here. It's a good bet, however, that someone from their embassy will show, as a sign of support.

He pointed, "They will all be seated there, in the front three or four rows, in the center. I don't yet know who else might be in attendance with them, but we doubt it will be the Queen.

"The Princess will enter through their private tunnel, and will go directly to her seat. None of the Royals ever linger in the corridors. They will walk from the upper Club level, where they visit, and then directly to their box. There is, by order of the Royal family, no visible showing of a security force around them. It does not mean we won't have members of their security service very handy, or that the SAS won't have members scattered throughout the seats, immediately behind the box, though.

"Because they are so well known around the world, they will be highly visible," Marley continued. "So, most of our security is focused on ensuring that no weapons but our own enter the facility, and that no one gets near the box, much less close to the patrons seated in there.

"All personnel entering that area are vigorously prescreened and known. An unknown face has no chance of finessing their way into the secure area, which extends all the way to the outer doors at the south end of the Stadium, right behind the box.

"All vendors are restricted away from that area, when any of the Royals are in attendance. So there will be access control measures and enhanced security presence buffering those points."

I could see where an attacker would have to find another way to get access to the box, other than merely trying to fake their way in. And forcing their way in would be very, very difficult, though not impossible.

I was going through various shock-attack scenarios in my mind, recalling executive protection protocols I had put in place for our corporate executives, in countries experiencing anarchy and routine kidnapping. My imagination went into overdrive, given the dedication of some extremists. I began to think in terms of suicide bombers, and attack squads, but there hadn't been any evidence of that as a tactic here, and I felt fortunate for Marley that Bishara's intelligence hadn't revealed a "team" approach to the recent attacks.

"Marley," I interrupted. "Do you think it is overkill to order up some additional ambulances, and place them on standby somewhere close, just in case we miss something? At least enough extra to transport high visibility types like Entire Royal box or the players?" I asked. "You can always triage mass casualties until ambulances arrive, but there would be hell to pay, if the Royals had to wait as well."

"Good thinking," he said. "You recall that we drove in on the east side of the stadium. If we had come down the west side streets, you would have noticed we have dozens of ambulances and medics spaced apart throughout the neighborhoods, so as not to cause undue suspicion.

"The fire director has that responsiblity and mustered them there as soon as we called him. Units are on standby throughout the county. If there is a need for so many units, it would be better to bring them in on the one-way streets from the west and to exit with the injured on the northbound one-way streets on the east side of the stadium.

There are eight hospitals within four kilometers,

or so, of here. Five can handle emergency trauma's but we have put the other three on alert as well, just in case."

I felt a little embarrassed making a recommendation that had already been seen to.

"I can see you have written a few disaster plans in your time, Michael. Maybe when this is over, you'll take a look at ours?"

I was flattered and felt better.

Marley continued with his explanation. "At the juncture of every section and row, there is a courtesy attendant who is matched up with a security officer. They are both unarmed, but each officer is more than a customer service representative. They are fully capable of engaging someone hand to hand, and even more so once additional help arrives."

What about a diversionary attempt?" I asked.

"No matter the distraction," Marley replied, "or how close to the Royal Box an incident may occur, their protection detail stays with the Royal Box. No distraction will serve as a diversion of resources from the Royals, each of whom who has been briefed on a rapid and safe evacuation from the box and into the tunnel to their cars, if necessary. So, we have that covered. Now, let's go outside," he said.

I was thoroughly impressed with the inside protection program, but the history of Wimbledon wasn't lost on me either. I was getting a private tour of the entire security protocol while inside Centre Court, at a tennis stadium that honored a sport whose Championship timeline went back to its first match in eighteen seventy-seven.

This was a building that suffered direct hits of

five, five-hundred pound bombs during the German carpet bombings of London, in nineteen forty-four. It stood as a testament to the will of the people of England, and I was standing inside it. I felt like I was on hallowed grounds, and I hoped it would still be standing, at the end of this tournament.

"C'mon," Marley said, shaking me out of my reverie.

■ ■ ■ ■ ■

BISHARA PULLED HER CAR IN behind Marley's and told her crew she'd join them inside in a moment.

The Imam was under her control now. She knew, from the moment he cooperated, that he had become her snitch for life. He would be killed if Hezbollah ever found out, and that is pretty powerful leverage.

She believed him when he said he didn't know much about the Messenger, who kept himself isolated from personal contact. Her direction to the Imam was simple to begin with, *find out where he worked or lived, and what he drove.* If Ayyad came through with any of that, the Imam's life would become even more complicated, not less, because the more your snitch delivers, the more you use him.

The Imam had provided the phone number he used to call the Messenger, but that belonged to a third party phone service and Bishara hadn't bothered trying to trace back its origin.

She knew that if they didn't locate him here at Wimbledon, then her informant Rasul Elqisi would indeed drop off their radar. That would give him the advantage of choosing the time, place and method of delivering his assault. That being the case, if he pulled off the bombing, his capture might only be after the fact, if at all.

As much as Bishara wished that there was no incident today, or ever for that matter, she knew that her best chance of catching Elqisi would be when he exposed himself to place or detonate the bomb. She had some of her best trackers out on foot at Wimbledon now, and they were all radio equipped, which would widen their response net if he was spotted. Her mobile demolitions crew was backing up Marley's team and the military munitions experts, if they found a bomb and had to defuse it.

Right about now, her technical team was in the control center, working to install facial recognition software on the camera servers, which should help scan the crowd more efficiently. It was a new tool to MI5's technology arsenal, and Bishara wished she didn't have to divulge its existence in this manner. But if it ever served a higher purpose, this was it.

Bishara was under orders from the Director himself, that this *Messenger* should be taken alive for questioning, if possible. The intelligence he possessed about Hezbollah in the United Kingdom could be priceless.

But if it wasn't possible to take him cleanly, Fairweather had said, then he must be taken out hard, before he could complete his attack. Slight collateral damage might be necessary, but that would be a small political sacrifice the Director could handle. Her crew was fully aware of their instructions.

But Bishara knew there was no option. She had to take him out, period. From the moment she saw Christian's suspect sketch, she knew it was Elqisi and she knew she was screwed.

There would be no easy way to explain how she had cultivated an informant, yet didn't have a good address or phone number for him. She only communicated with him through a series of drops that alerted him that he should call her, or that she would meet him at a mutually agreed location. Otherwise, he called Bishara. Her informant, right under her nose, was a terrorist who had become the subject of a major manhunt. While she should have been managing him, he had been manipulating her.

At this very moment, nearly every member of the Metropolitan Police and the British Intelligence Service were trying to keep her informant from killing the Princess and her young son on International television. It was a disaster of her own making.

Bishara had developed Elqisi early on, as a Muslim who entered the country seeking political asylum from Afghanistan, but not as a refugee. He came under a sponsorship from the mosque. It didn't take long for her to have Immigrations Services pull him in for a routine interview, under the guise of reviewing his work visa. Bishara stood in for the immigrations clerk.

Getting him to agree to report the activities at the mosque went easier than it should have, but Bishara didn't see that as a red flag. She missed that completely.

He turned in a few young men entering Great Britain under the auspices of the mosque and she was able to corroborate that they had indeed been trained in militant camps in Somalia. Elqisi seemed a good fit for her work on the *Muslim Desk* as it was called. And the fact that she was frequently gathering actionable intelligence from him, polished her luster even more.

Now she realized with bitter regret that Elqisi had been playing her all along. He got by with giving her tidbits, while he orchestrated a series of bombings throughout London. If he pulled this one off, Bishara did not know if her career, or she, could survive that. If he was captured and subsequently revealed that he had played Bishara, it would be all over for her anyway.

Bishara knew what had to be done. He would have to be taken out, not captured. And she'd have to be the one to do it.

She dialed Elqisi's phone again. No answer.

She took a deep breath of determination, checked her gun, and exited her car. It was time to find Marley and Christian, and Elqisi, The Messenger.

■ ■ ■ ■ ■

THIRTY THOUSAND PEOPLE WERE QUEUED up outside the stadium grounds at all the entrance gates. The ranks of people reached all the way back to streets alongside the high-rise apartments to the west of the stadium. Members of the security detail were walking along the lines and talking casually with those in attendance. Every now and then, I would see one of them glance down at a paper in his hand. It was the wanted poster. As customer friendly as they seemed to be, they were doing their job of screening the people in line. Despite the delay they were encountering, the ticketholders seemed polite and patient.

Marley explained, "Once they open the gates, the crowd will break into various groups. Some will head straight for the souvenir stands, while others head for the food and drink concessions, and others will head to the courts for the minor finals or practice sessions.

"Every one of the fifteen thousand fans who enters Centre Court must have a valid ticket with an assigned seat. There will be no open seating, and that validation process occurs outside the building at each of the entry gates, and again at the tunnel entrances. They won't be allowed into a section unless it's their assigned one. We can control most people who enter that way."

I said, "I don't really expect this guy to try to enter with a ticket. Not if his intention is to bring a bomb to the stadium. He'd have to be willing to risk getting caught. And based on his last attacks, it seems like his goal is to get away completely unnoticed and unidentified." Marley nodded as we walked.

We had exited the stadium through the short corridor behind the Royal box, and were standing in the courtyard near the ticketholder gate we entered, facing the "Last Eight Club" area. Marley pointed out that a Championship qualifier, who made it to the Wimbledon quarterfinals, received induction to the club and was granted lifetime privileges, including Court One and Centre Court seats.

"Even they will have special ID, but the gate attendees in this corner will still use dual authentication for them. These officers have been trained to recognize the players' faces. Nevertheless, they must also have current authorized credentials to enter the stadium."

"You know Marley," I pointed out, "the more you explain the security measures people have to go through prior to entering the stadium, the more I am convinced, the bomb will not be carried inside through a gate. There is no way anyone can get a device on his person, and into the stadium without passing through security."

"Right, especially not one of the size you think we might be dealing with. Our job is to make sure of that," Marley replied. "So, our plan is to break this external acreage and the adjacent public and private space, and the other court areas into segments, and to treat them separately.

"I'll walk with you around the perimeter of the other courts and venue areas open to the public, then I'll take you to the loading bays inside."

Even with the long lines of people surrounded by security forces, this still looked like any other major sporting event, not the scene of a possible mass murder.

■ ■ ■ ■ ■

MORNING HAD BROKEN FULLY ACROSS the All England Lawn and Tennis Club, melting away the evening shadows and bathing gathering fans in a warm, golden sunlight. The past few days of mist and rain had delayed some of the games, and there had been concern the final pairings would extend into the early week. Allah must have been smiling on the Messenger because today, the finals would proceed as scheduled.

Rasul Elqisi sat low in his truck. He had been wired with adrenaline and awake all night, with no desire to sleep. He had memorized the service vehicle timeline that had occurred every day, for the past twelve days. It was almost exactly the same each day. Being patient with it guaranteed him his free admittance to the stadium grounds, right on time. All he had to do was wait until the pieces fell into place.

His truck was one of dozens that were queued up in the open field across the east side of Church street from Centre Court and Court One. He got the job as driver through a reference made for him through a Hezbollah sympathizer at the mosque. His resume stated he had two years of experience driving a garbage truck in Germany. Having never done so in his life, nor having ever been to Germany, he had to learn how to drive it in one day, just before he was assigned here. But he got by, and after a few weeks, he was recognized and as accepted on the grounds as any other driver.

When his turn in line arrived, he would drive

south on the grass to the Golf Club service road and then west out onto Church. He would proceed north to the utility entrance north of Gate Five. Once he entered the trash storage area, he would then wait while Wimbledon volunteers loaded bags after bags of trash into his truck. All he had to do was operate the compactor until the truck was full. Then he could leave.

His original plan called for him to detonate the bomb alongside the stadium. It would most definitely destroy a quarter of the building and kill thousands.

Except today he had no intention of driving to the waste area or of removing any trash. He would crash instead through the rollup doors to the stadium's loading bay, then disable the truck. Those sheet metal barriers would provide no obstacle against the tonnage of this truck, and he would be inside before anyone could stop him. The explosive damage would be immeasurably worse inside than out.

He would still try to flee before the bomb detonated. If he could get outside the building, he would disappear amongst the thousands of tennis fans and workers.

The final round of the women's championship would be played within the hour. Before that, other finals had been played on several of the fourteen courts on the grounds. Besides those attending the women's final game, thousands of ticket holders would be milling about, entering and exiting through the outer gates.

He thought about the number of people who would be in the stadium today and, although he regretted that he did not have the capability to take the entire structure down at one time, he would not let that deter him from celebrating another successful mission.

This time would be different. He wouldn't have to remain anonymous any longer. Once he succeeded, he would claim responsibility for this and the other bombings. Then he would move to another country and take the battle there, safe and anonymous again.

The world would hold the British government accountable for the deaths of their government officials and for the lives of their tennis champions. All of England would mourn for the loss of their Princess and her child. The might of the British government, its military, its intelligence agencies and its law enforcement branches would be revealed as useless against the dedication of a single man. He smiled as he thought about it.

The statement he made here today, would serve to energize other operatives around the world. Thousands of single cells of dedicated men, with perseverance and determination, would be emboldened to action, all because of his success here today. He needed no rest. He was alive with a fervor he hadn't felt in ages.

His pleasant reverie was interrupted abruptly when he spotted someone he thought he knew. Yes, it was her! He watched intently as his handler walked from her car, leaving it parked on the sidewalk, and entered the stadium across from the Last Eight Club.

She was here, so she must suspect him. There could be no other reason. Certainly, a coincidence could explain why she was here, but he did not believe that important events were random.

He would have to be very careful not to be seen. As much as he wanted to kill her, he knew that his primary mission came first. Killing Bishara was merely an added benefit.

Hopefully she would be inside the stadium when he detonated over five hundred pounds of explosives. If he could do both today, he would. Otherwise, he would wait and kill her the next time she asked to meet. He checked his gun again.

His truck was in a queue and he would not reach the front of the line for at least another hour, when the crowds were at their peak. For the tenth time, he checked to see that the side panel was still wide open. That would release the force of the blast directly onto his target area.

He was totally focused on his mission.

From his position across the street, he could see where an unending trail of people, including the *Last Eight Club* members and members of the Royal Family, would be passing just inside Gate Five.

■ ■ ■ ■ ■

WE EXITED CENTRE COURT FROM the northwest corner and headed north past the four mid-courts. Marley explained that there were several dozen tennis courts at Wimbledon, many with either bleacher or stadium seating arrangements, and more practice courts.

"Television broadcasts," he began, "show you only the matches featuring players of note. It drives the ratings up and sponsors compete years in advance to buy the advertising minutes. But there are actually over 300 matches played in the two weeks leading up to today and tomorrow. They play as long as there is daylight, and nearly every seat in every court is filled.

"And throughout the day people are waiting in the queue for unused or partial tickets that get returned by their owners. They'll be resold at a significant discount."

"So not everyone here has a ticket to get inside?"

"No, and that is part of the problem we deal with. People can get right up to the stadium without ever having to go through security.

"So we monitor the entire ebb and flow of the crowds at every nook and cranny of the grounds."

I saw where securing the entire program was an enormous undertaking. And it had to be repeated each day for each individual match. Considering the larger scope of about twenty acres and a half million people these two weeks, it seemed even more complex. Marley's approach of breaking the grounds into sections began to make even more sense.

As we rounded the top of Number One Court, with the practice courts off to our left, the grounds seemed more open. I couldn't see this being the point of an attack. There wasn't enough opportunity for maximum carnage here. It would have to be Court One or Centre Court. I got my bearings and recognized the Wimbledon Pro Shop ahead of us and Church Road outside of that. We got about midway to the side of Court One, when Marley diverted us outside and onto the sidewalk alongside Church Road.

"Traffic from here northbound will flow pretty well as it leaves the area and it is all one-way outbound. So, we are focusing our attention on the one-way streets southbound, eastbound and the other inbound streets.

"What are those?" I asked pointing to a large open field that had been converted to a parking lot.

"It's our service staging area," Marley replied. "We have back-up vendors staged here. You can imagine the amount of food and beverages consumed here daily. Food handling and waste management are the logistics department's responsibilities, and we coordinate our security protocols with them. The food we can't get inside is stored outside in refrigerated trucks over there."

"But those look like garbage trucks."

"Yes, both types are queued up there. Rather ironic, isn't it? You can also imagine the amount of garbage thirty-five thousand people a day will generate after consuming a day's worth of food and drink," Marley said. "It all has to be removed from the site, or it would fill the loading bay area and the outdoor collection areas. We have hundreds of volunteers who do nothing all day long, but restock food stores from the trucks. And others who remove full trashcans and replace them with empties. They're mostly local high school kids.

"Another crew separates the waste from recycle materials, while yet another crew works full time emptying the waste bins into trash dumpsters, while other trucks haul our recycles. It's an ongoing process. When a series of dumpsters gets full," Marley nodded across the street, "those trucks are called from the queue to empty them and drive the trash off premises.

"Once they dump the trash, they return to the queue and start the process all over again. This goes on all day and evening long during the events. The trucks and drivers you see have been vetted and assigned, and have been here every day for the last two weeks."

Dozens of questions tugged at me about this set up, but I didn't want to embarrass myself again by asking a question Marley had already figured out ahead of me. As I tried to work it around in my head, a voice on the other end of Marley's radio interrupted. "Inspector Marley, what is your location?"

Marley gave him our location and the fact that we would soon be turning the corner to reenter at Gate Five.

"Right, sir," the voice acknowledged. "An officer says she will meet you there."

"Must be Bishara," I guessed.

Marley looked down at his watch and then advised his dispatcher, "Tell them it is ok to open the gates now, but each person and vehicle must be individually inspected, including any items they carry in. No slip-ups and everyone will be polite, but thoroughly diligent. Right?"

"Yes, Sir," came the reply.

It had begun. If the Messenger was going to try to enter the stadium, hopefully, he would have to pass the scrutiny of a very dedicated security team trying to keep him from doing so.

I wondered what any one of them might do if they encountered him, armed and carrying a bomb right up to a gate entrance. There was something that just didn't fit with that scenario.

"Marley," I said. "This just doesn't make sense."

"What doesn't make sense?" he asked.

"We have all these officers looking for a guy walking into the grounds, carrying a bomb that was so big, it likely took a lift to get it onto a truck. I just can't see that happening."

"It's the only way we can be sure he isn't getting on the grounds," Marley explained. "We have to start somewhere and that begins with an empty stadium and monitoring each person coming in. We've been checking all arriving delivery and service vehicles since this morning when we identified the Messenger. Even authorized official vehicles and the player's vans and limousines are being inspected."

Bishara walked out of Gate Five and onto the Church Road sidewalk. Seeing us, her hand rose in a slight wave of acknowledgement as we approached. Compared with the last time I saw her, she now looked frazzled and tired, and most of that erotic glow had faded. She got right down to business.

"Our facial recognition application has been loaded into the server software of the camera system," she said. "It's scanning everyone entering all the gates and seating areas. As the camera sees a face, it is converted into a digital map and run into the computer. Our artist has updated the sketch of our suspect to reflect the facial recognition points and features, and they have been converted into data points. Every face in this place is having the same thing done by our software to see if we get even a close match. We are also loading it now, onto the systems that monitor common outdoor areas. Unfortunately, they are on a separate computer system and have to be separately updated before the software can run on them."

"So, we are relying on Marley's team right now to keep an eye on the open areas?" I asked. I was thinking about the shortcut that Marley took to get us onto the property. If someone could make his way through a neighborhood, he just might make it right into a gate entryway.

"The facial recognition system is infinitely faster and much more accurate than all Marley's officers' observations combined," Bishara repeated.

I was impressed with all that technology, but every instinct I had convinced me we were missing something, but I was distracted by Bishara's state of agitation.

"You feeling alright, Miriam?" I asked.

"I'm fine," she snapped.

Marley looked at me quizzically. "The best we can do is head back inside to the camera command post. If you are likely to see him at all, Michael, your services are better used watching those places on a monitor, than trying to guess what gate he would likely use, and standing there."

Begrudgingly, I agreed. "Then I'll leave the general camera monitoring to the computers and focus my attention on the areas where we don't have the software loaded yet."

With that, we all headed back towards the entrance gate.

■ ■ ■ ■ ■

ELQISI JERKED UPRIGHT IN HIS seat, then quickly slouched back down, adjusting his cap down over his eyes. Bishara had just exited the building and joined two men on the sidewalk, and he recognized them both. One was the American and the other was the officer who was with Bishara in Putney, when he was on the roof.

There was no longer any doubt. They were here and they were looking for him. It was time to make an adjustment to his plans.

His original plan called for him to wait his turn to be called up to haul a dumpster away. This usually occurred early in the afternoon, which today, would occur about midway through the women's finals introductory ceremony. By then the stadium would be full. During the process, he would set the timer and walk away from the truck with its keys, rendering it unmovable. Now he would have to modify that plan and possibly take some risks he hadn't counted on. He set the timer.

■ ■ ■ ■ ■

BISHARA'S AND MARLEY'S RADIOS QUIETLY broadcast the simultaneous message, "Swan and Signet, ETA three minutes."

Marley interpreted for me, "The Princess and Prince William will be here shortly."

I began looking down the road for her entourage. "No," Marley said. "She will enter on the west side of the building at the gate directly opposite this one, and then proceed straightaway to the member's club area. The Duke and Duchess have not yet arrived, but we can expect them shortly, at the same entrance."

So, they'll be relatively safe from a blast in there?"

Marley and Bishara looked at each other. "Relatively," Bishara replied.

"Depends on the location of a blast and its intensity. They are on the second level, so it will be better than if they were on the ground floor." I was recalling the devastation of the explosions at Hyde Park, where two and three floors of brick structures had been blown to bits.

"They'll all wait up in the club, visiting others, until just before the introductory ceremonies begin, which should be in less than an hour or so. The players will warm up for about five minutes after that. The match is being broadcast worldwide, so they will be on a very tight start schedule."

"Would it do any good to have them move to their seats inside the stadium earlier than planned? That would limit their street side exposure."

"That's above my pay grade." But Marley spoke the request to someone from his radio.

"Yes," Bishara said, "We've done about all we can. Now we have to wait and watch, and hope we catch a break." She wanted to be closer to the center of the building, not so much to avoid any possible injury from a bomb placed outside, but to be able to respond from a central point if Elqisi was spotted anywhere on the grounds. "I have a seat near the Royal Box, just in case."

She needed to be one of the first command officers on the scene, so she could take him into her custody immediately. It was the only way to control him if he was arrested. And it would give her the best opportunity to be alone with him.

"Let's get inside," Marley said.

"Listen," I said, nodding up the sidewalk a ways, "when we get to your car, do you mind if I toss my jacket inside?" It was late morning and it was already becoming a hot and humid day.

"Certainly," Marley said. "I'd do the same, if I wasn't carrying this." And with that he patted the left side of his jacket, to remind me he was holstering a weapon.

I felt the emptiness on my gun side and sensed a twinge of disadvantage. We were looking for a terrorist, possibly armed, who had already killed at least one person, not to mention dozens of others with his explosive devices, and I wasn't even bringing a gun to a bomb fight. My only advantage would be to heighten my senses, and hope to spot the Messenger before he spotted us, or at least before he could place and detonate his device.

We continued down the paved walk another hundred feet to Marley's Jag. As I stripped off my jacket, I still couldn't help but think we were missing something.

"David, let me ask you something else about those trucks that are staged across the street," I said, turning and pointing to them. "Were they part of your enhanced vetting process this morning, or were they grandfathered onto the premises from earlier in the night?"

Bishara and Marley turned to look at the trucks, as he began his explanation.

■ ■ ■ ■ ■

ELQISI COULDN'T BELIEVE HIS BAD fortune. He had been spotted! How could this be?

From his vantage point, he could clearly see that the American was pointing at him, and Bishara and the cop were staring at him too.

He leaned across the center console of pneumatic controls and grabbed the satchel from the passenger seat. Hunched over, he reached into the bag, pulled the remote detonator from it, and reset the time to ten minutes. He uncoiled four more feet of wiring for the detonator, which allowed him to set the satchel under his seat. The bomb, the diesel accelerant, and a full fuel tank, were securely mounted in the rear of Elqisi's truck. The device sat next to the open side panel, obediently awaiting its remote signal.

He had planned every step so carefully, studying and conducting surveillance for weeks. All that preparation, only to be discovered at the last moment, and by an American who shouldn't even be here. He had not planned this to be a suicide mission, but he was prepared, if that became necessary. At all costs, he must uphold the motto of Hezbollah, emblazoned on their flag, *Lo, the party of Allah, for they are the victorious ones.* However it occurred, his mission must be a success.

Elqisi sat upright, engaged the gears, and pulled from his place midway in line, all the while, staring at Bishara. He retrieved the Luger from his hip and felt the heft of it in his hand. The magazine was

271

fully loaded with eight rounds and he had already chambered the ninth. When it came time, he would fire the first round with the hammer cocked, giving him a steadier first shot. All the rest would be fired with the same reduced trigger pull. He released the safety.

Elqisi was desperate now, knowing he may have to shoot his way out of there to make his way to his getaway car. And if that was not an option, he would meet Allah from the seat of this truck.

■ ■ ■ ■ ■

A FLASH OF MOVEMENT CAUGHT my eye about midway down the row of the big black garbage trucks. I could barely see through the windshield, but it appeared as if the driver had ducked down to hide from us as we looked back. I peered more closely trying to get my eyes to adjust to the combination of glare from the open field and the shadows from the row of trees lining the road. It was all complicated because the truck was across the street, and it wasn't my original intent to single out any particular truck anyway. I continued watching to ether verify my assumption or refute it.

Marley said, "I'm pretty sure all the vehicles on the property have been checked."

"Didn't you tell me that they are changing all day and night long? Could these trucks have gotten here before we began checking the oncoming and departing drivers?"

"Let me verify that," he said, keying his radio microphone.

Before he could get any farther with that effort, the driver of the truck sat upright in his seat. As if my eyes had played a trick on me, I scrunched them tight, thinking that would improve my vision.

He seemed to be wearing a baseball hat with a red logo on it. The eyes seemed to be the same cold dark eyes I saw on the rooftop. I couldn't be sure, but now was not the time to take a chance.

"Marley," I shouted, "I think that driver has the same hat on as the Messenger!"

"Where?" Bishara yelled, elbowing her way to my side.

I pointed again to the truck about midway in the row of waiting vehicles.

As I did so, we all saw the truck drive forward from the others and turn in our direction. He didn't appear to be speeding, just moving along the row, but out of sequence.

Marley's radio kicked on, "The Swan and Signet are in their nest," came the coded message. The Princess and her son were already in the Royal box awaiting the start of the ceremony. They had bypassed the Club and gone straight to their seats.

Bishara ran to the curb, looking to her right, waiting for traffic to clear, then ran on an angle across the street and toward the dirt road the truck was following towards us. I saw that her gun, a small semi-automatic, was already drawn.

Marley followed her, gun in hand also. And for some strange reason I followed too, empty-handed.

Marley had cleared the street, but I got caught up in traffic. People were slowing but not stopped, as they watched a man and a woman running with

273

guns. It obviously wasn't something they saw every day. As they slowed, they closed the distances between their already crawling cars. My attempts to get them to let me cross in front of them weren't having the same effect that Marley enjoyed.

I continued running up the shoulder of Church Road, waiting for my opening. Soon there was a break and I bolted across the street.

Bishara was closing the gap between her and the truck, when suddenly the driver swerved from the road and aimed the tons of steel he was driving right at her. I could see that he was aiming a gun outside the window too.

She dropped into a kneeling crouch and fired a shot into the front window that seemed to have no effect.

Bishara sidestepped and crouched behind a large tree on her side of the road and fired another shot into the windshield. As the truck swerved slightly to avoid hitting the tree, the driver fired three quick shots from inside the cab. He was practically right alongside her.

Bishara fell to the ground, hard. She'd been hit.

Marley closed in on the truck and was standing right in the middle of its path. He leaned into a standing combat-shooting position and braced his gun with his other hand. Slowly he squeezed off three shots in measured succession. I could see the windshield peppering with holes through the right–side driver's half of it.

The vehicle didn't alter course and as it passed Marley, the driver fired at him too.

Marley ran away from the truck but at an angle that made further aiming difficult for both of them. The driver fired more shots at Marley as he passed, and was now heading for me, as I ran towards Bishara and Marley.

■ ■ ■ ■ ■

ELQISI SAW THEM RUNNING TOWARDS him with weapons in their hands. He was mentally prepared for them and determined to finish his mission. He knew he held the advantage.

He was fairly protected inside tons of steel, while they were standing with no cover and no concealment. He had been trained in the Afghan desert on both of those protective concepts. There was nowhere for them to hide, and no protection from his weapon. All he had to do was remain calm enough to hit a moving target from a moving vehicle.

He didn't slow enough to be certain he had hit Bishara, but as his big truck passed her, he thought she went down. One of her bullets had blown a shard of glass into his left eye and it burned like hell. His vision out of it was partially blurry with blood. Despite the pain though, Elqisi fought to keep his right eye focused and clear, while he prayed to Allah that he had killed the bitch.

The other cop was more difficult. Elqisi could see that this one was trained and calm and taking direct aim. There wasn't much he could do, so he ducked below the dashboard and let the heavy metal of the truck serve as an armored vehicle for him. Just as he thought he would be alongside him, he raised up and fired at the detective as he passed him.

Again, there was no way to tell if he had hit him.

Interestingly, the American was standing in the middle of the road as well, unarmed! Elqisi swerved the truck at him and he leaned his gun out the window. This one would be easy.

■ ■ ■ ■ ■

I WAS STANDING THERE WATCHING Marley roll and rise as he limped toward Bishara. The garbage truck was not only heading in my direction, I could see the driver's determination as he aimed the steel monster right at me. He reached out his right-side window again and I could plainly see his gun in his hand, trying to line up on me. And when I saw the face of the Messenger, I realized how he was going to convey that bomb into the stadium.

In a tight crouching position, I ran at an angle to my right and toward the truck, narrowing his field of view from the cab and presenting as small a target as I could. Bent over like that also served to protect some of my vital organs from the shooter, who leaned further out the window, trying to regain his target alignment on me.

I broke hard to my right and ran between two large trees that had probably been planted in the early 1900s, when The Club acquired this land. I was now safely concealed behind solid cover. It was nearly impossible for the driver to get any kind of shot at me from the truck. If the Messenger decided to stop and get out, to finish me there, I was a dead man.

The big truck pulled by without stopping. When it cleared the street in front of me, I saw Marley kneeling awkwardly over Bishara, one hand pressing on a bleeding wound just over her hip, the other hand holding his radio as he barked into it. Bishara looked like she was about to pass out from the pain.

"Shots fired. Shots fired. I've got two officers down in the service parking lot between gates five and six. Send an ambulance."

Marley was bleeding from a wound in his leg. He wouldn't be chasing anyone. I looked around on the ground, found Bishara's pistol and grabbed it.

"You okay?" I asked him. Marley nodded and looked back to Bishara. I turned and ran after the truck, shouting over my shoulder to Marley, "Tell them not to shoot me!"

Marley continued talking into his radio, but I couldn't hear what he was saying.

■ ■ ■ ■ ■

ELQISI WASN'T SURE WHO HE shot and who he may have missed. He felt pretty certain he had hit Bishara, but he wasn't sure about the detective. The American had hidden behind a tree and seemed uninjured, but he was not armed and therefore, not a threat. If either of the officers survived, they would be on the radio broadcasting his description and that of the truck. He would have only a few minutes to execute his plan, and possibly make his escape.

There was no way for Elqisi to know whether or not anyone from the Royal Family would have entered the box yet, but he could not afford to wait any longer. Hopefully the blast would be powerful enough to hurl death across the bottom of the stadium into the member's Club area, if that is where they were waiting. He had to make a choice of where to immobilize the truck. He could do the most damage in the loading bay area under the stands. That would also align the open side of the truck out into the larger area of the stadium.

Approaching the drive that crossed back over Church Road, he encountered traffic blocking his turning lane, and cars were stopped the entire length of Church alongside the stadium bowls. He yanked the wheel hard right and tried to fit the truck between two old trees, but the space wasn't wide enough. He tried to force the truck through using its powerful gears and engine. The big tires spun, but couldn't gain the traction he needed to bully the truck through. Slipping it into reverse, he backed away from the trees and began looking for a small car to roll over or to push out of the way.

He was less than one hundred yards from the entrance but still out in an open area. If the truck detonated here, there would be plenty killed, but the blast wave would dissipate before it could wreak the destruction he had planned on. He had to get inside the gate. And he had only six minutes left to do it.

■ ■ ■ ■ ■

CLOSE AHEAD, I SAW THE big truck take a right turn, and try, without any success, to get between two trees. For a moment it seemed stuck there. I had a burst of adrenaline and picked up my pace. I glanced at Bishara's gun and saw that it was still on single action, meaning the slightest trigger pull would fire a round. She had apparently got some shots off, but I didn't know how many. I set the hammer back down as I ran, making sure the safety was off and in fire mode. I was gaining on him by the second.

The truck backed from between the trees, then drove through a queue of passenger cars, pushing one of them along the grass and out of his way. Angling back toward Church Road again, I could see the driver was going to try the same maneuver to get across the road and ram Gate Five.

I changed my angle of approach slightly and hoped to get to the truck about the time it got into the road. Once I intercepted it though, I had no idea what I was going to do to stop it.

The truck plowed into a small panel truck and pushed it over the shoulder of the road, but that didn't leave it any room to turn toward the gate. The truck backed up and turned north onto Church, but now it was in a non-moving lane of traffic. The truck slammed into the rear of the car ahead of it, trying to force its way through the procession of steel. He wasn't having any luck.

As the truck swerved back onto the narrow left shoulder of Church Road, I caught up with it. I saw the Messenger glance back at me, but he didn't turn out the window to shoot at me. He seemed

279

desperate to get the truck to Gate Five.

■ ■ ■ ■ ■

ELQISI GLANCED BACK AS HE slipped the truck into reverse, to disengage his bumper from the truck he had smashed into. That's when he saw the American running toward him, only now he was carrying a gun. He couldn't bother with the American right now, he had to get inside the stadium. He began crashing into the cars ahead of him, trying to get them to move.

Quickly realizing the futility of that, he pulled onto the shoulder of the road. It would be a lot easier to move cars laterally, than to push them into each other. Looking back again, he saw the American was nearly at the rear of his truck. Traffic was so slow, he could practically walk to the gate faster than he was going. But that would defeat his purpose. He began forcing car after car out of his way. He had less than fifty yards to go, and although he had lost track of time, he had to get the bomb inside the stadium, even if he was in the truck when it detonated. The American could not be allowed to stop him. He grabbed his Luger.

■ ■ ■ ■ ■

RUNNING TOWARD THE TRUCK, I looked across the street to the entrance of Gate Five. That seemed to be the closest way the Messenger could get inside the perimeter and close to Centre Court. There was a media crew standing in the driveway leading to the entrance. A former athlete, turned sportscaster, was holding a microphone in front of a lady tennis player, as he interviewed her. There were plenty of smiles all around, as they were completely unaware of what was going on a mere hundred feet away. She looked past the shoulder of the commentator and right at me, seeing me running with a gun in my hand. Her look went from pleasure to confusion, and then to fear. I didn't have time to see how she reacted beyond that.

The driver leaned out his window and aimed his gun at me. I wasn't waiting to hear the sound of a gunshot before I reacted. I again crouched as small as I could, while running toward the rear of the truck, reducing his angle, and making me an increasingly difficult target. I fired a round, hoping it would get into the window of the truck cab. If it didn't hit him, I hoped it would slow him down a bit. I heard two shots go off in rapid succession from the truck, but felt nothing strike me. I had no idea where in the crowd the bullets might have landed, but I vaguely heard screams from behind me.

The driver was moving slowly now along the shoulder of the road and was pushing cars ahead of him. He seemed to be gaining momentum.

Using the handhold on the truck, I leapt onto the back near the compacting bin. I was on the same side of the vehicle as the Messenger, but had nowhere to go. I couldn't get off and expect to catch up in time. I couldn't run around the back and hope to climb into the cab from the other side. I was running out of time and options. To move forward I could either climb along the side I was on and wait for the Messenger to lean back and shoot me, or climb on top of the truck.

Slipping the gun in my waistband, I grabbed the garbage bin loading mechanism tube, pulled myself up to the top, and shinnied onto the roof of the garbage bin.

The road was smooth enough, but every time the driver pushed into another car, I stumbled. I dropped to my hands and knees and crab-crawled the rest of the way to the front.

I dropped down between the truck's cab and the hydraulic pressure controls and landed with a loud thud as I crashed into the back of the cab.

The Messenger leaned back out the window, but didn't have any kind of decent angle. He fired a shot at me and missed. Everything seemed to unfold in slow motion in front of me and I could no longer hear any sounds. I knew that my next move could be my last.

I pulled out my gun, guessed where the driver's seat would be and fired twice through the back wall of the cab.

People on the sidewalk began screaming as they heard the shots and saw me with my gun out. Parents grabbed their children, looking for a place to hide. Some pedestrians ran off into the field to the east, and some hid behind the big trees, while others tried to crash through Gate Five security into what they thought was the safety of Centre Court.

Motorists, who looked out their rear view windows at the sounds of crashing cars, and who then heard the sound of gunshots, began crashing into the cars ahead of them, in their attempts to flee. Others drove their cars across the right hand shoulder of the road, pushing other vehicles and pedestrians out of the way, as they tried to get away through the field.

■ ■ ■ ■ ■

THE TRUCK JERKED HARD TO the left and crashed into the security bollard at the corner of Gate five. The impact was so severe, it nearly knocked me off the truck. Quickly, I leaned around, gun in hand and looked through the window.

The Messenger was leaning over the steering wheel as he tried reaching back toward his bleeding neck with his left hand. The other held his gun. When he saw me he hurriedly raised his gun, aimed it at my face, and pulled the trigger.

Out of instinct, I raised my hand in front of my face, raised my own pistol and ducked as I pulled the trigger as well. There was the sound of only one gunshot, and it was mine.

Quickly I reached over and grabbed the empty gun from his hand, but he resisted letting go. He wasn't dead, but he had been hit at close range, through the side of his chest, and it was obviously a critical injury. I yanked it from his hand, just to be on the safe side.

That action seemed to revive him, and he looked hard into my eyes, "I do not know who you are," he said, blood running from his mouth. "And it does not matter. I will be dead soon and so will you, all of you. It will explode before you can even find it, much less disarm it."

With those words directed to me, he managed to deliver his last message. The hard stare in his eyes turned glassy, and when his head slumped forward, I didn't need Cheri, the medical examiner, to tell me the Messenger was dead.

My attention focused on what he said. I may have no time left. I needed to find that bomb and get Bishara's munitions experts here to disarm it.

I pulled on the truck door and pushed the messenger over and began looking around in the cab. I wasn't sure what to look for, but I was worrying that there wasn't enough room in here to put any bomb of the size we were all thinking the Messenger had made.

Between his feet, I saw a canvas satchel. Opening the top flap, I saw the detonator device and the wires leading from it, through the back of the cab.

The bomb was in the back of the truck. All I had to do was separate the timing device from the bomb.

My plan was interrupted when I noticed that the entire device was wrapped in layer upon layer of duct tape to ensure that no one could separate it from the wiring coils without at least a little bit of knowledge, a knife and plenty of time. I had none.

I grabbed the Messenger by his collar, pulled him from the truck, threw him into the street, and climbed into the cab.

The engine was still running, but I had never driven one of these before, other than as a kid playing in the sand.

Looking down on the steering wheel knob, I saw

the order of the gears etched in to it.

I clutched and jerked the big truck into reverse, backed into traffic and bumped hard into the car behind me. I was surprised how easily the wheel turned, but how slowly the truck moved, as I slipped it into first gear. I needed to get this thing as far away from there as I could.

I steered the mobile bomb toward the crowded field where the service vehicles were parked. Looking into the passenger areas of those vans and trucks, I could see the eyes of the drivers and other occupants, wide with fear. I couldn't leave it here, where there were several hundred people staged.

I pulled the wheel right and worked only from the limited memory I had of the grounds. I backtracked the path the Marley had used to get us here only hours before.

That was when I heard the first ping of something slapping into the truck, followed by another and then another. They were shooting at me! Dear God, there were two things I didn't want hit. One was obviously me, but the other was the bomb!

I knew I was relatively safe because the shots were coming from the rear and not the sides. But I didn't know where the bomb was and how, or even if, it was protected.

My hands were slippery on the wheel, as I tightened my grip and guided the truck onto the path below the Wimbledon Golf Club and headed back east. I knew what I was looking for, but wasn't sure I would ever get there on time. The Messenger had said there wasn't enough time to find or disarm the bomb. Did I have a few minutes, or just a few seconds? I found myself wincing in anticipation of the explosion.

Up ahead I saw the driveway I wanted. It was more of a groomed grass road. I gunned the big truck and gave it another gear as it bounced and careened from side to side, brushing and snapping the tree branches alongside the path. I couldn't hear any bullets dinging off the truck any more.

I was trying to gage distance at this point and hadn't any experience to draw from. I knew I had to maintain, if not increase my speed, yet all my instincts said to slow down a bit. I didn't listen and gunned the engine even more.

The tree line stopped abruptly and gave way to a small parking area. I drove through the lot and past the cars with their empty trailers. I opened the door of the truck, leaned out with my foot still on the gas, and at the last second, I jumped. I did the best tuck and roll I had ever executed, having never done one before, yet I felt tree roots on the surface of the lawn, crushing against my side, as I tried to cushion myself from the impact.

My leap rolled me right into the marshy edge of Wimbledon Park Lake, as the truck lumbered by me. Its momentum overcame the water's initial resistance, and seemed to take an eternity to slide into the deep drop-off area of the boat launch. Within seconds it had sunk below the water's surface.

I did a brief physical inventory to learn that I was fine, other than some beginning aches and pains. Looking at the shoreline and the waves still lapping it from the disturbance of the truck, I didn't know whether to watch for a reaction, wait for an explosion, or to walk or run away. Dripping wet, I quickly backed away from the edge of the lake, not taking my eyes off it.

"Raise your hands!" "Drop to the ground!" "Don't move!" Came the shouting litany of confusing but seriously deadly orders. I tried to comply with all of them.

I raised my hands, knelt on the ground and stayed very still. Then I yelled out, "Don't shoot me. I'm Marley's Yank!"

There was a pause before one of them said to the others, "Easy lads. No mistakes here. He's one of us."

Then he said, "Good Lord, man. Where's the truck?"

I was about to reply, when there was an earsplitting explosion that pushed tons of water upward into a mushroom, fifty-feet in the air above the lake.

When it crashed back down on itself, it created a huge wave and spray that ballooned onto the shore with such force that the entire dozen of us were knocked down and drenched. We all watched from the ground, as secondary waves rolled back and forth over us, and across the entire lake, before dissipating.

I sat up, pointed to the lake, and said, "There's your truck."

■ ■ ■ ■ ■

THE LIEUTENANT FROM THE FAST Response Unit told me that Marley and Bishara had been conveyed to nearby Charing Cross Hospital. It was when I asked for a ride there, that he advised me that he *was asking me to go with him as a material witness*. In other words, they wanted to question me and take a statement from me first and it wasn't an option.

We drove in silence, with me in the back of the marked police unit. I was sitting behind the prisoner screen, and although I wasn't handcuffed, I knew the doors were on auto-lock, and I wasn't going anywhere but where they decided.

The lieutenant and his driver were pretty chatty with each other for most of the ride. They seemed to be releasing a lot of pent up anxiety about the earlier search for the Messenger, the threat to the Princess and her son, and the fact that there had been a shooting of a couple of their officers. I was guessing they were celebrating also that the bomb had been rendered harmless without killing or hurting anyone. I figured that there was a lot of fish-kill floating on Wimbledon Park Lake about now, who might disagree with that assessment.

To my pleasant surprise, the driver pulled in front of the Grosvenor Hotel. "Go grab a fast shower and get into something dry," he said. "We'll be waiting here, but make it quick. There are a lot of people who want to talk with you."

It didn't take long for me to get back downstairs. By then, people in the lobby were staring and pointing at me, as they whispered amongst themselves. It must have been the fact that it was the fourth time I had been either picked up or dropped off by the police in a matter of days.

The officers in the car were still in their wet gear, and I felt a bit odd to be warm and dry at their expense. I kept my thoughts to myself.

It didn't take long for me to realize where we were going. I was being driven into the secure parking area of MI5's Gower Street building. I was on my own now, without Marley or Bishara to stand up for me, and I wondered if I was going to need an attorney to represent me for possessing a firearm in Great Britain, and then killing someone with it, even though he was a *bad guy*.

Still in the garage, we went straight to what seemed to be a private elevator. Bishara had never used it when we were going and coming. We rode in silence for a few moments, until the car slowly and quietly stopped. When the doors slid open, we were in Fairweather's office.

"Christian, yes. Come in, come in," he said, as he greeted me. "That will be all, boys," he said to my escort. "Come sit. Can I offer you anything?"

I hadn't thought about it until then, but now I realized, I was famished. "No, thank you sir," I replied. "I'm fine."

"Well then, Since Marley and Bishara are out of commission at the moment, yours is the only total explanation of what happened."

I realized he or some minister was going to have to make a public statement, and would need to figure out how to explain what occurred and perhaps whom to blame. I didn't want it to be me.

Let's get right to it, shall we?" Fairweather said. "Just the highlights. I'll have someone take a full statement from you later. How did you happen to come across this *Messenger* and how did you stop him?"

I followed his instructions exactly and kept it all at a high level. I gave Fairweather as much detail as I could, though, about the bravery and heroism of Marley and Bishara, running right at the Messenger and keeping their forward momentum, even while taking gunfire and being hit. I wanted to be certain they were recognized for it, in case they were too humble to mention it.

I skimmed over the part about me running on the top of the truck. The more I thought about it, the more ridiculous it sounded. I did explain how I shot him through the cab wall, without knowing if the rounds would take effect.

"You drove the truck into Wimbledon Park Lake?" he asked, incredulously. "What possessed you?"

"Honestly, sir, I have no idea. All I could think of, at first, was getting the truck to a less populated area. When I made the turn into the field and saw all those people there too, I just continued driving further away. Then it occurred to me.

"I wish I could claim credit for a brilliant plan, but it was mostly luck."

"Brilliant," he exclaimed. "Just brilliant!" He continued with more excitement than I expected.

"You recall the three gentlemen in the room with me when you, Marley and Bishara were in here explaining your theory?" I knew whom he meant.

"Well, they are most pleased with the outcome, and we will soon be briefing her Royal Highness on the events that took place. They are already talking about awarding you some form of royal recognition, Christian. And I am a most enthusiastic supporter of their plan. Well done, Christian. Well done," said the man who regularly repeated himself to make a point.

I was flattered but didn't really care much about

that. These were the same three who just a day before were trying to downplay the threat, as well as minimize the value of the approach their officers were planning to protect their Princess. More likely, their jobs had been saved and they were preparing to take credit for preventing the attack. Tossing a few medals around would make them seem most generous.

I decided that no reply was my best reply.

"Would you mind, sir, if I gave that statement? I really want to get to the hospital to look in on Marley and Bishara."

"Yes, of course, of course," Fairweather said as he pushed the button on his desk. He called his secretary to the office and we stood. My time with Fairweather was over. As she explained that I would be taken down to an office where my statement would be taken, he grabbed my hand and shook it warmly.

"Christian, you seem to be taking all this in stride. Today's incident looms larger than you can imagine, on so many fronts. I know that you could have walked away from this at any time. And had you done so, today's outcome could have been tragically different. We are all very grateful. Thank you. Thank you."

I had no idea how to respond. "Yes, sir. You are most welcome," was all I could come up with.

■ ■ ■ ■ ■

IT TOOK ALMOST TWO HOURS for the officers

to complete their questioning of me. They weren't particularly interested in what led up to my being on the scene to begin with and I got the sense that a *proper* storyline was already being created to explain it. They asked me to draw the scene, but not to worry about being artistically creative. They had already cordoned off the area and would be looking for bullet casings and any other evidence they could find, but wanted some guidance as to where and how the events played out.

I wondered if traffic around the stadium would be snarled for a day while they examined such a large crime scene. Or, given the tidy way the case was wrapped up, if this would all be *managed* through a tightly woven cover story. That would keep questions and embarrassing policy matters to a minimum, and let the Championship finals proceed with minimal interruption.

I wondered if Marley and Bishara were in any shape to give statements, and whether or not theirs would align with mine. Given that I was at MI5 and not at the Putney Station, I felt that anything close to alignment would be good enough for this crew.

I signed several copies of the statement and then they asked me to sign a government secrets confidentiality notice. Somehow, I got the impression that I would be sitting in that chair a long time, if I didn't. I figured that since I wasn't a British citizen, it would be difficult for them to enforce it anyway. So, I made it easy on all of us and signed it.

They were most congenial in providing me with a driver to take me to see Bishara and Marley.

As they escorted me from the interview room and back to the parking garage, I received a couple

Here, here and *Well-done* remarks from staff. I found that terribly embarrassing, yet secretly gratifying.

Marley was in a private room, guarded by a serious looking police detail, at Charing Cross Hospital. A nurse was attending to the many bottles of fluids and electrical leads hanging on poles around his bed. He was sitting up in his bed, looking rather pale and seemed to be dazed. His leg was poking out from his hospital gown, slightly elevated, and wrapped in bandages from the knee to the ankle. Given the dreamy look on his face, I guessed that at least one of the intravenous lines was pumping painkillers into him.

The nurse looked up as I entered. There was a moment of confusion, and then she said, "You're him!"

I chuckled, "What do you mean, I'm him?"

The guy on the garbage truck!" She exclaimed.

She pointed to the television hanging on the wall, and there I was, bigger than life, crawling on the top of the garbage bin, as captured by the ESPN reporter outside Gate Five.

Seeing myself up there was an odd experience. I watched as if it was someone else. The truck crashed into a car in the line ahead of it, and I stumbled. The nurse exclaimed, "Oh my!" as if she was watching it live. And then there was the moment when I fired the shots through the back wall of the cab. And she gasped, "Dear Lord," and looked at me with a slight look of apprehension.

The cameraman was unable, of course, to get the rest of the action, where I pulled the Messenger's dead body out of the truck, but I was clearly visible driving it away and leaving a body in the street. Somehow that seemed a bit callous when watching it from that perspective.

He had trained the camera on the truck as it ran off in the distance, until he lost the close-up view where I turned onto the tree-lined path. The camera was still running and facing the Messenger, when we could hear the explosion in the background. I had no idea the sound had carried so far.

The cameraman had the presence of mind to point the camera at the direction of the sound and captured most of the large mushroom of water towering five stories into the air. It was impressive footage. The nurse gasped again as she watched the water rise over the treetops. "It's been playing all afternoon, and I can't stop watching it," she said. "You saved all those people."

I wanted to visit Marley, but now I was looking for a way out of there.

She could see that I was uncomfortable with the attention. I said, "Do you mind if we turn that off?"

"Yes, please," slurred Marley. "Been running over and over, for an hour." He seemed to be drifting in and out of sleep.

The nurse pressed a button on the remote and shut off the TV. She turned in the doorway on her way out of the room and said, "He'll be fine, but please don't be long. He's just coming out of his surgery anesthesia."

When we were alone, I wanted to ask him how he was doing, but I wasn't sure if he even knew yet. I wanted to tell him about the truck in the lake, or what was left of the truck. I wanted to tell him about meeting with Fairweather, but I could tell he wouldn't remember a thing. I knew I'd be leaving England soon, possibly the next day, and may not get to see him again. Somehow, I felt sad about that.

Instead, I opened with, "Want me to call Cheri?" As soon as the words fell out of my mouth, I wanted to pick them up and put them back where they belonged, in my thoughts.

Marley mumbled, "What did you say?" It was obvious he wasn't firing on all cylinders yet. "Did you just ask me if I wanted you to call Cheri?"

I wanted to say *no*, and figure out something similar sounding that I could say more clearly. "Yes," I said.

Marley seemed to be sleeping. Then he stirred. "Yes," he said.

"Yes, what?"

Marley looked somewhere between disoriented and frustrated.

"Yes," he whispered. "Call Cheri. Get her number from the officer out there. Please call her, Christian. I have something I want to tell her." Then he fell back into a drug-induced slumber.

Marley may or may not ever remember that I was there, but I knew. It was what cops do for each other. It doesn't matter if you are acknowledged, or even remembered. You just need to be there for each other.

I patted his arm and walked out.

I got the medical examiner's number from the officer, and called Cheri Monahan for Detective Inspector David Marley, my friend.

I asked the nurse what room Bishara was in.

She gave me the room number on the post-op recovery floor.

Bishara was in serious but stable condition. There was a uniformed police detail outside her room also, assigned with two plainclothes officers, probably from MI5. One of her technical team officers was waiting in the lounge down the hall. He looked exhausted.

As I joined him in the lounge, he said, "She'll be okay, they tell us." But he still had that worried look on his face. His partner had been shot. It is a gut-wrenching experience. It happens every time an officer is shot. It's almost as if the fabric of every blue uniform on the force has been torn with that single bullet.

"Mind if I look in on her?" I asked.

"Go ahead. She's in sort of a twilight sleep right now. She seems to hear, but can't answer yet. Still drugged." He nodded to the guys on the detail and they let me pass.

Bishara looked very tiny in that bed, child-like and fragile almost. This take-charge woman was now totally dependent on the hospital team for her life-saving care and recovery. It was probably better that she was asleep. I knew there was nothing I could have done to prevent this, but I wished there had been. As I stood over her bed, lost in my thoughts, she whispered, "Michael."

Startled, I leaned in and said, "Miriam?"

She raised her hand slightly and I took it in mine. She gave it a slight squeeze.

"Michael, dinner and drinks, yes?"

"Yes, Miriam. Dinner and drinks," I lied.

She smiled slightly and dropped off to sleep again.

Quietly, I left the room.

■ ■ ■ ■ ■

AGAIN, I WAS DROPPED OFF by the police, in front of the Grosvenor. This time, when the doorman saw me, he ran to assist with the door, "Mr. Christian," he said. "Welcome back."

I simply wanted to get my key and slip quietly to my room.

The desk clerk saw me, nodded discreetly, turned professionally to the key rack, and then handed me several message slips and the key.

I felt the heft of the key and noticed right away. "This is not my key."

"Yes, it is, Mr. Christian. It is to the Executive Suite, with the compliments of the house. We have taken the liberty of moving your things there. We hope you don't mind."

I was hungry and I was tired. I didn't mind at all. "Would you have someone bring up some snacks? I'm a bit hungry and don't want to go out for dinner this evening. And I will likely be returning some of these messages."

"Of course, sir. There is already a fruit basket in there, along with some champagne. If I may, however, I'll put together another selection and have it brought up shortly. Your elevator is right over there, sir." And he pointed me to a single-door elevator that I knew would have only an *up* and a *down* button, no other numbers.

The first message I returned was from Herb Lawrence at the embassy. It simply said, *Call me, as soon as you get this.* It wasn't his office number.

He picked it up on the first ring and I could hear the sound of glasses and silverware tinkling in the background. "Where are you?" he asked.

"I'm at the hotel," I answered, just as curtly. "I'm going to grab a quick snack, and I'll be in bed soon."

"Michael, the Ambassador would like you to meet with him tomorrow morning. Let's say eleven. Come to my office first. That was quite a move you pulled today and the Ambassador would like to meet you personally to thank you."

"That's not really necessary, Herb. I'm already getting too much attention and would just as soon lay low."

"Michael, what part of *The United States Ambassador to Great Britain wants to meet with you* don't you get? This is not merely an invitation. It's a nicely worded order!

"He wants to be seen in public with the American who saved the Wimbledon Championship, Princess Diana and her son, and he wants to brief you first. That briefing will take place tomorrow morning at eleven, the press conference will begin at noon, and you will be there for both of them."

The enormity of what he said finally sunk in. I reluctantly agreed to the meeting and was glad to have that call behind me.

The next message was sealed in an envelope. It was from my boss, Barry Brinton. *Expect a call from the U. S. Embassy. Nice work.* I didn't know if that last sentence was a compliment or sarcasm. Then he closed with, *See you tomorrow.* I had no idea what he meant by seeing me tomorrow. I hadn't even made any travel arrangements yet.

I wish I had opened his message first, because whatever the ambassador wanted, he had already coordinated with Brinton. I was glad I didn't try to push a hard denial to the ambassador. That would have been career ending. Regardless, I wasn't making it back to the States at any reasonable hour tomorrow. I'd have to call Barry in the morning to let him know.

The next was from Flannery and read, *Got a call, watched the video. I called you a badass earlier. Now I repeat myself. PS: Don't get arrested.*

The next note was from Alice. *Are you crazy? Call me.*

I called her right away. No answer. I looked at my watch and realized it was ten thirty in the evening at home. Where the hell was she?

While I was pondering that, there was a knock at the door. "Room Service," a voice called.

Two liveried men from room service, each pushing a cart with two tiers of food in warming pans, greeted me at the door.

They quickly rolled the carts to the center of the meeting room and began to efficiently set up an eating area on the conference table in there. There was enough food for a small group of people.

I was about to object when one of them said, "Mr. Christian, that was an amazing thing you did today. Thank you, sir."

Again, I had that rush of embarrassment. I told them I was just fortunate to be in the right place at the right time. They nodded politely and left when they finished.

Nearly half the conference table was filled with food and each seat had its own place setting, as if they were expecting a half dozen more people. I pulled out a chair and sat myself at the center of all that food.

I nibbled at the roast prime rib, and used the tiny fork to pry some lobster free of the pre-cracked tail. Took a few bites of the lamb chop and washed it down with a long sip of a buttery Guigal La Mouline. I looked at the spread and realized that even if I had only a sample of everything, I'd be stuffed.

I removed a lid that had condensation on it. Inside was a carved ice sculpture in the shape of the American Bald Eagle, just like the large golden one that perched on top of the U.S. Embassy building here in London. Nestled between its claws was a large dollop of vanilla ice cream. It was the creamiest I could ever recall. I sipped hot coffee from the carafe that said "Decaf".

In the center of the table was a full bottle of Crown Royal. I twisted off the cap and poured a small amount into a Waterford Crystal tumbler and downed it, letting the warm liquid soothe me.

The small notecard on the table read, "With Compliments. The Management of the Grosvenor Hotel and the City of London."

Enough was enough. I left everything right where it was, and retired to the bedroom for the night.

■ ■ ■ ■ ■

I WAS UP EARLY AND dressed for the day, when room service showed up again and cleared away the food from last night. If they noticed that nearly all the food remained, they never showed it.

300

They merely replaced it with a hot American breakfast of bacon and sausage, toast, bagels, and croissants, and scrambled eggs. There was also a European cold breakfast of rolls and butter, meats and cheeses, fruit, sweet rolls, and several decanters of juice and fresh coffee.

I had barely sat down to it, when the phone rang.

"Mr. Christian, you have guests in the lobby. A Mr. Brinton. May I send them up?"

Barry Brinton, Chief Executive Officer of Transeget Industries, was here in London. He must have taken his Gulfstream and left last night. He'd be tired and possibly hungry. "Yes, send him up. And please send up enough breakfast," I replied, as if there wasn't already enough food in the room.

I stood by the door and opened it at his knock. There he was. And there, also, was Alice, my wife.

She rushed into my arms and we hugged fiercely and kissed equally so. Brinton waited until that exchange ended, then he smiled and said, "Good morning, Michael. And please don't hug or kiss me."

They could both see the shock, the surprise and the joy on my face, and I think that was the effect they were hoping for.

Brinton started right in with the explanation, while Alice and I continued hugging and smiling at each other.

"As soon as the video came across the news networks, I had Flannery call to make sure that you were alright. Then I had your admin manager find Alice for me, so I could reassure her you were okay.

"By then, I had received the call from the

Ambassador's office. So, I decided to ask Alice to join me here with you."

"That was very thoughtful of you, sir." I addressed him formally in front of Alice.

"Let's dispense with the formalities, Michael, and let me tell you what's going on."

He basically went over what Lawrence had explained to me the previous night. More breakfast came as he was talking, and we all enjoyed it as he proceeded.

"The Ambassador sees an opportunity to lock in a good relationship with the British government. He wants to do it visibly, to make it a public debt of gratitude that he can leverage hard when he has to.

"Right now, emotions are running very favorably toward what you did. And he wants to convert the energy that is focused on you to the benefit of the *American People*, as he described it. I'm all for it, as well. And while I agree with those lofty principles, there's something more.

"I'm going to be expanding our manufacturing operations to the suburbs of London, this year. To further that goal, I'll be hitting up Barclays for a couple hundred million. I expect the Ambassador to leverage his goodwill for very good financing terms with Barclays."

And there it was. Now I understood why Brinton was so fast to get on board with the Ambassador, and why he flew over here in the middle of the night to do so. He wanted to be seen with him at the press conference. And since he would get a chance to make a statement, I am sure Barclays would be paying very close attention to every word they both had to say. It wouldn't hurt that image either, that I would be standing next to him and the

302

ambassador. I was sure Barclay's Mr. Finch would remember my face.

Brinton continued, "After the press conference, I'll be meeting with the ambassador. Why don't you take Alice then, and show her around London? Get into some casual clothes and maintain a low profile. In fact, stay a few days, or a week. Make a vacation of it and send me the bill."

I was about to decline, when he said, "That was a nice way of me giving you an order. You are now officially on vacation. And keep this room. I'll take care of it downstairs."

With that he rose and walked to the door. "I'll be heading back on the Gulfstream this evening, but I'll see you over at the embassy first. Meanwhile, I've got a few things to attend to. Enjoy your stay."

He closed the door quietly behind him.

I turned to Alice and held her close again. I could feel the heat of her body against mine, and I felt her tremble.

"Does this suite have a bedroom?" she whispered

.

Other Books
By
Mike Saad

THE FIRST of the Michael Christian Mysteries, **A DAY LATE,** is an international crime novel set in post-cold war Germany. Meet Michael Christian for the first time, as he takes on a smuggling-ring operating in Germany, Poland and Russia while using his plant's customs-paperwork, trucks and employees to seemingly legitimize their cross-border activities.

The bodies begin to pile up, while Christian works to solve the case before the Russians add his body to the count. Available on Amazon as a Kindle e-Book and in paperback format.

Released in August 2018, A DAY LATE enjoys all Five-Star reviews!
Here's what people are saying about it:

"Beautifully written"
"This book has it all"
"Sounds as if it has been ripped from some secret file"
"Great TRIP!"
"Interested the entire time"
"Intrigued til the very end"
Extremely suspenseful"

BOOK TWO **A DOLLAR SHORT**

Christian is in Russia for two reasons. One is secret...

"Maybe you are a spy. Is that why you are really here?"

Michael Christian, security executive, goes head to head with the Russian Mafia in Moscow, as he attempts to free his company's operations from their extortion. Realizing he is there to disrupt their business, they devise a plot to kill him.

Out of his league and in a country with no rules, he forms an unlikely alliance with the FBI legal attaché in Moscow, and with Vladimir Takhoyev, a wealthy former KGB officer, who proves every bit as ruthless and competent as the mob.

But Christian is also there, in a borderline espionage capacity, to gather intelligence for the U.S. government. Takhoyev seems completely aware of both of Christian's missions, and is a step ahead of him all the way, forcing Christian to decipher if he is a friend or a foe.

Christian runs full speed through a minefield of espionage, murder, mayhem and mystery as bodies pile up and time runs out.

Released in March 2019, here's what readers have said about **A DOLLAR SHORT** while awarding it their five star reviews:

"Didn't want it to end"
"The best one yet"
"Another gem from Mike Saad"
"A real page turner"
"Entertaining and gripping"
"Kept your interest until the final sentence"
"Must Read"
Exciting and fast paced"
"One of those books you had to finish"

About the Author

Mike Saad has been a security executive for several of the largest corporations in the world.

For the last forty years he has traveled extensively, investigating and "fixing" corporate problems, much like Michael Christian has. At the heart of each story lies a real investigation or two.

To further treat you, Mike draws on his experiences from over ten years as a decorated officer on the Detroit Police Department, in their Tactical Mobile Unit and in the secret and elite Wayne County Organized Crime Task Force, where he led complex international theft and fencing cases.

Mike has also spent a lifetime mentoring, teaching and supporting professional security practices in his field. Now he turns those experiences from education to entertainment. Through his fictional characters, Mike reveals what it's like to travel the world, responding to security emergencies. He shares his insights, ranging from his opinions to his reactions to real events, from classroom lectures to proven security practices, from his observations to his boots on the ground experiences.

He has been awarded the *Lifetime Designation of Certified Protection Professional* by ASIS International, the premier professional security organization in the world, who has also designated him a *Life Member.*

Mike is retired and lives with his wife in Michigan.

WANT TO LEARN MORE?

You can keep up with Michael Christian, sign up for advance notice of book releases, and learn more about the geographic and historical settings of these stories at http://www.mikesaadwrites.com.

You can also read Mike Saad's personal musings and professional biography, by visiting his blogs and webpages. In his blog section, you will also find his personal musings, and a few short stories, fact and fiction, about Mike's experiences as a decorated officer on the Detroit Police Department.

Access all this and more at
www.mikesaadwrites.com.

Made in the USA
Columbia, SC
07 August 2020

15841829R00193